betrayal

AN EMPTY COFFIN NOVEL

betrayal

BY GREGG OLSEN

SPLINTER
NEW YORK

NEW YORK

An Imprint of Sterling Publishing
387 Park Avenue South
New York, NY 10016

ISBN 978-1-4027-8958-8
ISBN 978-1-4549-0305-5 (export edition)

Distributed in Canada by Sterling Publishing
℅ Canadian Manda Group, 165 Dufferin Street
Toronto, Ontario, Canada M6K 3H6
Distributed in the United Kingdom by GMC Distribution Services
Castle Place, 166 High Street, Lewes, East Sussex, England BN7 1XU
Distributed in Australia by Capricorn Link (Australia) Pty. Ltd.
P.O. Box 704, Windsor, NSW 2756, Australia

For information about custom editions, special sales, and premium
and corporate purchases, please contact Sterling Special Sales at
800-805-5489 or specialsales@sterlingpublishing.com.

Manufactured in United States of America

Lot #:
2 4 6 8 10 9 7 5 3 1
07/12
www.sterlingpublishing.com

For Jamie Morris, the girl who opened the creaky door of an abandoned house in the dark, dark woods.

AUTHOR'S NOTE

LIKE SOME OF THIS STORY, the following is absolutely true: trust doesn't come in shades of gray. It's absolute and filled with power. When trust is broken, it's often not the act of betrayal that's most surprising. The real shocker is who in your innermost circle betrayed you—a best friend? A boyfriend? A sister? A parent?

Betrayal can appear small, like a little white lie, the whisper of a long-held secret in the hall at school, or the posting of a private confession on Facebook. Or it can be colossal and far darker, like a pretty young lacrosse player savagely murdered by her ex-boyfriend, or the mother with haunted eyes who drowned her babies in the bathroom tub. The truth is that big or small, betrayal cuts quite like no other evil. And when it comes for you, it finds its way quietly in the night like the slip of a knife at the base of the spine. As life fades to black, you ask over and over: *What did I do to deserve this?*

—*Gregg Olsen*

chapter 1

OLIVIA GRANT WASN'T EXACTLY SURE what she'd expected America to be like, but Port Gamble, Washington, most certainly wasn't it. As the sixteen-year-old foreign-exchange student had boarded the late summer flight from London Heathrow to Seattle-Tacoma International Airport and plunked herself down next to a smelly man and his chubby little boy, she daydreamed of palm trees and movie stars. The travel magazine in the seat pocket in front of her all but confirmed the glamour awaiting the redheaded teen in just a few short hours: the cover featured a big splashy photo of beautiful people living in sunny, USA splendor. She was almost giddy, but she held it inside. British reserve, of course.

Olivia immersed herself in American TV the entire way over the polar ice cap to Seattle and wondered if the little boy to her left was going to be a kid contestant on *The Biggest Loser*. His father definitely was destined for some kind of makeover show. He not only smelled vaguely bad—*garlic*—but his mustache hung over his lip like an inverted vacuum cleaner attachment. The stylist who cut his hair had apparently used a saucepan for the template. When he looked over, she simply smiled. Olivia Grant was always very, very polite.

As it had turned out, Port Gamble wasn't sunny Southern California. Not by a long shot. Instead, even in late August when she'd arrived, it was about as soggy and dismal as Dorchester was in the middle of winter. Gray. Wet. Windy. The people who lived there were average teachers, cooks, millworkers, nurses.

So *not* movie stars with golden hair and perfectly straight teeth.

OLIVIA PONDERED THIS WHILE SITTING in the living room of her first American party. Olivia conceded that her first American beer wasn't what she thought it would be either. Brianna Connors, her new best friend, had promised that her dad's favorite craft brew was no big deal, even at 11 percent alcohol content. Tonight at Brianna's Halloween party, Olivia—in full costume—had sucked down the amber liquid like water and at first felt great. Then all of a sudden, somewhere between fending off some geeky, eye-linered, pirate boy's cringe-worthy come-on ("Hey hot wench, you lookin' for a first mate?"), arguing with her host roommate Beth Lee, and trying to cozy up to Jason Deveraux, the hottest guy at Kingston High, a wave of nausea hit her like a mini-tsunami. With the party still in eardrum-splitting full swing, Olivia went upstairs and sought refuge in Brianna's acre-sized bed.

Olivia curled up for an hour, maybe two. If she'd been able to recount it later, it would have been hard to say exactly how long. Time came and went in the way that it does in a dream. Vapors. Mist. She wondered if she'd been drugged. She had only had one beer, two at most. She ran the scenario in her head. It was true that she had felt a little sick that morning. Maybe it was nerves? Maybe it was the onset of the bug that had been going around school? She hadn't really eaten a thing since breakfast. Could it be just the combination of really bad American beer and no food?

Where was Brianna? Olivia thought, feeling sicker by the minute as the room started to spin. *Was the party still going on?* She could hear loud music and some teen slasher DVD blasting from the TV downstairs. The bass from the two competing subwoofers pumped up through the gleaming, dark, walnut floorboards.

Slowly, slowly, and with great effort, Olivia sat up, pulled off the scratchy, sparkly costume, exposing her thin white Calvin Klein slip underneath, and looked at herself in the mirror across the room. Even in the dark and through her late-night drunken haze, she could see her red hair, her flawless pale skin, and her green eyes. Boasting was so tacky, but even then, sick as she was, she thought she looked pretty good. It was ridiculous that she had worn not one, but two silly costumes during the party. Yet it was her first Halloween in America, a country that apparently reveled in the weird, macabre, and cheesy. She wondered why every boy's costume was that of a superhero and every girl was dressed up as a naughty or sexy something.

America, land of the puritan posers.

Slipping Brianna's bedazzled "Lights out!" eye mask on, Olivia wrapped herself in the slippery, satiny duvet—the same one on which she and Brianna had spilled nail polish the previous week when they were ragging on their absent mothers. She felt the circular dry spot that had stiffened the fabric. She picked at the spot with her long, slender fingers. It felt slick and smooth.

It wasn't the last thing she would feel that night.

WHERE OLIVIA'S SLIP ENDED and the sheets of Brianna's bed began was impossible to pinpoint in the dark. Olivia tossed, turned, wriggled and, finally, started to get comfortable. As she drifted off to sleep, Olivia sensed movement in the far reaches of Brianna's expansive bedroom.

"Hello?" Olivia called out.

No response. Just the sound of a girl screaming on the TV downstairs.

Again, the air moved.

"Who's there?" she asked. Olivia unsuccessfully tried to lift her arms and head from the mummy-like yardage of sheets and the white fabric of her slip that had encircled her limbs and torso like a malevolent wisteria vine. She got one arm free and pulled off the eye mask. Olivia looked over. Silver glinted in the darkness as a shadowy figure moved toward her.

"Who are you?" she asked, still unable to see a face. Olivia was annoyed, but not unnerved. It was, after all, a party. Whoever it was might be looking for a place to crash just like she had when the beer hit her. Or maybe it was a Halloween prank? The living room and family room downstairs were full of kids looking to be the center of attention. Fighting to make an impression. Tweeted about. Facebooked.

"This isn't funny," she said, in her clipped accent.

It wasn't. Not at all.

It happened so fast, the way awful things almost always do. The mattress dipped under the weight of another person kneeling on the bed. The first cut wasn't the deepest. It was tentative, a slight jab through the snow-white fabric just above her navel.

"Hey! Stop!" Olivia cried.

Her voice, loud as it was, was lost in the sounds of the music and laughter downstairs. If anyone had heard her muffled scream, they might have mistaken it for that terrified teen with the fake boobs on the enormous plasma TV in the family room where half the partygoers congregated.

Yet there was nothing fake about Olivia Grant or the fear that seized her. Her manicured fingertips found her abdomen. She pressed it lightly with the heel of her palm and cried out in pain. She barely had time to process the fact that her hand was wet.

All too quickly, someone was on top of her, holding her arms down. Everything conspired against her. Her flowing slip, Brianna's bedding, the eye mask, and even her long red hair entwined in her attacker's fist gave her little hope of escape.

Is this a sick joke? Did the geek pirate not understand NO means NO?

Pain shot through the sixteen-year-old's body and she started breathing hard. This was no trick-or-treat prank. Her mind reeled. Olivia thought back to the self-defense moves she had seen on American TV. The key was to have a survival plan, a strategy to save your life. She worked up a scenario to use her knee to shove off her attacker, freeing her arms and scooting to the edge of the bed where she could—just maybe—get away.

But that damn sheet. It was a magician's endless handkerchief. Olivia couldn't move her feet. It was like she'd been spun up in a cocoon. The force of the continued onslaught pushed her, wrappings and all, crashing to the floor.

"Stop it! Stop!" she screamed. "That bloody hurts!"

Despite her beauty, Olivia Grant was no English rose. She was not frail, passive, or genteel. She was a fighter. Finally free, her arms and hands flailed into the darkness. Once, twice, she was hit by something sharp. Hard. It was hot and agonizing. Olivia realized what was happening was not a prank. She was fighting for her life and she knew it.

Was it a knife? Scissors? A box cutter? Something very sharp and deadly.

It passed through the teen's mind right then that she might never get to Hollywood. She'd never have a real boyfriend. She'd never get back to London. She'd never design that dress that every other girl in the world would covet. Her life and all her big dreams would be extinguished right there in her friend's bedroom.

With everything she had, Olivia lurched herself upright. She ran her bloody hands under her slip as she tried to extricate herself from the shroud, once white, now red.

Tears came as she thought of home. Her mind flashed to a memory. She and her mother were packing her suitcases for the trip in Olivia's bedroom back in London. Her mother implored her not to take her finest things to America, as she was all but certain that they'd be stolen.

"Everyone thinks that Aussies are descended from criminals, but I think there's a mix-up there. Take a look at America's crime rate," her mom had said. She sniffed in that superior-than-thou affect she used whenever the occasion called for it, which was always. "The U.S. is worse than Down Under by far."

She had been right. Her mother, with whom she'd battled about the smallest of things, had been absolutely right.

Just as the lightning bolt of memory passed, a pair of hands grabbed Olivia's shoulders and shoved her body backwards against the wooden floor. Hard and complete. So fast and so slow at the same time. She gasped.

I'm not going to die here, am I? she thought, though the answer seemed all too clear. *Am I?*

Olivia filled her lungs and screamed once more—only to have a wad of fabric violently shoved into her mouth. She started to choke, but she refused to give up. She had come to America to snag a boyfriend, be discovered for the rocking talent that she was, and to import everything she had learned back to the UK. She, most assuredly, had not come to America to die.

Get. Off. Me.

The teenager felt hot breath against her face. It came at her in quick puffs and it smelled of beer. *Jason? Kurt? All the boys had been drinking. It could be any one of a dozen or more.* As Olivia tried to roll away from her attacker, the blade of a knife flew at her, burying itself in her throat. It came with speed and fury.

Just like that.

Over.

Out.

In a second, blood soaked the fabric gagging her, slipping over her tongue with a peculiar metallic taste as it spilled from the corners of her mouth like candle wax.

In the final beats of her life, Olivia Grant caught a glimpse of her killer. Like a camera with a fading battery, her green eyes captured the image until they could no longer see.

Only her killer knew the irony of her last words.

That bloody hurts.

chapter 2

TAYLOR RYAN WOKE UP WITH A START. Something was very, very wrong. She gazed out into the blackness through her bedroom window overlooking Port Gamble Bay. It was *that* again. The feeling she could never explain to anyone. The same feeling that only her twin sister Hayley also felt: a gentle but unmistakable wave like low-level electrical current that most might not even notice. The last time it had come over her—or at least the most memorable time—was Christmas night the previous year. That was the night that Katelyn Berkley, just fifteen years old, had died.

Without reaching for her robe, the sixteen-year-old walked toward the window. It was so cold in her little upstairs bedroom that she could almost see her breath. She made a mental note to ask for a space heater for Christmas. At the foot of her bed, the family dachshund, Hedda, lifted her head and then dropped it back down. Whatever Taylor was doing apparently held no interest for the world's laziest dog.

The bay was empty and its surface was a stark sheet of glass. Taylor leaned closer, and her breath condensed on the wavy vintage glass of the house built in 1859. A perfect circle appeared. *A circle?* Then just as quickly as it had come, it vanished. That feeling, a strange urgency that came from nowhere, also evaporated.

Taylor went back to bed and let out a sigh, thinking back on the Halloween party earlier that evening. Brianna had billed it as the party of the year. Her dad and stepmom were away on a cruise, and she had raided their liquor cabinet. Virtually everyone from Kingston High was there and in costume, including a few crashers from another school. She and Hayley had gone as the Olsen twins and had lacquered on layers of mascara and eye shadow, never once letting on to their parents that they were going to sneak their first drinks that night. In the end, it wasn't as exciting as she had thought. Watching a few drunken teenagers act stupid and throw up everywhere wasn't exactly her idea of fun. She switched to soda pop early in the evening.

Around midnight, it became obvious that her best friend, Beth Lee, had seen better days. Despite the fact that it was Halloween, a quasi-holiday, they still had school the next day. The four of them—she; Hayley; Hayley's boyfriend, Colton; and Beth—had decided to leave even though it looked like the party would rage on for hours.

Taylor knew she was going to feel like crap in the morning. The only solace that came to her at that moment was fleeting. She figured Beth, who had a lot more to drink, would look far worse. The irony of that, of course, was that Beth Lee didn't give a crap what anyone thought about her.

She just didn't.

Taylor burrowed back under the heavy blankets and turned to the wall that separated her room from her sister's. With her free hand, she swiveled the plastic cover away from the spot where there had once been an electrical outlet. The outlet cover in her sister's room was already open.

"Something's happening, Hayley."

Taylor heard a shifting of sheets and felt the vibration of her sister as she rolled closer to the wall.

"I know," Hayley answered. "I've been thinking about it since we got home. Something's up. Brianna was in rare form at the party and Beth's definitely gonna be grounded for life, but it's more than that." She hesitated before saying it out loud. "The last time I felt this was when Katelyn died."

Just inches apart, Hayley faced her sister through the hole in the old plaster-and-lath wall. Her head was on a cloud of goose-down, a pillow that accompanied her on every sleepover she'd ever been to. Hayley was a mirror image of her sister. Winter-white skin. Long, messy blond hair. Blue eyes. At sixteen, the girls had a bond greater than mere sisterhood, greater than twinship and all that comes with being so, so close to another human being. The sisters also shared an ability to somehow see letters in signs or headlines rearrange themselves into words that revealed important messages. It always creeped them out a little when that happened. Even more unnerving, in the direst of circumstances, just by touching certain objects they could conjure images and memories that were not their own. They never told anyone about those incidents. *Who would believe them?*

And while they didn't understand it and were certainly unable to control it, the girls were digging in deep to find ways to accept whatever it was. They saw it as more than the ability to sense something; it was the ability to decipher what was happening now, and sometimes what had happened in the past, in a way that others could not. It was as if they were able to catch a whisper from the wind.

Freakish? Sure. Different from others? Absolutely. Whatever it was that passed through them bound them closer together and shut out others, including their best friend, Beth Lee, and Hayley's boyfriend, Colton James.

As the rain pelted the rippled windowpanes and the wind scraped a dead branch from an overgrown rhododendron against the espresso brown siding of house number 19, the Ryan sisters talked into the early morning hours.

All without uttering a single word.

THE 911 CALL CAME IN AROUND 2 A.M., the time the bars closed—always a busy hour for the Kitsap County law enforcement communications center in Bremerton, the region's largest city. The comm center's dispatcher on duty was Sally Marie Butterworth, a twenty-eight-year-old mother of two who liked working nights so that she and her husband, a navy yard pipefitter, never had to put their son and daughter in what they considered "prison for tots," or the local daycare center.

Sally had taken a number of 911 calls that Halloween, including a doozy about a tipped-over jack-o'-lantern that had ignited a two-alarm blaze and torched five cars at the Mariner's Glen apartment complex off Jackson in Port Orchard. A call from Chico had buzzed through around eleven o'clock from a woman who was suspicious about a homemade treat:

> CALLER: *My daughter brought home a popcorn ball that I think might be laced with something.*
> SALLY: *Is your daughter ill?*
> CALLER: *No, ma'am, she's not. I wouldn't let her eat it.*
> SALLY: *What makes you think the popcorn ball has drugs?*
> CALLER: *I just don't trust the person who made it. She's total trailer trash.* (Slightly muffled) *Amber Marie, get that cat off the stove!*
> SALLY: *Why don't you throw it away?*
> CALLER: (Long pause, the tinkling of ice cubes in a glass) *I guess I could do that. Good idea.*

Sally Butterworth disconnected the line and her eyes rolled upward in their sockets to the ceiling. She hated being called "ma'am" by someone who was probably her same age. She also wondered why people didn't just use common sense. The way Sally saw it, if she had a dollar for every idiotic call she received, she would already own that candy-apple red Nissan Juke she'd had her eye on.

The line buzzed again. Sally set down her Aquafina, adjusted her headset, and answered:

SALLY: *What's your emergency?*

CALLER: *It's really bad, I think. My friend is all bloody. Really, really hurt. Help me. Help us. This is really bad.*

SALLY: *Tell me your name and where you're calling from.*

CALLER: *Brianna Connors. I'm at 2121 Desolation View Drive in Port Gamble. Can't you just Google Map me or something?*

SALLY: *Help is on the way, Brianna. Can you tell me your friend's name and what happened?*

CALLER: *Her name is Olivia Grant. She's an exchange student from England. I don't know what happened. She was fine. Really. We were all at my house for a Halloween party. During the party, I went upstairs to check on her and to switch costumes. She was asleep on my bed. She didn't answer when I said her name. I figured she was drunk, so I went back downstairs again. When I came back to my room again after everyone left, she was on the floor and she wasn't moving. And then I saw the blood.*

SALLY: *Where is the blood?*

CALLER: *All over. I don't know what happened to her. I think she's been cut up or something. It's super nasty.*

SALLY: *Who else is there? Your parents?*

CALLER: *My dad and stepmom are on a cruise. My boyfriend's here. You want to talk to him?*

SALLY: *What is he doing?*

CALLER: *Watching TV, I think. I dunno. Just send someone.*

SALLY: *Can you check to see if Olivia's breathing?*

CALLER: *I already checked. She's not. I don't think she is. Hang on. . . . Drew, she wants you to check to see if she's breathing.*

BOY: (In the background, but audible) *I'm not going to do that. She's your friend and it's your bedroom, Bree.*

CALLER: *You are a lot of help, Drew.*

SALLY: *Brianna, are you still there?*

CALLER: *Yes. I hear the sirens. Do you want me to stay on the phone?*

SALLY: *No, you can hang up. Law enforcement is there. The ambulance is a minute behind the police.*

CALLER: *Ciao.*

Sally logged the end of the call on her computer screen.

Ciao? Really?

The 911 dispatcher wasn't sure exactly what was going on up there in the northern edge of the county, but if there really was a dead girl on the floor—and if this wasn't some teenager's Halloween prank—the incident was going to be newsworthy. The caller's attitude had struck Sally as atypical. She seemed more annoyed than upset. It was also strange that she wouldn't confirm if her friend was breathing. She had asked her boyfriend to do it. *Her boyfriend?* While Brianna Connors was on the phone making a 911 call, she said her boyfriend was watching TV.

Who watches TV with a dead girl in the next room? What was up with that?

MOST OF THE KIDS FROM PORT GAMBLE coveted a house like Brianna Connors's place on Desolation View Drive, a couple of miles outside the historic district off the highway to Kingston. Perched on a craggy bluff overlooking Puget Sound, it was a three-story mega-home built of the finest materials: western red cedar beams on a football field of travertine. Her father was a stub of man, a lawyer who apparently needed to show the world that he'd made it. Big-time. He wore a different Armani suit every day, and parked his Lamborghini in the three-car garage next to his two limited edition Porsche Boxsters that he only drove on rare sunny days. Yet none of that was what the Port Gamble crowd envied most about the Connors. It was that the house was new in a town full of vintage homes whose doors didn't shut tightly, whose uneven floorboards could send a skateboard across a room without even the slightest push. In Brianna's house, weather-sealed, double-paned windows held the heat inside where it belonged, instead of leaking icy air through handblown glass windows as it did in most of the houses in Port Gamble. Everything about the Connors's place, like Brianna herself, was unqualified perfection.

Everything, of course, except for the dead girl in the upstairs bedroom soaked in her own blood.

Brianna Connors and Drew Marcello huddled together outside in the damp air as crime-scene investigators went about their business inside the mega-home with the killer view. A reporter from the *North Kitsap Herald* had already arrived and was taping the goings-on with a tiny video camera, capturing footage he'd likely upload on the newspaper's website before sunrise.

Drew, wearing jeans and a dark-blue hoodie, slung his arm around Brianna. She was trembling and he kissed her gently at first on the cheek, then with more passion on the lips.

Port Gamble S'Klallam Tribal Police chief Annie Garnett was a dominating presence at just under six feet tall, with a cascade of black hair spun up under a knit cap to ward off the chill and to hide what no stylist could fix in a middle-of-the-night roust from bed. She interrupted the kiss as she approached the pair across the darkened lawn.

"Brianna, you told the responding officers that your parents aren't home?" Annie asked.

The crime scene was inside Annie's jurisdiction, but her police force was small. Kitsap County Sheriff's Department deputies and coroner's personnel were also on the scene to deal with the violent death of a teen girl. Annie knew that none of them was thrilled to be there—and it wasn't because it was so early in the morning.

None of them ever liked to deal with a murder of someone so young.

Brianna pushed Drew away and shook her head. "Dad and step-monster are on vacation. Acapulco or St. Croix. My mom lives in Seattle. I called her and she's taking the first boat over here."

"All right. When did you call her?" Annie asked.

Brianna watched a pair of uniformed county deputies unfurl yellow crime-scene tape and attach it to a post and then around the fountain and on to the Japanese maple tree that framed the view of the gazebo. "Right before I called 911."

"Why didn't you call for an ambulance first?" Annie asked.

Brianna looked at the police chief steadily, her large eyes the startling green of a traffic light. "Because I kicked Olivia pretty hard with my foot and she didn't move at all. She was probably totally dead. What good would an ambulance have done?"

The police chief made a note in a little black, leather-clad book. The book hadn't been used in a while, but she knew this case would require extra care. It was tragic and messy. Parents gone. Alcohol and possibly drugs. Decedent from another country.

Annie turned to Drew. "And you? Were you already here?"

"No way," Drew said. "Bree called me, and I drove like hell. I live ten miles away. Got back here in less than five minutes, which is my personal best." He gripped Brianna's right hand and she pulled away, flinching, before shoving it into the pocket of her fluffy Victoria's Secret Pink robe.

"Do you have Olivia's parents' phone number?" Annie asked.

"Oh, God, no," Brianna said, pulling her robe tighter to stave off the chilly air. A small bit of blood speckled the robe's trim. Brianna was a stunner. She had a heart-shaped face and big green eyes that somehow managed to be alert and evasive at the same time. Her hair was long, a dark shade of blond with—at least in that darkened light of night—an auburn cast. Not burgundy. Not red. "They live in London or Liverpool or somewhere. She's a foreign-exchange student. She's staying with Beth Lee and her mom in Port Gamble."

Annie knew all that, but she let Brianna go on anyway.

"I think I have Beth's number," Brianna said, tucking a long strand of silky hair behind her ear and scrolling through her phone list. "We're not close, not like me and Olivia. I really liked her." Brianna stopped briefly to respond to a text someone had just sent and then continued searching through what seemed like the longest contact list ever.

"Found it," she said, finally. She held up her phone to give Annie the number. The police chief tried very hard not to lose her patience with Brianna, who, as insensitive as she was, might have been the very last person to see Olivia before the murder. What Brianna had to say, what Brianna had *seen*, was crucial.

chapter 3

KITSAP COUNTY DETECTIVES SCOURED every inch of the Connorses' cavernous living room. It appeared to be more of a shrine than a living room. There were photos of Brianna everywhere. None of her dad. None of the woman in his life. None of her mother. There was Brianna on a horse. Brianna at the Venetian in Las Vegas. Brianna in pigtails. Brianna. Brianna. Brianna. Besides serving as center stage in *The Brianna Show*, it was obvious that the room had been built, designed, and decorated to impress. All the furnishings were white and modern. With its pair of white leather Barcelona chairs facing the inky night waters of Puget Sound, it almost had the vibe of an upscale dental office, the kind where teeth whitening comes free with the first visit.

Now, however, the room looked like a frat house after a Friday night. Someone had stacked up seven red plastic cups on a window ledge. The luxurious white leather couch with matching throw pillows (not too many to be annoying, but not too few so as to accommodate slouching) was thrown together by someone who didn't know that the zipper ends of the cushions should face inside. Pizza boxes, chip bags, and some kind of cheese dip that had congealed in its microwavable plastic container indicated that despite the tony address, the party was decidedly downscale.

As the detectives moved methodically through the still life of the party's aftermath, they photographed and bagged anything that might have DNA on it. Everything else was coated and brushed with carbon so fingerprint comparisons could be made. Their goal was twofold: collect evidence and find the murder weapon.

From the looks of the slash and puncture wounds on Olivia's body, the forensics team suspected that a knife had killed her. They found a potential clue in the kitchen. Next to the Viking range was a hand-oiled ebony and rosewood knife block designed to hold eight high-end knives. One slot was an open void, almost winking at everyone who came into the kitchen to notice a knife was missing.

"Big knife," a tech said, looking at the slot.

"Little girl," Annie Garnett replied, as she surveyed the huge white room.

A keg on the kitchen counter and more of those obligatory red cups indicated that the party drink of choice had been beer.

No surprise there.

"Seems like beer wasn't all that they were doing here," one detective said as he carefully put a clip with the remnant of a marijuana cigarette into a police issued evidence bindle, marking it with the time, place, and location of its collection.

"Yeah. Found a couple of them in the bathroom too," replied another.

"Jeez. In my day a party was a six-pack of beer, and when we ran out of that we watched TV."

"You're dating yourself. Kids today are different. They party hard."

"Mine don't," said a tech dusting a glass-topped coffee table near the fireplace.

The police officers glanced over in his direction but said nothing. It was well known in Kitsap law enforcement that the tech's eldest daughter *did* party hard and probably needed to be in rehab.

Despite the mess and garbage, there was one item that caught everyone's attention. It was the only thing that really looked out of place, the only thing that indicated that something might have been amiss at the party aside from the dead girl upstairs. On the honed travertine floor were several glittery shards of broken glass.

A tech wielding a camera looked down at the sharp splinters of glass against the coffee-with-cream toned floor. "Think a vase fell off the shelf?" she asked, flashing the camera's strobe. "Maybe a kid bumped into it."

Another tech standing nearby didn't think so. "Looky here," he said, sweeping his arms over the space where the glass sparkled like a Gaga headpiece. "There's no way someone just knocked a vase over. Someone threw it. And they threw it hard."

"Glass all the way over there," said another deputy. "There's a small dent in the wall too."

"Yup," said the tech with the camera. "That's right. Someone threw it like a bomb. Looks like we've got blood on this piece."

More photographs were taken. Each came with a tiny identifier so that later, when the crime wound its way to court, those images could be used for evidentiary purposes.

If it made it that far. And, of course, if the broken vase had anything to do with the homicide.

UPSTAIRS THREE PEOPLE STOOD next to Brianna's bed: a Kitsap County detective, a newbie crime-scene investigator, and Dr. Birdy Waterman, the county's forensic pathologist. Their eyes scanned every inch of the room, better, and with more precision than an Epson set at its finest calibration. No one said much of anything as they went about their work. They simply took it all in, made notes, and snapped photos, recording everything as it was—or at least as it appeared to be.

They couldn't help bringing their mundane observations to the scene:

I have a bed set like that. It's Ralph Lauren, Detective Sheila Walton thought. *Hated fussing with those pillow shams.*

Duane Bonner, the newest forensic tech, focused on the movie poster hanging on Brianna's wall and snapped a few shots.

Nice! She's a Hunger Games *fan!*

But to Birdy, who had seen plenty of bodies during her tenure in the coroner's office, this scene in particular was harder to take than most.

Tangled in the sheets on the hardwood floor, Olivia's body resembled a bloody and broken doll. The sheets were a deep crimson. The bloom of blood from Olivia's chest had wicked its way into nearly every fiber of the five-hundred-thread-count fabric. It was the smell that gave it away. A coppery, acrid odor permeated the room. Brianna Connors's room smelled of fresh blood. Lots of it.

The tech pushed aside what looked like a *Star Wars* costume and a sparkly white gown and picked up a lacy thong from Brianna's bedroom floor. He held it up like a frilly white flag of victory.

The detective's blood simmered. *That idiot picked it up with his bare hands.*

"You'd better hope that thong has nothing to do with this crime, because you just broke protocol big-time, Bonner," Detective Walton said.

He looked up with big, dopey eyes. "Right. Sorry," he said. "You don't have to get all technical with me."

Being technical was their job, but Birdy didn't say anything. So many people had traipsed through the crime scene that it was going to be difficult to sift out what was what. And, more important, who was who.

Everyone there knew that Bonner was the grandson of a former—and beloved—Seattle police chief. Bonner was the worst tech in Washington State, maybe even the whole West Coast, and had the job only as a favor to someone in power. Favor or not, if he screwed up again as he had with a drug case last month, he was out. The justice system will only tolerate a few screw-ups.

Birdy and Bonner continued to document the scene.

Flash.

Flash.

Flash.

And then Olivia's remains were maneuvered into the dark folds of a neoprene fabric body bag.

"What's in her mouth?" a husky voice asked.

Birdy looked up to see the concerned face of Port Gamble's police chief.

"Hi, Annie. I didn't hear you come in. Did you know the victim?" Birdy asked, now looking more closely at the dead girl's mouth. "Anything about her?"

Annie kept her cap on but loosened the collar of her heavy winter coat. Perspiration had beaded along her brow. She hated being over-heated, as it caused her hastily applied makeup to run. She'd always applied it with a heavy hand; she simply didn't have a lot to work with and needed whatever help Maybelline could provide.

"Olivia's from London. She's here with See America Studies. Staying with Kim and Beth Lee," Annie said. "We never really talked, but I heard she was a nice girl."

"They always are," Birdy said.

She reached for a small flashlight and pointed the beam of light directly at Olivia's bloodied lips. There was definitely a foreign object protruding. It looked like fabric.

"It appears she was gagged," Birdy said.

Annie inched closer. "Do we have a BTK type out here?" she asked, thinking back on the file of a serial killer from Kansas known for his tactics: Bind, Torture, Kill.

"Too soon to say," Birdy answered, though she highly doubted it. There had not been any obvious indicators that Olivia's arms or legs had been tied. There were no ligature marks on her wrists and ankles that she could see with the naked eye. UV light would be used back at the morgue when she did her exam.

The police chief bent down to get a better view of Olivia's mouth just as the bag was zipped closed. "Looks like the tail end of a man's necktie." Annie looked up at Birdy, then the cadre of investigators. "No one says a word about this. Understood?"

Her heart raced. In her years as the police chief, she had yet to handle a murder. Tragedy, yes. Deadly accidents, of course. But this was the first time in a long while that deliberate, violent evil had come knocking on a door in Port Gamble. As she pondered the reality of Olivia's homicide, she could only vaguely recall one other murder in the town's recent history. Fifteen years prior, a twelve-year-old newspaper boy named Joshua Archer had been abducted and murdered by a TV repairman. His mutilated body was found in an abandoned freezer in the earthen basement of the dreary, slate-gray house number 27.

ANNIE RETURNED DOWNSTAIRS to find Brianna and Drew on a bench in the foyer. The young couple had found refuge there from the chilly night air and the horde of investigators crawling around the house and yard. The two had expressions that were a mix of worry and fear colored by the greenish cast of a seedling hangover. Drew stood as the police chief came into view. Brianna kept her chin cradled in the palm of her hand.

"We found a shattered vase over in the den. Looks expensive. Do you know what happened to it?" Annie asked.

Brianna lifted her head and looked at Annie, tracking her with bleary eyes. "Yeah, one of those bonehead kids crashed into it at the party. It was my stepmom's fave too," she said.

"All right, an accident, then . . ." Annie said. "Were there any other accidents or fights I should know about?"

"Don't think so," Brianna replied.

No drama at a teen kegger? Not likely, Annie thought but said, "Well, we're just about done up there. Now I need you to tell me exactly what happened. Tell me how you found Olivia. Be as descriptive as possible. If you're up to it, it would be even better if you showed me."

"Showed you?" Brianna asked.

Annie nodded. "It would be extremely helpful in our investigation."

"Like . . . acting out what happened?"

"Not really acting it out, but pointing out where you were standing, how you found her, what you did."

The three of them headed to the staircase just as Birdy's team made its way down. As the teens hung back, Olivia's shrouded body was rolled onto a folding gurney at the top of the stairs. Bonner and another deputy carried her down the steps.

"Bye, Olivia," Brianna said and then skipped up the stairs, two at a time.

Moonlight poured all over the floor and onto Brianna Connors's bed. The bare branches of the maple outside the window made a spiderweb pattern on the mattress. Her Felix the Cat wall clock indicated it was after four in the morning.

The police chief studied the teenager. Like many girls with divorced parents, Brianna had learned how to command attention in any circumstance. With Drew hanging in the background, Brianna put her hand on her hip and surveyed her bedroom from the doorway. Her eyes landed on the bloody spot on the floor where Olivia had bled out.

"You guys are going to clean up this mess, aren't you?" she asked.

Annie shook her head. "Sorry. We don't offer that service."

"Don't you have a housekeeper?" Drew asked Brianna.

"Yeah, but she only comes three times a week. And she won't be here tomorrow. She said her mom or someone in her family is sick. I doubt it, though. She's a little liar."

"Brianna," Annie started to explain, "this is a crime scene. You won't be able to have your room back until we've done all of our work here."

Brianna made a face. "Oh, crap," she said, pulling the robe tighter around her thin frame. "That's just perfect. What am I supposed to do? This isn't fair. This is *my* room. Can I at least get some jeans and a new top?"

Annie nodded at the deputy.

"These okay?" he asked, grabbing a white sweater and a pair of brown-dyed Mek jeans from underneath a white ghost costume strewn over a chair on the other side of the room.

"Not those! I wore those yesterday."

"It will have to do for now," he said. "We can't compromise the scene."

"Can't I just get something from over there?" Brianna said, pointing to the dresser across the room.

"I'm afraid not. Maybe a little later. Let's zero in on what's important. Tell me what happened," Annie said, this time with an edge to her voice. "When did you come upstairs?"

Brianna thought for a second. "I came up to my room three times. The first time was early in the party—to ditch my mail-order bride costume and put on regular clothes. The bride dress was totally itchy—covered in all these scratchy little sequins, plus all the guys kept trying to put postage stamps all over me. The second time I came up to find Olivia. She was in my bed, and I thought I could hear her snoring. I called her name, but she didn't answer. Anyway, she looked okay to me, so I put on a different costume and went back downstairs. When everyone had left, I came up to make sure Olivia was okay, and that's when I found her on the floor."

"Do you know if anyone else came up here?" Annie asked.

"How would I know? I was the hostess. I barely had time to pee," she said. "Let me think a sec. No, I don't know if anyone else came up. Maybe Beth Lee. She and Olivia had a fight earlier in the night."

"Do you know what it was about?" Annie asked.

Brianna handed the jeans and sweater to Drew. "About my friendship with Olivia. About Drew picking up Olivia for the party. About whatever. Beth was jealous of us. It doesn't faze me. I'm used to it."

Annie nodded. *I'm sure you are.*

"Everyone's jealous of Bree," Drew said, tucking the clothes under his arm, and looking like he'd rather be just about anywhere else right then. A safe bet for sure.

"You said you kicked Olivia to see if she was asleep," Annie said to Brianna. "Was that the first or second time you came up?"

"The second time," Brianna said.

Annie positioned her body between the bed and Brianna. "Did you kick her hard?"

"Yeah, I think so."

"Why did you kick her? Why not just tap her on the shoulder?"

Brianna held up her left hand. Her glossy nails gleamed with an icy-blue hue. "Because I'd just done these, that's why."

Annie looked at Brianna's hand and nodded. *Who does their nails at two in the morning?*

"What about you, Drew?"

"Like I said before," Drew answered, "I wasn't here. I went home with everyone else. I didn't find anybody dead. That's all on Bree."

chapter 4

THE PORT GAMBLE S'KLALLAM TRIBAL Police Department had been housed in the same building for more than forty years. It was in the basement of what the locals called "the old post office," a large wood-framed structure that at one time or another accommodated not only the post office but also the morgue, the town's first hospital, and even the community theater. Annie Garnett's office was one of three dedicated to law and order in the historic town. The other two belonged to her deputy, a part-timer named Stephen Shields, and an office administrator and records clerk named Tatiana Jones.

Chief Garnett had driven Brianna and Drew to the police department so they could provide full statements while the events were fresh—and hopefully before anyone had a chance to change a story or make up a new one. Neither teen had liked being in the back of her police car, and their separate interrogation rooms weren't giving them the warm fuzzies either.

Annie started with Brianna and offered her a soda, but she declined.

"I'm tired, and this whole thing has been a total nightmare," Brianna said. "Like, I just want to get this over with. This wasn't how I wanted my party to end, you know?"

Annie ignored the comment. No one wants a party to end in a bloody stabbing. She placed a yellow legal pad on the table at the exact moment Brianna's phone buzzed.

"Is it your mother?" she asked.

Brianna scrolled through her text messages. She made a face. "No surprise. She missed the boat. She'll have to take the next ferry."

"Do you want to wait for her?" Annie asked.

"No," she said. "I want to go to bed. But not my bed. My entire room needs to be taken to a landfill." She put down her phone. "I was ready for a change anyway."

"Is there anyone else I can call for you, Brianna?" the police chief asked. Her concern for the girl was genuine. Besides her work in law enforcement, Annie had given her time to coaching, mentoring, and speaking at conferences on behalf of young people whenever she could.

Brianna shook her head. "No. Dad's off with dumb-dumb and my mom will get here as soon as she can. I just want this night to end."

"I know this has been a terrible ordeal for you."

"It has been the worst. The worst *ever*. The party was so fun and then this happens. It just isn't fair."

"Murder is never fair, Brianna."

"I don't need a lecture. Don't misconstrue what I'm saying here, officer."

"Chief, please," Annie said, gently.

"People are so hung up on their titles," Brianna said, her tone a little smug, living up to her stereotype of an entitled rich kid with as much warmth as a vodka luge.

"About Olivia," Annie said, getting the interview back on track.

"She was cool. I liked her accent. She came to my party, and someone killed her. That's all I know."

"Fine," Annie said. "Let's dig a little deeper. You said Drew and Olivia came to the party together?"

Brianna fiddled with her phone. "Drew picked her up," she said. "I was busy getting things ready. She didn't want to wait for Beth and the other Port Gamble losers."

Annie kept her expression flat. "Which Port Gamble 'losers' are you referring to?"

"Colton James, Beth Lee, and those genetic copies, Hayley and Taylor Ryan."

"Was she not getting along with them?"

"She told me Beth was miffed that she wouldn't wait for her little clique. They had a big fight."

"All right. Do you know if Olivia had any enemies?"

"She wasn't here long enough. Look, she was pretty. She was smart. All the boys thought she was a supermodel in the making, and the girls wanted to talk fashion with her. She actually had an Alexander McQueen purse. That's the Holy Grail. Harder to get than a Birkin, you know."

Annie nodded, though she really didn't know. Her idea of designer goods was what she could find on the clearance table at Shelly's Tall Girl shop at the mall. "She sounds like a nice girl," she said.

"She was nice. I liked her. We were best friends. Well, I was her best friend anyway. She was so new, you know?"

"Kids at the party were using drugs and drinking, right?" Annie asked in her calmest, most nonjudgmental voice.

Brianna flinched. "You can do whatever you want in your own home. I didn't provide any booze or drugs. If kids were drinking and getting baked, that's not my fault. I provided snacks and stuff. That's not against the law."

"This isn't about your party and what snacks you served, Brianna. It is about the death of your friend, Olivia."

Brianna looked at her phone again, fingers almost twitching to touch the screen. It was clear right then to Annie that Brianna's phone was an extension of herself. It reminded her of her last visit to the Olive Garden in Silverdale. Two girls sat across from each other, but barely spoke. Instead, between all the breadsticks they could eat, they texted and Facebooked.

"Yeah, I get that," Brianna said. "I just don't like the way you're treating me. You're being inappropriate and making me uncomfortable. I know when I'm being bullied. Bullying, in case you haven't heard, is a serious problem. I've watched some videos on YouTube."

Annie tried to ignore the remark. *This girl is a self-centered, condescending brat.*

"At some point in the evening," Annie said, "Olivia went upstairs to your room? Tell me about that once more."

"She said she was feeling sick. I don't know why. She wasn't *that* drunk. My dad's wife, Shelley, is a total boozer. I know what wasted looks like. Are we done now?"

Annie pushed a pad and pencil toward Brianna. "Almost," she said. "I need a list of all the kids who attended the party."

"Look, I can give you some names but not all of them. We had some crashers. People always want to come to my parties, and when they show up uninvited, I sometimes let them in. It's my way of giving back. You know, inspiring kids who don't know what to aspire to."

Annie smiled—a forced one, but a smile nevertheless.

Brianna jotted down a list of names, then stopped a beat. She looked Annie in the eyes before going on. "Don't get me wrong. I like to help everyone, even those who live a little on the fringe. I don't mind the fringe. Though, I'm sure some people do."

"What happened to your hand?" Annie pointed to a thin red gash on the palm of the teen's right hand.

"Oh, that? That's nothing. Paper cut," Brianna said flatly. She looked Annie straight in the eye as if daring her to push further.

The two sized each other up for a long minute before Annie ended the discussion.

"That's all for now, Brianna. You can go," Annie said.

"How am I supposed to get home?"

"You can't go home right now. Your house is a crime scene."

Brianna glared at the police chief. "Great! I didn't do anything and I can't even go home."

"Can you stay with a friend? Drew's folks?"

Brianna, distracted by the vibration of her phone, shook her head. "Never mind. I'll figure something out. I always do."

"I'm sure you will. Let me know if I can help."

Annie wrote down Brianna's answers while the teenager turned her attention back to her phone and immersed herself in Twitter:

> @ police dept. Totally sux having a murder committed at
> your party! Please RT. #partyruinedbymurder

After she finished, Brianna stood up, stretched, and did a couple of yoga poses in the small, cramped office.

"Crap," she said loud enough for anyone to hear. "This whole thing has really upset me. I'm completely out of it."

Annie watched as the teenager dropped into the Downward Dog pose. While a zillion things were competing for focus in her mind as they always did in the first moments of a criminal investigation, one thought decisively shoved all of the others aside: *Who on God's green earth does yoga when their friend has just been killed?*

AT LEAST ON THE SURFACE OF THINGS, Andrew Marcello was one of those kids others couldn't help but envy. He had his own car, a traditional family, a nice house, and, probably most important, a hot girlfriend. His mother, Marsha, was an administrator for the North Kitsap School District and his father, Chase, was a three-term Kitsap County Superior Court judge. Although Drew spent most of his childhood in the Kingston area, there was a period of two years in which he lived in California with an aunt. He called it his "So Cal sabbatical from Kidnap County." Although he was eighteen, Drew told everyone that he was a year younger. He didn't want the other kids to know that he'd been held back and had to repeat the second grade.

Drew was attractive, but the bleary, fluorescent overhead lighting in the interrogation room didn't do him any justice. He had dark hair, dark eyes, and a pug nose almost too small for his face. Over his right pec was a tattoo of a fleur-de-lis, a gift to himself in honor of his Italian heritage. His parents didn't have the heart to tell their less-than-brilliant son that the design he'd had inked permanently on his body was French, not Italian. No one in the Marcello household liked to push or prod Drew. When he was calm, he was much easier to deal with.

"Yes, Chief," he said to Annie Garnett's request to take a seat for the interview. He waited a beat for her to sit first.

Annie was unsure if the teenager was trying to be polite or if he was using her title in sarcasm.

"All right, Drew," she said. "Let's talk about what happened tonight."

Drew shrugged and pulled on the zipper on his hoodie, revealing a Kingston High Buccaneers red and gold T-shirt. "Fine, but, if you don't mind, my dad says that kids don't have to talk without their parents being here. My dad's Chase Marcello, the judge. Maybe you've heard of him?"

"I've heard of your father. You're not a minor, Drew," Annie said. "You're eighteen."

"My dad says it's never good to talk to the police without a lawyer."

Annie kept her emotions in check. The kid was a piece of work, but he was right. "Understood. Are you requesting a lawyer? Or would you like me to phone your father at this hour?"

Drew glowered a little. "Nah. Not really."

Annie dropped a new pad on the table and reached for a pen. With her perfect, deliberate penmanship she recorded Drew's version of the events of the evening: who came to the party, who shouldn't have been there, and if he knew of any reason why Olivia Grant had been murdered.

After a series of answers that varied from "I don't know" to "I don't remember," and to "I was kind of wasted" to "I didn't see anything freaky," Drew said, "I wish I could help. I know it would be the right thing to do. Really, I do get that. But I don't know anything." He paused and surveyed the room. "There were a couple of kids dressed up as

Occupy protestors. Tim and Ken or something like that. Maybe they know something. I've seen them around at school."

Annie wrote down the names. "Did they cause any kind of trouble?" she asked.

"Nah. They drank some beer and, if anything, bored a couple of girls."

"Did everyone get along that night?" she asked.

"Yeah. There wasn't anything out of the ordinary. Not for a party. A couple of guys got into it over something, a girl, a car, I dunno. No one punched anyone. Brianna asked me to get them out of there, and I did. They said something about Bree being totally mean, but I didn't argue. Sometimes she *is*. She even accused me of having a thing for Olivia— totally ridiculous. Olivia is so not my type."

"When was the last time that you saw Olivia?"

Drew fidgeted with the drawstring of his hoodie. "I hardly saw her at all. She was talking with her friends from Port Gamble—the Ryan twins, Colton James, and Beth Lee, the girl she's been living with. They didn't look like they were having much fun. Especially Beth. I think she had plans to come to the party with Olivia, but it didn't happen. Whatever. It wasn't that big of a deal."

"Olivia was supposed to go with Beth?"

Drew nodded. "Yeah, but I picked her up at the Lee house early. Bree asked me to."

"Was Olivia all right when you got there?"

"To be honest, not really. I'm not sure what it was about. I didn't ask."

"If you didn't talk to her about it, what makes you think something was wrong?"

"She was mad at somebody, all right. That's totally for sure. She said something along the lines of 'If looks could kill, I'd be a dead girl.'"

Annie's pulse quickened. "Kill? Did somebody threaten her?"

Drew shrugged again. "Honestly, it was pretty much a joke. We laughed about it on the way over."

"What else did she say?"

"Nothing. She said nothing. Can I leave now?"

Annie stood and indicated the door. "Thank you, Drew. I know this has been hard."

Drew grinned. "Not that hard. You should try going home late from a party and having my old man question you. *That's* hard. Being questioned about a murder? That's cake."

chapter 5

THE DAY AFTER HALLOWEEN at Kingston High usually saw a mix of nerdy boys bragging about the awesome pranks they'd played on some unsuspecting sap (frequently involving dog poop in a paper bag, toilet paper decorations, and stealing candy—bowl and all—that trusting neighbors left on their front stoops), dorks with taffy stuck in their braces, and weight-watching teachers complaining that they ate their entire leftover stash of Fun Size (or rather, ton-size) Snickers and were now beyond sorry for doing so.

Not this year. Not by a long shot. The morning after Brianna's party, Kingston's gleaming halls were abuzz with decidedly sinister talk. The news started off with a text message from Beth to Hayley and Taylor:

> **BETH:** OMG! OLIVIA WAS KILLED LAST NIGHT.
>
> **HAYLEY:** WTF?
>
> **TAYLOR:** JOKE?
>
> **BETH:** NO. POLICE CAME. KILLED AT BRIANNA'S. DON'T KNOW DEETS. MOM IS CRYING. I AM 2. THIS IS MY FAULT.
>
> **TAYLOR:** NOT UR FAULT.
>
> **BETH:** I SHOULDN'T HAVE LEFT HER. SHE WZ MY RESPONSIBILITY. I SHOULD HAVE BROUGHT HER HOME. I SHOULDN'T HAVE FOUGHT W/HER.
>
> **HAYLEY:** WHAT HAPPENED TO HER? OVERDOSE?
>
> **BETH:** WORSE. STABBED.
>
> **TAYLOR:** HOLY C.

That was followed by a Twitter post, a Facebook firestorm, and mass texting from and to nearly every kid who went to Kingston High

School. While many didn't know her personally, they all had heard what happened and knew who she was: Olivia Grant, the British girl:

KID WITH ASPERGER'S: SHE HAD A NICE SMILE.

JEALOUS GIRL: SHE WAS PRETTY, IN AN OBVIOUS, UNORIGINAL KIND OF WAY.

HORNY BOY: SUCH A WASTE OF HOTNESS.

TEACHER'S AIDE: ☹ SHE WAS SO YOUNG.

Hayley and Taylor stood by their lockers, feeling sick and scared. They had learned the news by text as soon as Beth and her mother had been awakened by police to say that their houseguest would not be coming home. Beth's text was confirmation of what Taylor and Hayley's nighttime silent chatter had been about: something very, very bad had happened. The circle on the windowpane hadn't been a circle, but the letter O.

O for Olivia.

As other students went about their preclass business with the almost electric energy that gossip creates, Hayley and Taylor reviewed everything that had happened the night before. The party. The drinking. The argument.

"Things like that don't happen here," Taylor said.

"You sound like a dimwit who claims that the serial killer next door was nice. Things like this *do* happen here. They happen everywhere, Taylor," Hayley responded.

"I guess you're right," Taylor said.

"The question is, who could have done this to Olivia?" Hayley asked.

"No idea," Taylor said, stowing her swim-team duffel bag in her locker. She stopped and scanned the crowd in the halls. She waited to see if she picked up on anything weirder than usual in the jostling group of high schoolers. Nothing. "The one thing that really scares the crap out of me is that whoever did it is probably someone we know."

"I was thinking the same thing," Hayley said. "We sort of knew everyone who was there. Brianna bragged that hundreds of kids were coming, but really, I'd be surprised if more than fifty were there."

Taylor did a quick mental count. "Forty, I'd say."

"Anybody could have done it—but who did, and why?" Hayley asked. "I don't think I'm going to learn a single thing in class today. Can't concentrate."

"You, me, and the rest of the school."

It was then that the first text message came through to both twins' cell phones. Neither teen recognized the texter's handle or the phone number the message came from:

CASE FILE #613-7H: I KNOW WHO KILLED HER.

The girls read their screens in disbelief. Time froze in the tiled halls of Kingston High. The air stopped moving. It was like a lid had been dropped over them and they were completely and utterly alone.

"Who do you think sent this?" Taylor whispered, an edge of panic in her voice.

"Could be anyone," Hayley said, looking around. "Maybe it's *him*—her killer." She pressed her palm into her stomach. She was sure she was going to hurl and that would not be something she would want to ever, *ever* do at school.

"What should we do? Should we tell someone? Should we text back and find out what they want?"

"No. Remember Dad's rule about texting strangers."

Hayley rolled her eyes at her sister. Their crime-writer dad, Kevin, had drilled it into them in fifth grade when they got their first cell phones. It was a cardinal rule, though the specific number—as he actually and annoyingly numbered his rules—she couldn't recall just then:

"Never respond to someone you don't know. By your answering him, the creep knows that the message was received and could get more aggressive."

"You're right," Taylor said. "It's better not to tell anyone and hope

Text Creeper doesn't text us again . . . the freak. And as much as it unnerves me to get his—"

"—or her," Hayley interrupted.

Taylor nodded. "Right. As much as it unnerves me to get his or *her* texts, we need to figure out who killed Olivia."

"Who," Hayley added, "and why?"

"Are you going to do that all day?" Taylor asked.

"Maybe. I like precision and you know it."

Even if they weren't going to tell their parents about the texter, the girls decided they should share the news about what happened to Olivia before it reached their parents, Valerie and Kevin, through Port Gamble's super-speedy grapevine.

Fifteen minutes before the first bell rang, the twins made the calls. Taylor called their mother, a psychiatric nurse, who was on the ferry headed toward her job at Puget Sound Hospital near Seattle. Because she worked such long hours, it was more like her second home. As the ship's engines roared, Valerie Ryan soothed Taylor the best that she could.

"Are you girls all right?" she asked. "You just saw Olivia last night. You must be so upset. I wish this ferry was coming home."

"It's all right, Mom," Taylor said. "There really isn't anything you can do."

Hayley had their father on her phone.

"Did they arrest someone?" he asked.

"I don't know," Hayley said. "I don't think so. Beth didn't say much."

"How is Beth?" Kevin asked.

"I don't know. We haven't seen her yet today."

Hayley told their father they'd check in later if they heard anything. He said he'd do the same. On her phone, Taylor made the same promise to her mother.

"Love you, Mom," Taylor said.

"Love you, Dad," Hayley said.

The girls put down their phones and started for the restroom. The noise of kids talking was closing in on them, leaving them feeling shaky. They needed a place where they could pull themselves together and regroup.

Taylor, who internalized anxiety and was all but certain she would have an ulcer one day, splashed water on her face. The towel dispenser was empty, and she wasn't about to stick her face in front of the hand drier.

"I can't believe a kid could kill Olivia like that. I didn't think she was here long enough to make enemies," Taylor said, blotting the water with the sleeve of her purple fleece pullover, which was nearly like running a dry paint roller over her face—soft, but not absorbent.

Hayley swiped some concealer at the dark circles under her blue eyes. "I know," she said. "And whoever did it is probably walking the halls right here, right now."

"Maybe," Taylor said. "Maybe not. If I killed someone I wouldn't show up for school twelve hours later. I mean, if I did something that terrible, I would run away or at least need some serious downtime to get my act together."

"Agreed. You would."

Taylor looked at her sister. Sometimes, as smart as Hayley was, she just didn't get the obvious.

"You work in the attendance office, Hayley," she said, pushing the bathroom door open. "Find out who didn't make it in today."

ONE OF THE REASONS HAYLEY RYAN liked working in the high school attendance office was that it appealed to her slight tendency toward OCD. Every day, she got to run through the list of students and check off who was there and who wasn't. The work was mundane but detailed, and Hayley found it extremely satisfying to keep her lists orderly and neat, much like the way organizing her french fries in perfect rows on the plastic tray at McDonald's made her feel. Taylor thought it was a weird, annoying habit. But then again, she had her own food preferences, being a vegetarian who ate chicken and all.

The other reason was that the job was like being in the middle of a reality show. The attendance office was next to the school nurse's office, which afforded the bonus of knowing who was sick, who had cramps, and who was trying to get out of giving a presentation in front of the class. Each morning brought just enough drama to keep the boring parts from being overly so. Kids who had missed the previous day were required to provide a written excuse signed by a parent, a guardian, or in rare cases in which the student had missed five days or more, a doctor.

It didn't take a forensic handwriting expert to figure out when notes were forged:

> *Please excuse Sarah's absence from yesterday. She had the flew.*

The "flew"? What did she do, sprout wings and fly?

When Hayley made the calls to check on kids who weren't in school, following the state law, sometimes she got the kid on the phone. When that happened, the call was predictable. The kid would say their mom was either in the shower, off getting meds at Rite Aid, or asleep. Hayley had been trained not to take no for an answer, but every once in a while she'd let one slide. You never knew when you might need the favor returned. "Attendance Chick," as some boys called her, was decidedly better than "Attendance Bitch."

Hayley sat down in her ergonomically molded chair in the cubicle in front of the vice principal's office. The blonde administrator with an unflappable smile waved a cheery hello to Hayley through the glass and went about her business trying to make everything at Kingston High run as if perfection were a possibility—which, given the daily megadoses of high school drama, it wasn't. Clearly, as indicated by her friendly smile, she hadn't heard about Olivia's murder yet. That was not surprising since the thorny tendrils of gossip tended to stay on Hayley's side of the glass partition.

Adults, Hayley thought, *are always the last to know just about everything.*

Hayley thumbed through the roster of who had been reported absent that morning. Most of the list made complete sense. Alana, the girl who almost never came to school on time, was late again. Her mom was a total freak and never took care of the younger kids, so Alana pulled mom duty at the ripe old age of seventeen because someone in that family had to. Also on the list were a couple of stoner kids who rarely made an appearance—and when they did, they were usually mentally absent anyway. A freshman boy named Cody who was fighting leukemia was out again. Hayley's already gray mood immediately darkened when she saw his name. Cody was a nice kid, and she had heard he was getting better.

She continued her way down the list while the girl she worked with, Tammi Mars, chatted with her college boyfriend like she did every day. Hayley was sure Tammi was checking up on him, because she initiated every call and kept the poor guy on the line for at least twenty minutes every morning.

Hayley's eyes scanned the paper slips that came from each first-period class.

Brianna Connors was a no-show. That made total sense, considering she was the one who had found Olivia's body.

Definitely an excused absence.

Drew Marcello was also gone. That fit. He was probably off some-where consoling Brianna.

Hayley's boyfriend Colton James was marked absent, which she already knew about. He had a dental appointment scheduled that morning.

Beth Lee was out sick. That would have made sense even without a murder. She was probably at home trying to pull herself together after a night of pre-funking with some plum wine and beer at the party.

There were three others, none of whom Hayley recalled being at the party: Susan Finholm, who was getting a nose job *(deviated septum, such a liar!)*; Jacob Wexler, who was competing in the Science Olympiad Nationals in Spokane; and Meghan Aynesworth, whom Hayley had just seen heading toward the mall in her pale green VW bug.

After going through the list of that morning's absentees, Hayley started losing faith in her sister's theory. If the person who killed Olivia was a Kingston High student, then he or she wasn't stressing out too much and skipping class.

chapter 6

FINANCIAL WORRIES WERE A NOOSE around her bony neck and Brianna's mom, Brandy Connors Baker, preferred a strand of pearls over a noose any day. A double strand, ideally black, would be her choice—that is, if she could still afford a choice. Judging by the state of things in her life right then, she couldn't. Brandy had pored over the paperwork that Gloria Piccolo had set out in front of her. It had been an early morning meeting on a gorgeous day in mid-October. The Seattle law office smelled of Starbucks and pastries. Brandy had waved them all away. None of that for her.

Gloria, Brandy's latest lawyer, had marked with bright yellow stickers cut in the shape of arrows all the spaces in which her client needed to sign.

"Sign here, here, and here . . . and over here," the lawyer had said, pointing with a gold Cross pen.

Brandy looked past Gloria, through her expansive window as a familiar white and green Washington State ferry glided through Elliott Bay to Colman Dock. The sight was stunning from the high-rise—even better than the view from the condominium a few blocks away that Brandy could no longer afford.

"I see where to sign, Gloria," Brandy had said, her voice holding a sharp edge.

Gloria ignored the tone of her client's remark. She hadn't worked with Brandy long, but the woman had come with a Ryder truck of personal baggage and was well known in Seattle legal circles as a client who made them earn every second of their billing. Calling Brandy "demanding" was the polite way of calling her impatient, aggressive, and completely unaware that anyone else existed. Because of her obvious and maddeningly overt sense of entitlement, Brandy's downfall had been met with more glee than tears.

"Great," Gloria had said. "But still, as you know, I'm not advising you that this is a good move for you, Brandy."

Brandy stopped the sweeping loops of her signature in midscrawl.

"I don't recall asking your advice a second time," she said.

Gloria had tried to smile, but it wasn't easy. "I'm just doing my duty, Brandy."

"Who pays your fees?" Brandy asked, pretending to think. "I believe that's *me*. I hired you for your services. This is how it works. I ask you for something, you do it, and then I pay you."

Gloria could have said something about the fact that Brandy hadn't paid her for anything for three months, but she thought better of it. She'd leave that to the law firm's collection department. Brandy Baker was experiencing hard times like a lot of people since the housing bubble burst and the disastrous economy followed.

The documents were stacked in neat and perfect order. Her will, insurance policies—both personal and homeowner's—were pushed across the mahogany table that served as Gloria's desk. Brandy's financial portfolio had been hit hard. She didn't need an accountant or a lawyer to figure out that part.

Brandy got up and grabbed her coat from the silver hook next to the heavy glass door. "How long until all this is settled?" she asked.

Gloria looked at her watch. "Should be in the system this afternoon."

Brandy nodded. "That's fine. No real rush. It just feels really good to move things along."

Her phone vibrated, indicating a text message.

She looked down. An annoyed look swept over her face and she started texting.

"What is it?" Gloria asked. "Is everything all right?"

Brandy shook her head. Her eyes were no longer full of condescending ire. She just looked hassled.

"My daughter, Brianna," she said as she rolled her eyes. "I'm supposed to go shopping with her for a Halloween costume. Teenagers can be so needy. If you were a mother, you'd understand that."

Brandy pushed open the door with a whoosh and disappeared down the hallway toward the bank of stainless-steel elevators, where she would check her hair and makeup. No matter if her ship was sinking, Brandy cared about appearances.

She always did.

A part-time clerk named Ted came into Gloria's office.

"Jeesh," he said, setting the day's mail down, "that woman's a real piece of work."

Gloria took off her glasses and flipped through the stack of mail he'd delivered. "Look, Ted, I know you're only twenty-four and from Idaho, but that's no excuse. That's not the way we talk about our clients in this office."

"Sorry," Ted said, his face reddening as he backed out of her office. "Just *saying* . . ."

Gloria put her glasses back on and returned to the files arranged in front of her. Ted was right. She'd thought the same thing, of course. Everyone in the office did. Brandy Connors Baker was nothing if not a piece of work.

chapter 7

BETH LEE PUT DOWN HER PHONE after texting most of the day away with Hay-Tay, her singleton name for the Ryan twins. Fittingly, Halloween night had, indeed, been a nightmare. She was definitely too sick to go to school, and it wasn't because of the alcohol. Or puking at the party. It wasn't from the monster fight that she'd had with Olivia or Brianna after the hostess with the killer party had stolen Olivia right out from under her nose. It wasn't any one of those things but surely the combination of all of them that had kept the sixteen-year-old home. The sum of each item had conspired to make her feel sicker and sadder than she had in a very long time. Above all of it was Olivia's murder. Olivia Grant was dead. Beth was sick, devastated, and sad. Beth never, ever wanted the world to see that side of her. She was Tough Beth. Unpredictable Beth. Retrendy (a word she'd tried—and failed—to coin to describe a mash-up of retro and trendy) Beth.

She was the girl who didn't ever want anyone to see the hurt behind her lovely almond eyes. Luckily, Hayley and Taylor knew that about her and always, no matter what, just let her be. That's exactly why when Hay-Tay texted and asked to come over after school and Taylor's swim-team practice, Beth had answered:

WHAT'S TAKING U SO LONG?

She sat on her bed in her small room in the Lees's daffodil-yellow house number 25 and faced the drawing that she'd completed the day before—the day before the whirlpool that was her life sucked her down into the darkness. Again. Beth had always been a doodler, but over the summer as she agonized over the parallel parking mishap of her Driver's

Ed training (she knocked the cones over and somehow managed to run over a chipmunk at the same time), she took up drawing. Sketching turned into a full-on hobby. At first, it was a series of drawings of chipmunks pleading for their lives, which then morphed into scenes from Port Gamble, and finally, into images that depicted a kind of otherworldly sensibility that she called Gotharamic.

"Think what Freddy Krueger would paint if he had paintbrushes stitched on his fingers instead of knives," she once explained to Hay-Tay.

The picture in front of her that late afternoon showed two figures in the middle of a forest rendered in moody charcoal and black crayon.

Beth took her eyes off the drawing as her mother, Kim, entered her bedroom. Beth's eyes were nearly fused from crying. She hated how her eyes looked when she cried.

"I brought you a Red Bull," Kim said.

Beth looked surprised—*shocked*, actually. According to her mom, Red Bull was practically a gateway drug. She knew her mother would never have offered an energy drink if she didn't think her daughter was in a bad way. A very bad way.

Beth took the slender blue and silver aluminum can from Kim's outstretched hand. "Why do the people I care about keep dying, Mom?"

Kim, an impeccably groomed Chinese American woman who almost never went anywhere without heels (mostly because she was just shy of being five feet tall and hated being asked if she and her daughter were sisters), moved her head sadly.

"Don't say that, Beth," Kim said. "It isn't true."

Beth was close to tears, but she wasn't about to cry again. Tears did nothing for anyone other than the Kleenex manufacturing company, in her opinion. There had been so much death in her young life. "Christina," Beth said, her voice splintered with emotion, "then Dad and Katelyn, now Olivia."

Kim considered listing all the names of people who were among the living, but she thought better of it. It seemed a little too defensive.

"I have no answers, baby," she said, finally. "No one does. Tragedy isn't a stalker. It doesn't come looking for someone. There's no reason for it. It just happens."

Beth didn't care much for her mother's platitudes. She'd heard them over and over, whenever something terrible happened. It didn't matter if it was a catastrophic event like 9/11 ("We can be grateful that there were only four airplanes") or something smaller, like a house fire in Bremerton that killed a little girl ("Her little sister got out alive, a real blessing"). Kim always had some kind words that she wrongly assumed could help her daughter get through the hard stuff.

"Then why does it happen to us every few years?" Beth asked.

That was, Kim Lee knew, a good question. She pondered it while she watched a flock of seagulls hover and drop a discarded bag of Doritos in the backyard. Orange triangles like mini-road-warning signs scattered on the messy, wet grass.

"Christina . . . The bus crash was an accident," Kim said. "Your father died in a—" she paused a moment, her throat catching a little, "in an accident. There was nothing anyone could have done. No one could have done a thing differently."

"And Katelyn, too," Beth said, adding the name of her friend who'd died in a bathtub accident the previous Christmas.

Kim nodded. "Right, Katelyn's death was another accident."

"Accident, not so much, Mom. Not really. That one could have been prevented." Beth looked into her mother's damp brown eyes. "You know, if Mindee Larsen wasn't such a bitch."

Kim let the b-word slide. She'd read in O magazine that venting was good, cheap therapy. While it had been only the two of them for almost a decade, they'd never been able to dig into the hurt. Kim would try, but Beth would shut her out with sarcasm or a cold shoulder.

"Maybe so," she said, finally. "Changing one little thing can change everything."

Beth sipped the Red Bull. "What happened to Olivia wasn't an accident, Mom."

Kim nodded. "You're right. What happened to Olivia was evil and it should never have happened. This time there will be someone to blame. It won't make anyone feel any better, Beth, but at the end of the day, someone will be held accountable."

Kim picked up the drawing. She held it by the corners and turned it into the light from the window for a better view.

"I like this one," she said, trying to shift the conversation to something pleasant.

Beth sucked down the rest of her drink and looked back at her drawing.

Kim put down the artwork, her eyes, soft and full of worry, lingering on it.

"You need to get some rest. Olivia's parents will be here tomorrow."

Beth could see her mom starting to crumble and whenever she did, it only made Beth mad. She wasn't sure where the anger came from, or if it was really anger at all.

Beth looked sceptical. "Some rest? Then why give me an energy drink?"

Kim took the empty can. "It was the only thing I thought would cheer you up."

Seriously? Beth thought. *Our exchange student is murdered and the best you could come up with is a Red Bull. A Red Bull? If I didn't hurt so bad, I'd so be tweeting that.*

The doorbell rang, and a moment later Taylor and Hayley rushed into Beth's bedroom and threw their arms around their friend.

"I'm so sorry," Taylor blurted out. "I know you were close to Olivia. She didn't deserve this."

"Yeah, Beth," Hayley said. "How are you holding up?"

Beth shrugged, feigning nonchalance, though her cried-out eyes told a different story. "Oh, you know. Not great, but what else is new? Nasty hangover. Oh, and Olivia's parents will be here tomorrow."

"You want us there?" Hayley asked.

Beth nodded. "Wouldn't have it any other way."

"School was weird," Taylor said, switching to full report mode. "Everyone was talking about what happened. All the kids, anyway. The school still hasn't officially acknowledged Olivia's gone. Brianna skipped today, of course. Drew too. Don't worry. We'll be there tomorrow."

Beth knew she could count on them, and that was a good feeling. They never let her down. Yet, as much as she loved Hay-Tay, Beth was also envious of them. They had each other. In some ways, they *were* each other. Beth was alone. She looked over at her drawing. She wondered if she had drawn a picture of herself and Olivia.

Or maybe it was two other girls she knew?

ONCE AGAIN THE DOORBELL CHIMED at the Lee house. Kim Lee emerged from the third bedroom, which she'd converted to an office, and went to the door. Like her daughter, she'd also taken the day off, knowing she would have been too distracted to focus on her job in the accounting department at the Port Gamble mill. The day had started with tears and high anxiety, and it was about to end with something even worse.

Fear.

In the emerging light from the porch lantern, a tall figure in a dark-blue Macy's Woman suit loomed on the front steps. It was Annie Garnett, the only police chief who could wear her badge like a Tiffany brooch. Her dark eyes, underscored by the circles left by a sleepless night, met Kim's.

"Annie," Kim said as she opened the door. The two had talked on the phone several times throughout the day as Annie gathered up information about Olivia and her family, and how to contact them.

"May I come in?" Annie asked, tamping her oversized feet gently on the Lee's jute welcome mat. "It's more about Olivia and the Halloween party. I need to talk to you and Beth."

Kim motioned the police chief inside.

"Beth!" she called down the hall. "Chief Garnett is here to talk to you."

Kim offered tea, but Annie declined. She was jittery from endless cups of coffee, and one more drop of caffeine would make her unable to focus. She smiled when Beth emerged. Annie sat down in Park Lee's favorite recliner. Kim joined her daughter on the sofa.

"Have you caught whoever killed Olivia?" Beth asked, wondering what Hay-Tay were up to in her room and if they could hear what was being said.

Annie shook her head. "No, not yet. We will. I know you and your mom are quite understandably upset."

"Yes, we are devastated by the loss," Kim said, starting to cry. "I should never have let Olivia and Beth go to the party—on a school night, no less. This is my fault. I know it is."

Annie put up her hand to stop her. "It isn't your fault, Kim. I'm sure you thought she was safe."

Kim, still crying, looked at her daughter who she now knew had lied to her about Brianna's parents' whereabouts during the party. "I thought there was an adult present," she said.

Beth deflected her mother's gaze. "Olivia was almost like a sister to me," she said, her eyes gliding over the urns that held the remains of her sister and father above the TV. It was a reflex more than anything, but Annie followed the trajectory of the teen's eyes. Everyone in town knew that half of the Lee family was on a shelf in the front room.

"You had a fight with Brianna last night," Annie said, a touch abruptly. "I just want to know more about what happened at the party."

Beth looked at her mom, then back at the police chief.

"It wasn't really a *fight*," she said. "It was just over-the-top banter. I might have gotten a little bit out of line."

"You hit her?" Kim asked.

"No, Mom!" Beth said. She turned to Annie. "Absolutely not. I just told her off. She made some remark about my costume."

"What kind of remark?" Annie asked.

Beth shrugged a little. "Something catty. I can't even remember what it was."

"What was your costume?" Annie asked.

Beth fired off her response a little too rapidly, a clear indicator that guzzling a can of Red Bull before meeting with the police chief would never fall anywhere on the list of good ideas. "Geisha. Nothing special. Just a costume."

Annie asked, "May I see it?"

"I guess so." Beth got up, ducked into the hall closet, and returned a moment later with the kimono on a platinum gray Huggable Hanger she'd purchased from QVC.

Kim shook her head. "Something else I didn't know about, Beth. You should have asked."

"You would have said no," Beth said.

Kim didn't answer. Her daughter was right.

"Pretty," Annie said. The silk folds of the kimono swirled as Beth turned the hanger.

"It was a gift from my father when he went to Japan," Kim said.

Annie took the hanger and spun the garment around. "I see some loops here for a belt. Do you have that?"

Beth glanced at her mother, and then turned to face Annie. "No," she said. "I used a couple of neckties from my dad's closet."

"You what?" Kim asked, trying to keep her cool. While Beth's mom could conjure a poker face when needed, this was not one of those times. She was mad.

Beth knew what was coming, but she didn't feel like backing down. Her mom treated the remnants of her sister's and father's lives like they were precious artifacts. She didn't see it that way. She didn't understand why she couldn't use Christina's Holiday Barbie for an art project or why her mother hung onto her dad's clothes as if he were going to come back one day and wear them.

"It isn't like Dad needs them," she said. "They were skinny ties anyway. In style for about five minutes then back out again. Besides, I put them back."

"Can you get those for me, too?" Annie asked.

Beth left the living room and returned with two silk ties. Her eyes were downcast, and her hands were shaking a little. She stood there, not saying anything.

"What is it? What happened?" Kim asked, rejecting the urge to add "now" to punctuate the litany of disappointments hurled at her daughter since Annie's arrival.

"I can't find the third one," Beth admitted. "I used three."

"What color was the third one?" Annie asked.

"Pomegranate," Beth said.

Annie looked a little confused. "Pomegranate?"

"Deep red." Beth reached over and pressed a fingertip to a frilly chrysanthemum painted on the bottom of the right sleeve. "This color right here."

Annie's eyes swept across the hem of the kimono's sleeve. She felt sick to her stomach, and it had nothing to do with her all-protein diet. A speck of dark red pigmentation, a different shade from the chrysanthemum, stood out against the garment's silk pattern. Port Gamble's police chief recognized the color and shape: blood spatter.

Oh no, Beth, not you.

Trying to maintain her composure, Annie kept an even tone to her questioning. "I see. Can I borrow all of these? I promise to return them, but it might take a while."

Kim Lee's anger dissipated. Something bigger was afoot, and she knew it. "Why do you want them?" she asked.

"We need to examine all the evidence," Annie said.

"What kind of evidence?" Kim stopped and waited, but Annie didn't answer right away. "Is Beth some kind of a suspect?"

Annie, who'd known Kim through the worst possible times—the bus accident that killed Christina and her husband's suicide—looked down at the floor. It was a moment of awkwardness that sucked the air out of the room.

"I can't really say," she said.

Beth wondered if she was in trouble. If so, it had to be big trouble. The police chief didn't come around collecting evidence because she had nothing better to do.

Beth stood up. "You didn't answer my mother. Am I a suspect here or something?" she asked with both force and fear in her voice. "I admit that I drank. I admit that I had a fight. But that's it."

Pulling on a pair of latex gloves, Annie took the garment off the hanger, carefully folded it, and slipped it into a large, clear bag that she retrieved from her eco-friendly canvas tote. "Just procedure," she said, her eyes fastened on Beth's worried stare with a look she hoped conveyed reassurance.

"I wasn't even there when Olivia died," Beth said. "I got sick, and we left the party early. Hayley, Taylor, Colton, and me. She was alive when we left. She was having a blowout with Bree."

"Just procedure," Annie repeated.

Annie tried to diffuse the drama by asking Kim how things were going at the mill.

"I hope you're not one of the layoffs I heard about," she said.

Kim, her worried expression undiminished by the casual tone of the conversation, stood and strode decisively toward the door. Turning her hand on the knob, she said, "No. Not me. At least, not yet. But housing starts are down, and if things don't get better, they won't need an accountant."

Annie took the hint and said a hasty good-bye. Kim managed a smile and shut the door after her.

Three rooms away, two worried twins waited for their friend. The walls were thin in Port Gamble's historic homes. As a breeze blew the Doritos bag into the neighboring yard and darkness shuttered the sky over the bay, Hayley and Taylor heard every word.

What had Beth Lee done?

chapter 8

LIKE ALL VICTORIA'S SECRET STORES in the world, the one at the Kitsap Mall in Silverdale, a few miles south of Port Gamble, was an eruption of pink, a tidal wave of lace, and a ginormous Slip 'N Slide of satin. Amid the thongs, French-cut panties, lacey bras, and whatever else a girl thinks she needs or a boy hopes she wears, Drew escorted Brianna toward a table next to a white-and-black mannequin with a bored-to-tears expression. That her bedroom on Desolation View Drive was drenched in Olivia Grant's blood seemed far from either teen's mind.

"You'd look so hot in that," he said, indicating the microscopic panties and sheer bra.

"I look hot in whatever I wear—or don't wear, for that matter," Brianna said. "I'm glad you understand that, Drew." She kissed him, held up a light-pink thong and grinned.

"I had a slingshot like that once," he said.

"If you did, then you're a total dork," Brianna said, as she sorted through thongs and bras in various shades of pink.

"Do you like carnation or rose?" she asked.

Drew raised his brow. "They look the same to me," he said.

"Don't be dumb," Brianna said. "Carnation is lighter, a more pure shade."

"I guess so," he said, checking her attitude. "Whatever you say, Bree."

Brianna nuzzled her boyfriend again as they made their way across the store toward the cashier. Neither of them knew they were being watched, but they were. Certainly store security personnel always keep extra alert around teenage shoppers. But aside from the video camera fixated in their direction and a skeezy man who was shopping for the "wife" he didn't have, there was one more set of eyes riveted on them.

Watching the young couple from across the store was classmate Starla Larsen's mom, Mindee. Like everyone, she'd heard what had happened at the Connorses' home. Instead of concern, she actually felt a little relief. Maybe now the people of Port Gamble would stop their incessant finger-pointing in her direction? It wasn't *all* her fault that Katelyn Berkley had died in her bathtub last year. Certainly, she accepted a small, itsy-bitsy, teeny-weeny part in the events that led to the death of her daughter's former best friend. Yes, Mindee had faked those bullying e-mails. Yes, she had written terrible things about the fifteen-year-old. But she'd had a good reason. She was defending her daughter. All those judgmental moms who had stopped being her clients at the hair salon would have done the same thing. She was sure of it. Yes, she played a role in the whole mess, but it was tiny, and Katelyn's electrocution was proven to have been an accident. Mindee's part in it was merely a bad decision.

A bad decision just like those thongs Brianna Connors was buying with her embarrassingly horny boyfriend in tow.

Brianna's and Mindee's eyes met briefly, and Mindee waved from behind a rack of padded bras.

Brianna pretended not to see Starla's mother and hoped she wouldn't turn her in for skipping school. She considered Mrs. Larsen a total loser, one of those moms who never understood that she was older and should stop trying to dress like her daughter. Her chance had come and gone. The way Brianna looked at it, over time hotness turns to lukewarm, then to cool, then to cold. Sadly, Mrs. Larsen had her home-manicured claws dug in, clinging to the lukewarm zone.

"Buy one more and you get a free one," said the clerk, who wore a top so sheer that some shoppers wondered why she bothered to wear it at all.

"Drew," Brianna said, "go fetch another apricot one."

Drew scampered off like a puppy and came running back.

"Here you go," he said.

Brianna put a hand on her hip and shifted impatiently. "That's not apricot," she said. "That's peach. I said *apricot*."

"Sorry," Drew said, "I guess I got my fruits mixed up."

Brianna turned to the clerk. "Thank goodness he's cute, because he sure is dumb. Meet Drew-without-a-Clue."

"Umm," the girl said, "you want to skip the freebie? I can give you a sample of this season's signature fragrance, Hot and Juicy, instead."

Brianna laughed and shook her glossy dark hair in a can't-be-bothered manner.

"Gross! It sounds like a hamburger," she said.

The clerk laughed. "I don't name 'em. But, yeah, it is gross."

Brianna took out a credit card to pay, then turned to Drew and gave him a kiss.

"I know you're trying your best, Babe," she said. "I guess I have to teach you everything."

They walked to the front of the store, where Brianna stopped to check out a rack she had missed.

"Are you still staying at the Silverdale Beach Hotel?" Drew asked.

"Of course I am. My mom always stays there, and she took care of everything," she said.

THE SILVERDALE BEACH HOTEL had undergone a recent remodel, with a cadre of designers and carpenters coming together to yank the venerable hotel out of its mauve and taupe cloud and forest of oak and ferns and into a more modern vibe—the dark wood, cool glass accents, and the tasteful carpets of a modern hotel. Even so, the Silverdale Beach Hotel wasn't the W, not by a long shot.

Brianna sent a Platinum American Express card sliding over the black granite counter like a silver streak.

The clerk, a chinless man, looked over his round-frame glasses.

"I need to extend my stay. I'm an authorized user. Call if you have to," she said.

"Um, how long will you be staying?" the clerk asked.

Brianna slammed her purse on the counter. "How the hell should I know? Indefinitely."

The clerk blinked. "That might be a problem. I don't know how to put that in the system," he said, scratching his head while pecking at the keyboard in front of him.

Drew looked at the card. It had Bree's father's name on it.

"Your mom didn't set up the room for you, did she?" he asked.

Brianna shot him a sideways glance, one that he'd seen plenty of times since they'd started dating last year. It meant back off. *Now.* She punctuated the look with a few words this time—in case Drew-without-a-Clue didn't quite get it.

"I don't want to talk about it," she said.

"Figured it out!" the chinless clerk said. "You need help with your luggage?" He looked over at her purse and the little pink bag from Victoria's Secret.

"I can manage," Brianna said.

"Oh, okay then. Enjoy your indefinite stay."

As they walked to the elevator, Drew nudged her, snapping her out of whatever was preoccupying her mind.

"What's the deal with your mom anyway? First she missed the ferry and then said she'd come over later. *Didn't happen.* Then she said she'd take care of your room? No mom. No room."

"Look, Drew. I might have the perfect life. But I have the worst mom ever. I know that. She left me when I was a kid. She didn't have time for me back then. She doesn't have time now. But don't ever get me wrong. I wouldn't trade her in for step-monster Shelley any day of the week. Don't dog her. Don't put her down. That's my job. Because when I do it, I know that it doesn't really mean anything. She's my mom."

They got off the elevator, and Brianna inserted the key card to unlock the room.

"What happened to your hand?" Drew asked, eyeing her cut palm.

Brianna slipped her key card into the front pocket of her jeans, dark-dyed from the Gap of all places, because that was all the Kitsap Mall had that was halfway decent. Being booted out of her house without a complete wardrobe and no time to order anything decent online had cramped her style.

Big-time.

"Nothing," she said, pulling away. "I slipped when I found Olivia. I'm okay."

Drew followed her into the room, pulled off his fleece and flopped down on the bed. He tucked his hand inside the waistband of his jeans.

"Want to fool around?" he asked, arching a brow in a way that he was sure was sexy.

Brianna barely looked at him. "Okay," she said. "After I post on Facebook."

She typed on her wall:

BEEN THINKING ABOUT OLIVIA. ALL THE TIME.
DON'T KNOW HOW I'LL GET THROUGH THE REST OF THE DAY.
HEARTBROKEN. ☹

MINDEE LARSEN DID NOT HAVE a blue ribbon or a trophy for completing her community service, and frankly, it ticked her off a little that Kitsap County authorities didn't give her one. She did more than was required. She talked to two extra classes about the dangers of cyberbullying and about the warning signs that kids and parents should look for if they suspect someone is being victimized online.

While she easily could have, Mindee never told her audience the number-one tip for saving someone from being cyberbullied: *"Be mindful* of all jealous, overprotective, stage-mother wannabes. If her stunning daughter—the one who will bring her riches, fame, and a place in Palm Springs—is threatened and might lose everything, there's no telling how far the mother will go to protect her future assets."

That would have been good advice, the kind that only personal experience can bring. Compelling stuff in front of a group, indeed.

Finally at home, Mindee looked at the clock. It was 5:30 p.m. She kicked off her vintage Wild Pair heels, poured a glass of box sangria, and guzzled it like she was a camel heading into the Gobi. Doing five heads at Shear Elegance salon, talking to a group of smelly kids in Bremerton, and visiting her son, Teagan, at the detention center made for a very hard day.

She poured a second glass—the one she usually let sit half-consumed, a prop to indicate she wasn't drinking too much. Not today. Mindee played back her conversation with her son as she sipped:

TEAGAN: *Mom, I still don't know why I'm the only one who's in big trouble.*

MINDEE: *Honey, maybe you'll think twice next time before climbing into a girl's bedroom and scaring her to death.*

TEAGAN: *Sometimes I kind of hate you.*

MINDEE: *That's all right. That means you're getting better. You're getting in touch with your feelings.*

As Mindee sucked down the last pinkish drops in her wine glass, her daughter flounced into the house. She barely gave Starla, in full Buccaneers' cheerleader uniform, a second to put down her book bag and drop her pom-poms before jumping in with, to her mind, earth-shattering news. Mindee was one hundred percent certain the latest turn of events at the mall would help her get back into the good graces of those who judged her.

"On my way to Port Orchard to see your brother," she said, "I stopped at Victoria's Secret. Guess who I saw there?"

Starla brightened a little. She didn't care who her mother saw, but the fact that she went to the mall always put her in good cheer.

"Mommy, what did you get me?" Starla asked, lapsing into I-love-you-so-much-because-you-buy-me-stuff mode.

Mindee set down her glass. "God, Starla, however did you become so selfish? It isn't all about you, twenty-four-seven."

Starla appeared a little confused. She thought it *was*. She flipped her long blond hair. "You're so harsh! But get to your point."

"This is good. Pay attention. I saw Brianna and Drew, and believe you me they weren't acting like they were sad about their friend being butchered in Brianna's bedroom. They were practically making out by the Angel Wing thongs. It was really, really inappropriate. It was like they were celebrating or something."

"Those thongs are pretty nice, Mom," Starla said, her blue eyes flashing. "I wish you would have bought me some."

Mindee reached for her glass. "Don't you ever listen?"

Starla made a face. "Don't you ever buy me anything anymore?"

"Considering that we have hardly any money because of legal fees for me and your brother, I think we're doing all right."

"Maybe Jake should get a real job," Starla said, referring to her mom's younger bad-boy boyfriend. "Where is he anyway?"

Mindee looked at her phone. It was after six. "He's over at Sheila's helping her repipe her laundry room," she said.

The teenager rolled her eyes with such overt exaggeration that she was lucky they stayed in their sockets. "Is that what he calls it now?" she asked.

"Starla! That's not nice," Mindee said, shaking her head. "The Victoria's Secret thing could be big for me, for *us*."

Starla, still annoyed, always liked to hear how something could benefit her. "How?" she asked.

Mindee took a dramatic breath. "If Brianna—who I've always thought was as cold as her mother—killed that British girl and gets caught for doing it, everyone will forget all about what your brother did."

Starla gathered her hair and made a messy ponytail. "Or really, Mom, what you're saying is no one will think about what *you* did."

Mindee let the gibe pass. If Starla had learned how to ignore and put herself above others, she'd learned it from her mother.

"I'm telling Chief Garnett tomorrow," Mindee said. "I can't withhold this crucial evidence. It just wouldn't be right. I'm all about doing the right thing." She sipped the rest of her wine and looked longingly in the direction of the sangria. *I think I'll treat myself to a third glass tonight. I deserve it.*

chapter 9

TUESDAY AT KINGSTON HIGH was far from normal. With the news of Olivia's death moved far beyond teen Twitter to the Seattle news channels, Principal Andrea Sandusky knew she had to respond in an appropriate and sensitive manner. Gone were the days when kids were told to buck up and shut up, like they had been when she was their age. Andrea took off one of her wide looped gold earrings and dialed the number of Phoebe Cooper, the district's designated grief counselor, a woman who seemed to relish the role a little too much—as if she were sucking in tragedy like a vampire.

Empathetic? Sort of. Always available? Definitely. For a price.

"Tell me, how does it make you feel?" Dr. Cooper would say over and over.

"It's all right to cry, dear," she'd offer, her lips a straight line. "Crying is a gift, a present all wrapped up in tears. Let it go."

And finally, the zinger she'd always end on—no matter the occasion. It could be a car crash that killed someone's parents. A kid buried in an avalanche and yet to be found. It didn't matter to Dr. Cooper.

"Life isn't fair," she would say, "though we wish it could be."

Students were encouraged to seek help from Dr. Cooper at any point during the day, and teachers were asked to give even the most misbehaved some latitude during a very trying time.

Beth and Brianna were both at school, although they stayed on opposite sides of the hall whenever possible. Beth, who'd barely slept—thanks to chain-guzzling Red Bull—was jittery. She was trying her best to cope with Olivia's death as well as the aftermath of Annie's visit to the house. Brianna let out some tears but mostly spun around her rapt circle of friends telling the gruesome story of discovering the body.

"You don't even want to know how gross it was, but if you really, really want me to tell you . . ."

Colton and Hayley watched her from the other side of the hallway.

"She sure doesn't seem upset," he said. "I mean, not like you or your sister or Beth."

"I've always kind of felt a little sorry for Bree," Hayley said.

Colton set his backpack on a bench and searched it for his homework.

"Sorry for her? She has everything."

"Yeah, she has a big house," Hayley said. "The biggest house we've ever seen. She has her own car and everything, but she always seems a little lonely to me."

Colton pulled out his English paper, relieved that he hadn't left it at home. "You mean like some attention is better than none at all?" he asked.

Hayley nodded as they started for class.

"Yeah," she said. "Just watching Brianna makes me want to figure out what happened even more. We owe it to Olivia."

UNFORTUNATELY FOR TAYLOR, Mr. Hayden, her hipster wannabe "Family Life" teacher who didn't realize that skinny jeans only work if you're actually skinny, was plowing ahead with their latest project, right on schedule. Olivia's death, apparently, only put a dent in *her* "Story of My Life in Words and Pictures" assignment—not anyone else's.

"People, I want high points and low points," Mr. Hayden pontificated from the front of the classroom after saying a few words about Olivia's death and Dr. Cooper's availability for counseling. "Gather up photos and family mementos. Scan them, provide explanatory text, and above all make sure your presentation shows creative edge and breadth of discovery."

As he walked, Mr. Hayden's loaf-sized muffin top jiggled over his low-risers and the reek of his Aqua Velva cologne made its way down the aisles, jolting awake the sophomores sleeping at the back of the room. Turning abruptly on his heel, Mr. Hayden stopped and leaned on Taylor's desk. He looked her straight in the eye, giving her a too-close-for-comfort view of the sandy-gray plume of hair emanating from his shirt collar like a Mount St. Helens eruption.

"I really need to see you in words and pictures. Your real self. Your authentic being. Each and every one of you is totally amazing. Each of you is dipped in awesome sauce," he said.

Taylor shot an incredulous look over at Beth, who was marooned with her in the worst class ever.

"Is he asking us to be scrapbookers?" Taylor whispered as soon as he trotted away to torture a new victim.

Beth rolled her eyes. "Yeah, too bad I got rid of those scalloped scissors in third grade."

Taylor couldn't agree more. "I'm still gagging on the idea that we're dipped in awesome sauce."

DURING LUNCH PERIOD, Taylor approached Brianna by the student-run latte stand in front of the cafeteria. Brianna had been holding court there off and on, retelling the horror of her discovery to all who would listen, which was just about anyone with a heartbeat. It was, after all, not only a ghastly story but also the kind of thing that usually only happened to people on TV.

"Bree, I know you've been through a lot. I'm really sorry," Taylor said.

Brianna did a hair toss and paid for her drink, a mocha with cherry syrup and a mountain of whipped cream.

"No kidding," she said. "I have been getting dozens of requests for interviews. Seems like finding a dead girl in your bedroom is newsworthy. Maybe your dad will want to interview me for one of his books."

Taylor took her latte, a vanilla soy, no foam. "Maybe. My dad usually only covers stories after the perpetrator has been caught and brought to justice."

"A semi-journalist with ethics," Brianna said. "That's ironic."

Taylor let it go.

"Well, I'm sorry about what you're going through," she said.

"I guess someone had to find her, and we were practically best friends. So really, what choice do I have? I'm being victimized right along with Olivia."

Not exactly, Taylor thought. *Olivia is dead. You're drinking a disgusting cherry mocha.*

"What do you mean, *victimized*?" Taylor asked.

Brianna ate the cherry off her whipped cream. "People talk," she said. "They say nasty things. I get it. I've been thrust into the public eye. The TV reporters are coming around. Everyone wants a piece of me. I feel like one of the Kardashians, except, thank God, I have a smaller butt."

"What do you think happened to Olivia?"

"Besides someone stabbing her, you mean?"

"You know what I mean," Taylor said, trying to conceal her annoyance. "Why her? Why your bedroom?"

Brianna shrugged. "You ask a lot of good questions. I guess you're the daughter of a question-asker so you just do it without thinking about how rude it might sound."

Keep calm. She's a twit. A rich twit. A traumatized twit.

"Without thinking?" Taylor asked. "What happened to Olivia was either random or intentional. In any case, whoever did it *will* get caught and go to prison. I just want to know who did it. Beth is my friend. I care about her, and this has really hurt her too."

"I'm the one that this mess has hurt. Olivia and I were tight. I adored her. I wanted to spend Christmas with her in London."

"Hey, Baby."

Taylor turned to find Drew practically leapfrogging over her to get to Brianna. He didn't acknowledge Taylor at all.

"Hi, Drew," Taylor said.

He ignored her. "Cops keep bugging me for another interview," he said to Brianna.

Brianna shook her head in disgust. "You, too? Mom texted me during Spanish that they want to talk to me again, too. Can't they just take decent notes?"

"I guess not," Drew said, sticking his finger in Brianna's whipped cream and then offering his finger to her.

If she licks it, I'm going to hurl, Taylor thought.

Which, of course, is exactly what Brianna did. As her tongue rolled over his finger, Drew shuffled his feet and squirmed in ecstasy.

"Hey guys, nice talking to you," Taylor said, backing away, wishing there was antibacterial spray for the brain so she could forget the last couple of minutes.

WITH DREW GONE OFF TO CLASS and the bevy of curiosity seekers and fake friends dissipated, Brianna smoked an electronic cigarette in the bathroom stall. It was against school rules to smoke on campus, of course, and in doing so a kid risked the same sort of wrath the FAA might bring down on a smoker on an airplane. The beauty of the electronic cigarette was that the wispy vapor was water, not smoke. There was no worry about tripping the smoke alarms, plus the price of cigarettes was sky high—too pricey for the average teenager's allowance. Money wasn't an issue for Brianna, but she liked to steal a little. In her circle, she wasn't alone in that regard.

Brianna had managed to snag her dad's phony cigarette and assorted cartridges—including the disgusting menthol ones that he ordered through the mail by mistake. He never even knew that they were missing. And there she sat, not really smoking, but really mad.

Sure, she was enjoying all the attention of Olivia's death, but at the end of the day, all this left her with was Drew (who was fun, but not exactly a life partner), her good-for-nothing parents, and even worse, her nicey-nicey stepmother. Her dad and stepmom had cut their cruise short, which out of everything that happened, provided the biggest ray of sunshine.

Serves them right, she thought. *They are so selfish*.

When it came to her mother, Brandy, Brianna had always talked a good game. She'd defended her mom's abhorrent behavior to the wall whenever someone suggested that Brandy Connors Baker was less than Mom of the Year material. When Brianna was in elementary school, Brandy ditched her husband and only child for another man. Lawyer Robby Baker was younger, more handsome, and far richer than Brianna's dad. At first Brianna made her father the heavy, blaming him for her mom's unhappiness. In time, she turned her blame on Robby, first wondering what self-respecting man would still call himself *Robby* and not Rob or Robert, and then focusing her hatred on him as a home wrecker. Whenever Brianna tried to make plans with her mother, Robby would step into the mix and ruin everything. Brandy would be full of apologies and promises of rescheduling, but nine times out of ten, things ended the same way.

"Robby has made other plans, Honey. I just can't get over to the peninsula this weekend after all. Rain check. You understand, sweetie."

When Brianna was twelve, her mother had said that she couldn't come and pick her up at the ferry for the weekend of shopping she'd promised. Brandy had left a message on Brianna's cell. Again, Robby was to blame.

"Honey, forgive me. Robby's sick and is being a big baby. I have to spend all weekend taking care of him. I love you. Rain check."

Brianna's heart sank. She heard something familiar in the background.

She had played the v-mail over and over until she was sure. It was there all right. There was no mistaking it.

"Flight 253 service to Miami boarding now at B-8."

It wasn't Robby who had screwed things up and continued to keep them apart. It was her mother.

After that, Brianna took her mother on her mother's terms. Whenever she had time, whenever Robby didn't have more exciting plans, and whenever Brandy felt guilty enough, mother and daughter saw each other. Brianna told everyone she had a great mom and that her mother was always doing special things for her.

"My mom got me this cool top from Saks in Bellevue," she'd lie to friends, when, in fact, Brianna had purchased it herself online.

"My mom is taking me to Italy in August. I'm so lucky," she'd tell teachers when they asked about her summer plans. The following fall she'd be back in school with an expensive Italian leather purse.

"My mom and I saw it in a shop in Milan and she just had to get it for me."

It was only a half-truth. Her mother did buy it in Milan, but she was there with Robby and had shipped the package to Brianna in Port Gamble.

Every time she carried the soft Italian leather bag, she'd say "Ciao," explaining, "It's something my mom and I got into when we were in Florence. It felt so right there and, well, I just love the way it sounds."

Brianna out-and-out lied about her mother. She told nearly everyone that her mom was the best mother in the world.

"She's always getting mistaken for Demi Moore, you know," she once told a group of girls hanging around Pretzel Time at the mall. "She's the prettiest mom in the world. I'm so lucky that I favor her side of the family. What a total relief! If I looked like my dad's side of the family, I'd kill myself right here and now."

When she had called her mom about Olivia's murder, Brandy had said she'd be right there. A few minutes later, Brianna had gotten a text message:

HONEY, CAN'T MAKE THE BOAT. MISSED THE LAST CROSSING.
LUV U.

Brianna knew that was a lie. There were two more boats early that morning. Even when she needed her the most, Brandy just couldn't rise to the occasion. She could send money. She could send false promises. She could even look the part of the adoring mother when the camera zoomed in on the rare outing together. Deep down, it was painfully obvious that Brandy Connors Baker just wasn't the mommy type.

While Annie Garnett and all the other cops had collected evidence after the big Halloween party, Brianna had held back her blackest feelings and had texted a reply to her mother:

OKAY. I'LL BE FINE. DON'T WORRY ABOUT ME.

Her dad, Brian, for whom she was named, wasn't much better than her mom. She loved him, but she hated Shelley, her stepmother, whom her dad always seemed to put first. She wondered if Shelley was good for him or merely better than nothing. Brianna couldn't understand why her mom would just go off and leave them. It was so selfish. Couldn't she have waited until her daughter was out of high school to trade in her life like all the other moms?

Brianna could feel her anger swell, just as it had during the Halloween party. Puffing on wet air in the stall, Brianna remembered how she had picked up the crystal vase and flung it against the wall. Glittery shards had rained down on the room. Her hand was cut, but she didn't care.

Good.

Shelley's favorite vase, Waterford. A wedding present, no less.

Gone.

Just like all of them.

As she sat in the bathroom stall thinking about her fake mother, Brianna Connors wondered what she'd done to deserve a life that was so pretty on the surface but so ugly deep inside.

So fake.

Brianna didn't feel sad that Olivia had died. Not really. She was kind of in awe about the irony of it all. Olivia Grant was a nobody in life and all of a sudden she was the girl everyone was talking about. All it had taken was the sharp edge of a knife.

chapter 10

AFTER THE MURDER, the Port Gamble S'Klallam Tribal Police Department was an uneasy blend of business-as-usual with petty thievery, lost dogs, and a smattering of post-Halloween vandalism calls filling the dispatcher's log sheet—and, of course, a murder investigation that had just swung into full, tragic gear. The department's phones hadn't stopped ringing from the first mention of the crime on a Seattle TV station.

"How are you holding up?" records clerk Tatiana Jones asked Police Chief Annie Garnett as she emerged from her office.

"I've had better days. You?" she asked.

"I've talked to six news outlets and at least a dozen parents wanting to know if alcohol was served at the party and, if so, would Brianna's parents be charged with a crime."

"They're mad about *that*?" Annie looked over as the fax machine rang. She knew what was coming.

Tatiana, a slender African American woman with a luxurious, plump black braid that ran halfway down her back, had been taking criminal justice classes before she came to work at the police department seven years ago. She was analytical and direct.

"Yup. They want to lash out at Brianna's dad for something. They're upset that their kids weren't being supervised during the party."

Annie shook her head. "But they're not concerned about Olivia Grant and what happened to her?"

Tatiana's console started to flash like a row of ambulances. "Not really. Oh, they *say* they are, but as far as I can tell, not really. They're just mad that their kid drank beer and they want to make sure that—"

"—*that* never happens again," Annie concluded.

Tatiana's braid swung like a pendulum, and she swiveled and picked up the phone.

"Yes, ma'am, the party was a bad idea," she said, her eyes on Annie's. "Yes, ma'am, I agree . . ."

Annie shook her head and returned to her office. She looked down as pages of forensic pathologist Birdy Waterman's autopsy report rolled off the fax machine one by one. Her stomach was in knots. Looking at that sort of paperwork was never easy, and deep down, she was glad for that. The day that reading autopsy findings didn't break her heart was the day Annie would need to find a new career.

It struck her that every time she studied one of Birdy's reports, she couldn't help feeling an overwhelming sadness that a person's life had been reduced to nothing more than words on a page. They became evidence in a criminal case. She knew Birdy had a deep and abiding respect for crime victims and their families, but none of that was ever translated into her reports. Like Birdy's autopsies, her paperwork was professional, clinical. No judgments. No tears. Just facts.

Before the Halloween party, Olivia Grant had been a lovely, vital young woman. It was hard to reconcile that with the reality of what was in front of Annie, rendered in clinical black and white.

Annie's mind flashed to her recollections of Olivia: the first time they crossed paths in the General Store when Olivia had arrived in town in late August, Olivia with Beth Lee in line for ice cream, and Olivia at Kingston High's fall safety fair where Annie was the featured speaker. The pretty, slender redhead with the charming British accent had been talking to someone, but Annie couldn't remember who it was. One of the Ryan twins? Starla Larsen?

Annie had never spoken to Olivia. And yet in her mind's eye, she could still conjure her up, alive and well, before she'd been cut open with a saw under the cool light of an autopsy suite in an old house-turned-morgue in Port Orchard. It was a world so far from London in every way. The only British things in the place were packages of salt-and-vinegar flavored potato chips from the Walmart on Bethel Avenue belonging to Birdy's assistant, Terry Morris.

Grabbing the complete report from the beeping fax and taking a seat behind her desk, Annie read through each page, occasionally pausing and thinking about the dead girl's tragic end in a place so far from home.

OLIVIA WARRINGTON GRANT

MANNER OF DEATH:

Homicide.

CAUSE OF DEATH:

Exsanguination due to multiple stab wounds.

TIME OF DEATH:

Between 1 a.m. and 2 a.m.

FINDINGS:

1. Generalized pallor and evidence of exsanguination.
2. Multiple stab wounds of neck, trunk, and upper extremities with one (1) stab wound penetrating the throat in a left to right direction; three (3) stab wounds penetrating into chest cavity and right lung in a slight right to left direction; and multiple wounds of upper extremities consistent with defensive injuries.
3. Stab wounds are consistent in size and shape, indicating one weapon, most likely a knife or thin-edged blade—although a double-edged blade cannot be excluded.

GENERAL APPEARANCE:

The body is that of a well-developed, well-nourished, white female who appears the stated age of 17 years. Body height is 68 inches. Body weight is 105 lbs. At crime scene, the body was warm to touch. There is obvious evidence of multiple sharp-force injury.

IDENTIFICATION:

The identity of decedent, Olivia Warrington Grant, was established by Brianna Connors at the time of the discovery of the body.

CLOTHING AND VALUABLES:

The body is admitted to the morgue wrapped in a sheet, within a body bag, and with the hands bagged. Clothing and sheet are very bloody and have tears and punctures matching those at the trunk. In addition, prior to removal of clothing, the body was examined concurrently by me and by crime scene technicians from the Kitsap County Sheriff's Department, and trace evidence was collected from the body and clothing. See "TRACE EVIDENCE" section at end of report. The clothing consists of a slip, brassiere, and underpants. Valuables on or with the body include three gold rings, a pair of earrings, and a purse with $225 in US currency. The valuables will be released to the parents of the decedent while the clothing is retained as evidence by the law enforcement agency.

HEAD AND NECK:

The head is normally shaped. Scalp hair is long, red, and wavy in nature. The irises are green; the pupils are equal and round. The teeth are natural, and oral hygiene is good. Irregularities: A man's tie, red in color, was extracted from the victim's mouth.

TRUNK:

No natural abnormalities. No visible prior injuries. No evidence of sexual relations.

EXTREMITIES:

The extremities are symmetrical and without natural deformities. No bruising or evidence of bondage. The legs have no significant peripheral edema and no skin atrophy. The fingernails are all of medium length and coated with a silvery white nail polish.

SCARS, INCIDENTAL FINDINGS:

Old scars at the left knee.

INJURIES:

Multiple incised and stab wounds are present on the neck, chest, upper extremities, and hands.

PROCEDURES AND SPECIMENS:

EXPEDITED TOXICOLOGY: Blood, bile, urine, ocular fluid, and nasal swabs. Alcohol found present in blood, but less than the legal limit, the equivalent of one (1) beer. No other drugs were present.

TRACE EVIDENCE: One (1) black nylon fiber on right shoulder/chest; small, possibly glass fragment from left upper chest, three white, iridescent sequins in hair, and two frayed white polyester threads. Neither the threads nor the fiber match the deceased's slip (Calvin Klein), which she was wearing at the time of death, or the sheet she was wrapped in.

Annie shut her eyes and took a deep breath. A pause. Almost a prayer. It was obvious that Olivia had fought for her life. The defensive wounds on her hands had been proof of that. But she hadn't fought long. Annie wondered if the tangle of the slip and sheets was the impediment or was it something else? Was someone holding her steady while someone else stabbed her? There was one weapon, but had there been two attackers?

One thing Annie knew for sure: even with one beer in her, with each plunge of the knife, Olivia had known exactly what was happening.

And she had had no chance.

BRIAN AND SHELLEY CONNORS LOOKED WORSE for the wear, despite the golden tans they'd acquired while sipping rum drinks from coconut shells in Acapulco. Brian, in his late fifties, had a deeply etched face and alert blue eyes. Shelley, his second wife, was a good ten years younger, a brunette with a short, sassy bob that made her look even more youthful than her years. They met Annie in her office. It was two days after Olivia's murder, and neither had a warm greeting for the police chief.

It was easy to see where they were headed.

"I'm sure you must be exhausted," Annie said. "I appreciate your being here."

She pointed to a pair of chairs, but neither took her up on the offer to sit.

Brian folded his arms across his barrel chest. "Here's the deal. We're here to tell you that we understand the dire circumstances of Sunday night's tragedy and the importance of interviewing Brianna."

"I appreciate that," Annie said, feeling a chill in the air.

"And we are not going to make any complaints about the county's handling of the matter, nor your role in it."

Shelley looked down at the floor and said nothing.

"I'm afraid I don't understand," Annie said.

"I'll get to the point. No more interviews with our daughter. She's done."

Annie didn't want to give up. She needed Brianna. "She might know something that could help the investigation. Something that could lead us to Olivia's killer."

"I seriously doubt that, Chief Garnett," Brian Connors said. "Bree is just a girl. She doesn't know a damned thing."

Outside in the 7 series BMW that was Brian Connors's proof to the world that he'd made it—much like his house—Brianna sat slumped in the backseat. She texted Drew, who was out doing whatever it was he did:

DAD AND DUMB-DUMB ARE TELLING THE GIGANTOR COP TO
TAKE A HIKE. THEY ARE SO LAME. GLAD I RUINED THEIR VACAY.

chapter 11

OLIVIA GRANT'S PARENTS HAD TRAVELED ALL night and yet the dark circles under their bloodshot eyes owed more to too many Bloody Marys on the flight from London to Seattle than to actual jetlag. Edward Grant, normally an effusive man in his fifties with a suspiciously perfect head of sandy hair and blindingly white teeth—a kind of perfection that suggested veneers—crumpled in the sofa in the Lee's living room. The fireplace crackled, and Kim Lee had set out tea, milk, sugar, and some cookies, but everything went untouched. Edward Grant could barely get a word out.

Winifred Grant looked a good twenty years younger than her husband. While she had a lovely figure, her face, Beth thought, was indeed as Olivia had once described her mother—a little horsey. Her hair was thick and black and could only be termed by any reasonable person as a mane. Her teeth, also impossibly white, looked a bit large for her mouth, like a row of old-school refrigerators in the Bremerton appliance dealership that Beth and her mom shopped at when their dryer's element had burned out in July.

Olivia had called her mother Winnie, rather than Mum, and her name resonated in Beth's mind as the equinely ironic "whinny," her name as horsey as her face.

"My husband adored our daughter," Winnie said, before offering a correction. "We *both* adored our Olivia."

Beth highly doubted that. Olivia hadn't exactly been a fountain of information about her family life, but she'd never indicated a deep devotion to her mother. Nor did she mention her with even the slightest trace of affection. The way Olivia saw it, everything Winifred Grant did was for herself and the advancement of whatever her agenda was at the moment. She'd been nurturing to Olivia when she was a toddler, but after a time it appeared that Winnie—whom Olivia occasionally referred to as "Winnie the Loo"—was a climber. Her husband had a chat show on British television, and she'd wormed her way into his life first as an assistant producer, back then with a hook baited with sex appeal and promises of devotion. A family life too. Edward was a surprisingly easy target: a workaholic with an ego the size of Buckingham Palace. He needed constant reassurance, and Winnie was extremely efficient in that endeavor. She showered Olivia with attention in the early years of childhood, all the while biding her time for the freedom that came with boarding school. The program that brought Olivia to study in America had been Winnie's idea.

"We are so sorry for what happened," Kim said, holding up a plate of orange jack-o'-lantern and white ghost-shaped cookies that had been left over from the mill office's Halloween potluck.

As the four of them sat in the living room, the Lees on one side, the Grants on the other, the mantel clock over the fireplace ticked like a bomb. The air could not have been any heavier. Heartbreak and grief had returned to house number 25. Indeed, it had returned with a vengeance.

"Liv was everything to me," Edward finally said. "I didn't want her to come here. America is dangerous. There are shootings and sex scandals all the time. This was no place for our daughter. Perugia would have been so much safer."

"She wanted to go, darling," said Winnie, who somehow managed to eat the heads off two ghost cookies. "The biscuits are charming, Mrs. Kim. A traditional recipe, I imagine."

Kim nodded, but didn't say that the cookies were traditional only if one shopped at Safeway's bakery department. "Thank you. Lee is my last name. Kim is my first name. Please call me Kim."

Winnie patted her husband's slightly quivering knee to stop it from vibrating the deep red velvet camelback sofa. "Of course, Kim," she said. "Sorry."

The clock ticked some more.

"Edward used to have a TV show in the UK," Winnie said. "You'd never know it right now, of course. He's let himself go, I'm afraid. And what's more, he's just so devastated by what's happened. I hope you will forgive him. He's normally not nearly this rude."

Beth, who had remained mostly silent while the adults struggled to make polite conversation, didn't know what to say. But in her mind, she hurled insult after insult at the stuck-up woman.

YOU are the one who's rude, Mrs. Grant. Your daughter has been brutally murdered. You expect him to be a charmer right now? I can see why Olivia never said a freaking nice word about you, she thought.

"I love your bracelet," Beth said, just to fill the gap in the conversation. She thought it was hideous.

Winnie jangled the loose chain around her wrist and murmured a thank-you.

Kim pointed to the teapot, but there were no takers for a refill. She tried to give her guests the benefit of the doubt and connect with them in the only way she thought she could. "It is beyond devastating. Years ago, I lost a daughter, too."

Winnie looked up from her cup. "I'm very sorry to hear that," she said. "At least you have another."

Stunned into silence, Kim held her tongue. Without knowing exactly how much alike she and her daughter were at that very moment, she mentally picked up the teapot and dumped the hot liquid all over Winnie's matching travel outfit. Imagining her guest drenched and in pain, Kim churned an internal response: *Beth is not a spare for Christina!*

Beth watched her mother for a reaction but saw none and chalked another notch on her belt of disappointment. The sixteen-year-old was certain that Christina had been her mother's favorite daughter. It wasn't that Beth didn't think her mother loved her. She knew she did. Her mom showed her love every single minute of the day. Deep down, however, Beth was sure that if given the choice and the biggest do-over in the history of the world, her mom would have put *her*, not Christina, on that bus for the Girl Scout Daisies picnic that ill-fated day.

Beth returned the gaze of Edward Grant. "I packed all of Olivia's stuff for you. She might have some things at school," Beth said. "I can check her locker tomorrow, if you like."

Edward nodded. "That would be nice. Thank you, Beth."

"Do you want to see where she was staying?" she asked.

"Please," Winnie said.

They all got up and followed Beth down the hall to Christina's old bedroom—Olivia's during her stay. On the floor next to the crisply made, canopy bed—a sunny yellow and white affair that was too young for a teenager but certainly appropriate for a little girl—were Olivia's four Louis Vuitton suitcases. Stuck in the mirror frame above the dresser were magazine pictures of Hollywood stars, American singers, and a single photo of Olivia and Beth. It had been taken the day Olivia died, with Beth's Polaroid camera, her mom's latest garage-sale find. In the photo, the girls were smiling, carefree, and utterly unaware of what the next eight hours had in store.

At the time it was snapped, Beth and Olivia had just returned from costume shopping at Spookaporium, the former mega-bookstore turned Halloween superstore across the street from the decidedly unglamorous Kitsap Mall. Both had ruled out trampy and skimpy, including a naughty nurse and a slinky mermaid number with a clamshell bra and chiffon fins.

"How is one supposed to walk in that?" Olivia had asked, laughing at the ridiculous and impractical costume.

"I don't intend to walk. I'm going to just sit on the couch with a drink and flip my tail at cute boys," Beth had joked back, feeling happy for the first time in a long, long time.

Olivia would never replace Christina, but living together, she provided Beth with a reminder of what it was like to have a sister.

In the end, Olivia had chosen a simple ghost costume, complete with cutout eye holes. Beth had just stuck a pair of chopsticks in her re-dyed black hair and snapped off an arm-length Polaroid of the two of them just as Drew arrived to whisk Olivia to the party early, ruining everything.

THE DOORBELL JANGLED BETH back to the present, and Kim Lee hurried off to answer it. A moment later, Hayley, Taylor, and Colton entered the now-exceedingly crowded bedroom. They introduced themselves, and Edward nodded. Winnie managed a smile as she studied the teens. Colton spoke up. "We're all really sorry for your loss."

"I imagine you would be," Olivia's father said. "I heard you were the one who took her to the party, didn't you?"

The tone was a tad more than accusatory. Indeed, right then it seemed Olivia's father had an interrogator's spotlight on Colton and he was doing his best to sweat out the truth.

Colton shook his head. "Actually, no," he said. "She went to the party earlier with Drew, Brianna's boyfriend. Brianna asked her to come early to help set up. We got to the party later."

"Oh, I see," Edward said. "You were at the location of my daughter's murder later. All of you were there."

Awkwardness permeated the sad little bedroom.

"Yes, Mr. Grant," Hayley finally said.

Edward's face reddened and the veins in his neck thickened. "You were supposed to keep her safe. Treat her like she was part of the family. That's what the website promised, right, Winnie?"

Winnie didn't have a chance to respond.

"We really liked Olivia," Taylor said, her face turning pink with anger. "We came over to tell you that what happened to Olivia was vile, worse than the worst thing that could happen, but if you think for one second that we are responsible in any way, then you are dead wrong."

Bad choice of words, Hayley thought, though she didn't say so.

She liked it when Taylor was provoked into standing her ground. She needed to do more of that. Pushing the father of a dead girl into a corner probably wasn't the best practice of a needed skill, though.

Like a bantam hen, Kim Lee, the shortest person in the room, huddled the teens together. They were good kids and there was no way, even in the depths of their grief, that the Grants should be unkind to them. Not in her house, anyway.

"I don't know what more we can tell you," Kim added. "I'm sure the police can tell you more."

Winnie spoke up. "Our first stop was the constable's office in Port Orchard."

"Anything encouraging in the investigation?" Kim asked.

"Nothing yet," Winnie said, letting her words hang in the air. "Nothing we can really say. We don't want to impede their efforts by disclosing any details of the investigation."

"Of course not," Kim said.

Edward scooped up the two largest suitcases. "I'd like to meet Brianna."

"I could take you to her," Colton said.

"No need. We have a rental car with GPS," Winnie said, picking up the rest of Olivia's luggage. "I'm sure we can manage. We managed the long drive from Seattle to this," she paused, "—this charming outpost." Her words, of course, didn't match her sentiments. Without saying so, it was clear that she'd thought very little of Port Gamble.

Taylor wondered what Olivia's mom would have really liked to have said just then.

"*We found our way to your insufferable little hamlet in the middle of nowhere.*"

Or, maybe:

"*I would have rather had my daughter die in Seattle than here. In Seattle, at least, they have some decent hotels.*"

"I think we'll be going," Hayley said, looking at her sister and Colton.

"Thanks for coming," Beth said.

Kim put her hand on her daughter's shoulder. "We've had a very long, sad day."

"You haven't the slightest idea what long and sad is," Edward replied, in his clipped British accent.

Kim did, of course. She let it slide, however. There was no point in arm wrestling to see whose loss was greater. Things like that could never really be measured. There's no getting over it. No setting it aside. She knew that Olivia's father's bitter affect was all about his deep, unabated grief.

As a final parting shot, Winnie turned to Kim and commented, "I told that girl to take a different set of luggage. But she didn't listen. She never did. I warned her that American people get killed every single day for wearing status shoes. I told her she'd be a target walking around the airport with her Louis Vuitton. I saw on the news that a couple from Germany was killed outside of Disneyland for the husband's Rolex. America is a very dangerous place."

Kim wanted to defend her country and point out that no one killed Olivia for her designer luggage.

The truth was that no one, not Kim or the police, knew why Olivia had been savagely murdered Halloween night.

And only one person, maybe two, knew who the killer was.

BRANDY CONNORS BAKER FANNED OUT the bills that had piled up on the copper-topped dining table of her Seattle condominium. All around her, boxes of her belongings sat in three neat piles: SELL, GIVE AWAY, and KEEP. The SELL boxes had dwindled over the past few months. She'd put everything of true value up on Craigslist and watched as her assets dwindled. She had nothing left. No second husband. Though she hadn't told a soul—especially her daughter and ex-husband—Robby had left her months ago. No youthful face and not enough money for Botox.

In the place of what used to be her perfect life was a stack of bills and a kind of emptiness that she'd never imagined. Her emotions swung back to something more familiar: disappointment and unbridled anger.

How could things have turned out the way they had? It was so unfair.

She surveyed the mess all around her and then picked up her phone. Brianna had put her photo on the contact button, and Brandy pushed it with her glossy red fingernail.

There was no answer. The call went to voice mail.

"Hey! This is Bree. Leave a message. But make it short. I get bored easily. Bye!"

Brandy left a message. "I hope you are all right, Honey. . . . I love you so much."

It was a brief message. But it was also as long as it needed to be.

Brandy got up and passed by the mirror as she went to the bedroom. She barely glanced at herself. Seeing her reflection in the afternoon light was so unforgiving, and it made her feel even more bitter.

The bedroom was in complete disarray. The bed was unmade; the nightstands were littered with the obvious remnants of a party for two. A pair of Diesel jeans, a black T-shirt, and Armani Exchange underwear were scattered by the door to the bathroom. Brandy wasn't alone, but it dawned on her that being with someone didn't mean an end to loneliness.

chapter 12

DESPITE THE LATE AFTERNOON DOLDRUMS and a protein energy bar that was doing flip-flops in her knotted stomach—like the tasteless snacks always did—Annie Garnett offered a sincere smile when she looked up from her desk and saw Mindee Larsen shoehorned into dark-green razor-cut jeans and a black leather top with four buckles that was part motorcycle chick and part purse. Mindee, with her shock of too-too-blond hair and exaggerated slash of red lipsticked pouty-mouth, definitely knew how to dress for attention. No doubt about it. Mindee succeeded in being a halogen light among a world of incandescent bulbs. No one ever looked away from her without blinking.

Or gawking.

Annie believed in redemption and giving people second chances. She even continued to go to Mindee at the salon when many of the other women of Port Gamble dropped her for another stylist. Mindee never made Annie feel self-conscious about her size or her not-so-great hair. Annie was never sure if it was because Mindee embraced all people, or if it was that she was so completely self-absorbed she didn't care about anyone else's backstory.

Only her own.

"How's Teagan doing?" Annie asked, caring but really more interested in the murder case at hand than the accidental electrocution that had shocked everyone in Port Gamble. It was a death for which Mindee's son, Teagan, took responsibility.

"Fine," Mindee said, applying lipstick and blotting with a tissue from the chief's desktop dispenser. "He's learning how to manage his disappointment and anger. Most of it, if not all, is caused by his absent father."

Annie resisted saying something about the boy's mother and her role in the boy's situation.

"That's good," Annie said. "I'm happy to hear that. Teagan will come out of this all right."

"I know," Mindee said, fishing a Tic Tac from the depths of her purse, a wet-look leather satchel that was so shiny, she occasionally used its glossy surface as mirror. "He and I are a lot alike. We're both deep. We care so much about everyone and everything."

Again, Annie held her tongue.

"I understand that you've done a great job with your community service, Mindee," she said.

Mindee checked her makeup. "Don't call it that. That makes it sound like I'm a criminal."

Too easy.

Mindee snapped her purse shut. "I'm not here about me. I'm here because I saw something that was very disturbing and it is my civic duty to tell you about it."

"Your civic duty, yes," Annie said. "What's it about?"

Mindee tilted her head as if she was about to say something she didn't want anyone else to hear, though, of course, that wasn't much of a worry. No one else was listening.

"Brianna Connors and the murder of that beautiful girl, Olivia Graham."

That was one response Annie hadn't expected to hear.

"Olivia *Grant*," Annie corrected. "What do you know?"

Mindee leaned forward, revealing cleavage in major need of a push-up bra. She wanted to make sure that all of what she was about to say was completely understood.

"Okay," she said. "You might want to write this down." She pointed to a pad.

Annie nodded and picked up a pen. "All set," she said, halfway humoring Mindee, but also intrigued.

Mindee cleared her throat. "I'm not a gossip, and you know that. You know from sitting in my chair at the salon that I never, ever speak badly about anyone." She stopped when she caught the look of disbelief in Annie's eyes. "Not unless it's true, anyway. Here's the deal. Yesterday I was at Victoria's Secret at the mall and I saw Brianna and Drew carrying on like they were completely oblivious about what had just happened at her party. They were practically making out by the thong bins. Something's wrong with that girl."

Annie thought of the yoga poses Brianna did the night of the murder. That was strange too.

"Wrong?" she asked. "Just what do you mean by that? Be specific, Mindee."

"Who carries on like she was shopping for her honeymoon when her girlfriend was sliced like a Benihana hibachi steak the night before?"

"That isn't fair. People handle shock in different ways."

Mindee nodded. "I know. But I Googled it. She's a sociopath. You should Google it too. And besides, it isn't just me," she said. "Others think something's up with her too."

"Others? What others?"

Mindee shrugged. "I'm not sure. Just others. You know, kids at school."

"Did Starla tell you something?" Annie asked.

Mindee looked away for a second. "Starla isn't talking to me right now," she said. "Not much. You know, we're so close that sometimes we just don't get along."

Annie nodded. "Right. So what others told you things, and what things?"

"Just people," Mindee said, clearly backpedaling.

Annie looked down at the pad. She hadn't written a word.

"You should go to Victoria's Secret," Mindee said. "Investigate or something."

ANNIE GARNETT HAD NEVER been inside a Victoria's Secret store, though she'd always dreamed of doing so. It took a criminal case, not desire, to get her inside of the Pepto-pink store at the Kitsap Mall. She made her way past the displays of the things that would never, ever fit her right. *Look. Don't touch. This isn't for you.* The big-boned police chief longed to feel silk on her skin, not the stiff weave of polyester, staticy granny panties that she had to buy from Penney's on the other side of the mall.

It took a murder and a visit from Mindee Larsen to bring her into this lingerie dream/nightmare.

Doralee, the manager, was a pretty, 40-ish woman with soft curls, a sugar voice, and a name to match. She set up Annie in her office to watch the video surveillance tape from the time Mindee had said she'd been shopping.

"Chief," Doralee said, "you'll want to watch this tape here. Counter numbers actually match the time stamp."

"Thank you," Annie said as she settled in.

"If you see something you want to keep, let me know. You'll need a subpoena for that, but no worries. I'll guard the tape with my life."

The tape was HD-clear, which surprised Annie. She expected it to be as fuzzy as one of those black-and-white convenience store films that made it on to the evening news whenever there was a holdup in Tacoma or Seattle. After ten minutes of searching, right there in living color Annie spotted three familiar faces. Mindee was lurking off on the edge of the frame, looking a bit like a crazed stalker (doing her "civic duty"). Nuzzling each other like they couldn't wait to get a room were the stars of the tape: Brianna and Drew. They were kissing. Laughing. They didn't appear to have a care in the world.

As her heart sank lower into that PowerBar–churning stomach of hers, the word Mindee had uttered, had Googled, came to Annie just then: *sociopath.*

They'd just come from being questioned by the police about a murder in Brianna's bedroom, but it didn't faze them a bit. Olivia was . . . what was it that Mindee had so indelicately said? Benihana-ed to death.

A few minutes later, Doralee returned carrying a big pink shopping bag. She put it on the table next to the video player and set it in front of Annie.

"I don't have a subpoena yet. I'm fast, but not that fast."

Doralee smiled and shook her head. "I saw you admiring our Angel line on the way in, Chief Garnett. We tried some sizes last year for bigger girls, but they didn't sell. Big girls just don't come in here. We try, you know, but nothing works. Anyhow, I'm tossing them out, and, well, I thought you might like to have them."

Annie looked into the bag. It looked like a parade of pink and white silk ribbons. She could have cried just then; she was so touched by the gesture. But she didn't. Not when she had a murder to solve. It was against department guidelines for her to accept gifts of any kind, but just then she decided to forget about that particular point in the handout that came with the job.

Victoria had her secrets. Annie was entitled to a few of her own too.

In her car on the way back to Port Gamble, she dialed the numbers she had for Brianna and Drew. She didn't care that Brianna's folks had said their daughter was off-limits. She just needed to talk to the young couple. Just one more interview.

She had a tape to show them.

Both calls went to voice mail.

Damn, where are those kids now?

KEVIN RYAN WAS A NEWS JUNKIE, and his girls had picked up the habit. No matter what was going on in their lives, the Ryans always seemed to find their way to the living room for the evening news. With the tail end of *The Ellen DeGeneres Show* emanating from the TV, the twins were doing homework on the couch, Valerie was listening in the kitchen through the doorway, and Kevin was not-so-successfully multitasking, scrolling through his iPad.

At six o'clock sharp, the news closed in on its blonde anchor, a Seattle legend who had been on the air almost since the time media moved from radio to TV. She stared right at the camera with her all-knowing and sympathetic eyes.

"In other news, we bring you this special report on the murder of Olivia Grant, a foreign exchange student from the United Kingdom . . ."

Kevin stopped scrolling through his Twitter feed and looked up as Mindee Larsen, of all people, came into view. She was standing in front of the Kingston hair salon, holding a pair of scissors and shaking her head.

"I couldn't believe what I was seeing. I reported it to the police," she said. "It made me sick to my stomach."

The camera cut to a Victoria's Secret salesgirl.

"Yeah, that girl was basically bumping uglies with that boyfriend of hers when she was here."

Next rolled the store's video footage of Brianna and Drew cuddling by Thong Mountain before the producers cut back to Mindee.

"What kind of a person acts that way when a girl is killed in her house? I don't get it. I really don't know what's wrong with people these days."

The segment concluded with the mention that "while Brianna Connors and Drew Marcello were not named suspects by any law enforcement agency, they were considered 'persons of interest' and sources indicated an arrest warrant was imminent."

"Dad?" Hayley asked. "What's going on?"

For a change, her crime-writer dad Kevin didn't know. He had been following the case ever since the twins had told him about it, but from a distance. "They must not have anything on Brianna and Drew. They need more evidence to arrest them than just tacky, bizarre behavior."

"What reason would they have for killing Olivia? I mean, unless it's a random mall shooter, Dad, don't killers usually have a reason?"

Kevin shook his head. "Motive isn't something we can ever really be sure about, unless it's for greed or power."

"But that wasn't the case with Brianna and Drew. *If* they did it, they didn't benefit by killing Olivia. I can't think of a single good reason."

"There's always that other category of killer, the one who does it because in his twisted mind, he thinks it's fun. We call those sickos 'thrill killers,'" he said.

Taylor slumped on the sofa next to her dad. "Brianna isn't like that. And Drew is a moron. So I don't think that's possible."

"Maybe it was an accident," Kevin said. "Maybe they were doing something and it went too far."

He left the phrase "doing something" appropriately vague.

Neither of the twins knew Drew or Brianna all that well, so a creepy scenario of some kind couldn't be ruled out.

Taylor had read online about the horrible things some kids had done when messing around: eating spoonfuls of cinnamon, the so-called choking game, and consuming vodka in ways that were disgusting and wrong.

None of them involved the sharp edge of a knife.

chapter 13

TAYLOR RYAN STOOD NEXT TO HER LOCKER, pulling some books out of her backpack and shoving them into the tight metal space. She was pretty sure that her right shoulder drooped a little because of the strain of carrying around her thick door-stopper of a geometry book. That was the worst offender.

Beth Lee saw her from across the pod and hurried over, earbuds still jammed into her ears.

"Hey, we have to talk. I need to tell you something, and I don't want you to broadcast it to your sister. She'll tell Colton. He'll probably tell his mom. Follow me," Beth said, tugging Taylor toward the girls' bathroom.

"Colton wouldn't do that," Taylor insisted. "He can keep a secret."

Beth shook her head. "Whatever. This is big, and I'm freaking out."

The bathroom looked empty, except for a freshman girl named Tia Malone who was messing with her long black hair and retro Goth makeup in the broad mirror over a bank of sinks.

"You're gonna leave now, Tia," Beth told her.

Tia kept her eyes on the mirror, barely glancing at Beth. "Who's going to make me?"

"I am," Beth said, her fierce eyes now glowering.

Tia spun around and faced the girls. Taylor, in her dark-dyed Sevens, pale-blue North Face jacket, and cream-colored pullover, didn't seem like much of a threat. Beth's eighties-style acid washed jeans, SAVED BY THE BELL T-shirt, biker boots, spiked hair, and scowling face, however, told a very different story.

Tia fumed as she went for the door. "Beth, you're such a poser."

"I'll pose you," Beth shot back.

"What's the matter with you?" Taylor asked. "Since when did you become trash-TV mean? I get that you're upset over Olivia, but you've got to get a grip."

Beth didn't answer. Instead, she looked around the perfume-bombed utilitarian bathroom to make sure they were alone. She checked the first stall for feet. *No one.* The rest of the doors were open a sliver. The school had removed the latches because they were getting stuck. That was the principal's story, anyway. New ones were supposedly on the way. Until their installation, girls had to use their toe tips to push the door shut if someone was lurking in front of their stall.

Satisfied, Beth grabbed Taylor's shoulders and looked squarely into her eyes. "I'm in trouble, Taylor. Big, life-changing trouble. I'm totally scared right now."

Taylor didn't blink. Beth *was* terrified. It was all over her face and in her eyes. "Scared about what?"

Beth took a gulp. "That police chief called again about Olivia's murder."

Taylor's blue eyes widened. "What about her murder?"

Beth ran her fingers over her spikes and looked around again, making sure that her only audience was Taylor. "They found one of my dad's neckties from my costume jammed into Olivia's mouth. It was, you know, used to, like, shut her up."

"Ugh. That's so sad. That's gross too."

Beth clamped both hands onto Taylor's shoulders. "Sad? It's a nightmare. I think they think that I killed her."

"You? That's crazy. You wouldn't hurt a spider," Taylor said, randomly and unfortunately pulling up a mental picture of Charlotte, the homemade spider tattoo that Beth had inked on her inner thigh in middle school.

"Someone must have taken your dad's tie. Do you remember leaving it at the party?"

"No. But there's something else that also looks kind of bad."

Taylor thought she saw some movement on the door of the last stall, but she put it aside.

"What is it, Beth?"

The bathroom door swung open. It was a freshman named Sassi or Cici or something like that.

Beth pointed an index finger stacked with four silver rings she'd made from her mother's flatware service in the seventh grade. "You have to leave," she said to the intruding girl. "My friend here might be pregnant."

Sassi or Cici looked at Beth, and then shot a judgmental gaze at Taylor before turning around and leaving.

Taylor's jaw practically skimmed the floor. "Beth! Why did you have to say *that*?"

Beth brightened a little, but only for a second. "Just came to me. Never mind. No one will think it's true." She waited a beat. "No offense, you know, but for obvious reasons."

Taylor wasn't sure what obvious reasons she was talking about. *The fact that she didn't have a boyfriend? Or was it that she couldn't get one?*

"Do you think you're a suspect?" Taylor asked. "That doesn't make any sense."

"Well, there's the tie business. And we had a big fight. Me and Olivia. Queen Bree summoned Olivia to the party early. We got into it. Words were said. It was, well, not good. I was so angry about her wanting to hang out with Brianna. They'd gotten so close, and I felt left out."

Tears started to roll down her cheeks. *Actual Beth Lee tears. Until the last few days, that had been a rare occurrence.*

"It's okay," Taylor said reaching over to the tissue dispenser and offering one to her friend.

"You don't get it," Beth said, taking the tissue. "Of course you don't. You've always had someone. I had Christina, and then she died. Then my dad died. I just thought that Olivia would be mine, you know? My mom and I arranged for her to come. We Skyped all summer. I thought we were getting kind of close."

Taylor hugged Beth. "I'm sorry," she said. "But I'm sure that the police know you didn't have anything to do with, you know, the stabbing."

Beth pushed away and looked at the mirror, her eyes still tracking Taylor's. "You must think I'm pathetic," she said, dabbing her eyes and turning the tissue black with mascara.

"I don't. And I do understand. Lately with Hayley always hanging out with Colton, I'm alone most of the time too. I don't like sharing Hayley with him. I really, really don't. But Colton is a decent guy and, well, I know that relationships change."

"I said some awful things to Olivia that night about British food—yuck—Pippa's overrated butt, and something mean about Nicki Minaj. I told Olivia that I wished she'd go back home on the *Titanic* and hoped it would hit another iceberg. I don't think she heard me, but I might have said something to the effect that I wished she would drop dead."

"No! You didn't!" Taylor said, her voice rising. Her mind reeled, wondering who, if anyone, had heard Beth say those scary, prophetic words.

Taylor grabbed another tissue and provided it to Beth, who took it with a quick nod. "Who knows that you fought with Olivia?" she asked.

Beth ignored the question. "I had it out with Brianna at the party too." She stopped herself. "Do I look like I've been crying? I don't want anyone to think I'm a big baby."

Taylor patted her softly on the shoulder. Beth liked everyone to think she was aloof, tough, sardonic, and above all of the stuff that teenagers obsess over. She wasn't, of course. No one at Kingston High was. No teen *anywhere* was.

"No, you look fine. No one will know. Now, please, answer me. Who knows about the necktie and that you fought with Olivia?"

Beth looked directly into Taylor's eyes. "No one but the police," she said. "You're the only other person I've told."

"All right, I swear to keep it confidential. You and me, Beth, we're like sisters."

Just then Beth gave Taylor a quick hug, which surprised her. Beth had never spontaneously hugged her before. Sure, it was a quick, hard little gesture, but it was Beth genuinely letting her guard down. Letting someone on the inside. It made Taylor smile.

Beth gathered herself together, put her earbuds back in, and the two of them went for the door.

"What are you listening to?" Taylor asked.

Beth shook her head. "Nothing. I just don't want to talk to anyone. It's a defense mechanism, I guess."

"I'm glad you talked to me," Taylor said, her own blue eyes glistening with emotion. Not tear territory, but the kind of dampness that comes when something good happens.

"I'm glad you're not pregnant," Beth said.

STARLA LARSEN PUSHED OPEN THE DOOR to the very last stall. She had chosen it because it was the farthest away from the well-used bank of mirrors, and she didn't like anyone to hear her pee. As she sat there, she took in every word Taylor Ryan and Beth Lee had been saying. She understood why some musicians said they'd practiced singing in the bathrooms. In a place where no one really wants to hear what the next person is doing, it was the ultimate irony that one could hear the sound of a pin drop against the tiled floor of a girls' bathroom.

And one could certainly overhear Beth Lee spill her guts about Olivia.

Starla went to the mirror, her crystalline blue eyes focused not so much on what she was doing as she washed her hands, but what she was thinking. Starla reapplied some cinnamon gloss to her lips and fidgeted with her halo of blond hair. When Katelyn's death was tied to her mother and brother last year, it was more than embarrassing. Starla had to work double-hard to maintain her in-crowd status. Like her mother, Mindee, Starla was looking for a little redemption. Served with that? A side of revenge, of course.

As she threw a million-dollar smile at her reflection, Starla thought about what to do with this tantalizing tidbit. Her mother had already gone to the police. So scratch that. Going to the police was so yesterday.

LATER, WHEN HER KILLER REPLAYED the night Olivia Grant was stabbed to death, it brought a sense of euphoria that hadn't been expected. Murderers had long talked about the thrill that came with stealing another person's life. There was something darkly magical about seeing the eyes of a human being move from fear to anguish and then to peace. It was like being God, creating a storm of terror and letting it wash over another person, and then, just as quickly, allowing the terrified to find complete and final peace. The killer liked that. No, *loved* that. It was a rush better than any pharmaceutical could provide. It was far above the mix of adrenaline and laughter that comes from the scariest and best amusement park ride. Tower of Terror in Disneyland? Forget it. Skydiving with an unreliable parachute? Not even close. Skiing down a mountain in front of an avalanche's white wall? Nada.

Even better than sex.

The murderer had a specific intent, a purpose that really had nothing to do with the rush that came with the act of doing it. That had been a surprise. As the water ran in Brianna's bathroom sink and the blood flowed downward into the swirling cyclone of the drainpipe, the feeling was undeniably good.

The sensation of being all-powerful on that Halloween night had been an unexpected bonus.

chapter 14

THE WASHINGTON STATE CRIME LAB IN OLYMPIA, the state capital a hundred miles south of Seattle, was a kind of way station for all major criminal court cases—the midpoint between the crime scene and the courtroom. All of the evidence collected by Annie Garnett and her team from the Connorses' house at 2121 Desolation View Drive in Port Gamble in the early morning hours of November 1 was processed at the county's lab in Port Orchard and then sent to Olympia for further analysis. The fact that the victim was from another country had flagged the case as one with "special sensitivities."

A slaughtered American girl would warrant great care, but the Olivia Grant case required just a bit more. International incidents were an albatross for any jurisdiction.

Fourteen containers, each holding pieces of potential evidence collected from the four-thousand-square-foot Connors residence, were checked in and sent to the appropriate lab for additional analysis. Most of what was gathered the night of the murder and throughout the morning after Halloween was mundane, however, and would likely never be part of any court proceeding. Case in point: thirty-two red plastic drinking cups, taking up the space of two boxes.

It, without a doubt, had been *some* party.

Seven objects, however, were of special and considerable interest: the multiple pieces of a broken crystal vase; Olivia's slip, which was literally a bloody mess; Brianna's robe; Beth Lee's kimono; and three men's neckties—one of which had been retrieved from the victim's mouth.

Cheryl Raines, a veteran lab worker with twenty-one years of experience to her credit, carefully removed all seven items from their plastic packaging and logged them into her evidence ledger. It was crucial that from the minute these items were recovered from the crime scene, each time the evidence was handled was noted on the tag. Chain of custody was important because if the evidence was compromised by less than attentive supervision, it was akin to handing the perpetrator a "Get Out of Jail Free" card, especially if he or she had a good defense attorney. And judging by the crime scene photos it was clear that much of the evidence had been disturbed by the throng of investigators. Compromised evidence was a defense attorney's best friend.

After Olivia's slip was hung on a clothesline to dry in a lab designed to preserve blood on a garment, Cheryl carefully spread it out on a stainless steel table. Although now stiff and wine-brown with dried blood, the fabric was once a shimmery white sateen. The tech could also see a scattering of loose sequins caught on the slip in various places and threads that didn't match the fabric.

Next, Cheryl turned her attention to the slices in the material. She counted the number of slashes at three, although it was hard to tell if another irregularity in fabric had been caused by a knife or was simply torn as the British girl tried to get away from her killer. None of the cuts went all the way through to the other side.

Birdy Waterman's accompanying autopsy report indicated that Olivia Grant had been stabbed once in the throat and three times in her chest and abdomen. The wounds were consistent with the incisions in the slip.

Cheryl snapped photographs of a small ruler placed along each of the slices in the blood-drenched fabric and by the thread and sequins before running each item underneath a microscope.

Through a magnifying lens, Cheryl easily confirmed her hunch. Neither the sequins nor the ivory-colored thread came from the slip. They'd come from another garment.

What else had the dead girl been wearing that night?

The shards of the vase, it turned out, were easier to re-assemble than Cheryl had originally thought. Almost all of the pieces had been recovered, and it was immediately evident that none had been used to murder Olivia. The pieces were thicker than the wounds noted in Dr. Waterman's report, which meant the murder weapon was still out there. *Somewhere.*

Seeing a single red smear along one edge of a splinter of crystal glass, Cheryl tested for blood. *Positive.* A quick run through the samples of the principals collected by Kitsap County provided a clear and indisputable match to Brianna Connors, the hostess of the party.

The blood on the trim of Brianna's robe was a match to the victim, but it was much too small an amount to have been worn during the violent attack that left Olivia on a slab in the morgue.

The final thing Cheryl did before clocking out was photograph and examine the kimono and the three ties under ultraviolet light. Under her examination, Cheryl noted a red spot on a sleeve of the kimono. She also noted that two of the three ties were without any blood, DNA, or anything. She found a single black fiber on the third one, the one marked with Olivia's saliva, which tested positive for blood.

It was Olivia's, of course.

AT FIRST, BRIANNA CONNORS, and to a lesser degree Drew Marcello, seemed to revel in the swarm of attention that came with the glow of the media's unblinking spotlight. Everyone wanted a sound bite from the not-so-grieving best friend. Overnight, the Kingston High School student had become bigger than Paris-Lindsay-Nicole-Winona-Snookie-Britney and all of those annoying TV Teen Moms combined. It wasn't for a good reason, either.

The hashtag #WORSEBFFTHANBRIANNA started trending on Twitter almost immediately after the story hit the news about Brianna's indifference to what had occurred in her bedroom:

My BFF stole my boyfriend. #WORSEBFFTHANBRIANNA

One time my BFF borrowed my car and smashed it up and stuck me with the bill. #WORSEBFFTHANBRIANNA

My former BFF stole my mom's jewelry and hocked it. #WORSEBFFTHANBRIANNA

"Look," Brianna told a reporter in a sit-down TV interview that she insisted was her last until the mess sorted itself out, "I get that I'm not all crying about it like you want me to be, but it isn't like I don't have feelings. I don't know what you all want from me. I feel like I'm being attacked for being different. I'm not a lawyer—my dad *is*—but criticizing me for the way I grieve and how I look could be considered a hate crime."

The story played even better in the UK. Fleet Street in London trumpeted the tale of the British girl murdered in a tawdry sex game in the US as an example of American culture gone wrong. A reporter who knew her way around the Internet better than her American counterparts found an old online journal that Brianna had kept in the dark ages of social networking—on MySpace. Before Facebook, before Instagram and Pinterest, she had posted pictures there, mostly of "hot shirtless" (as if there were any other kind) Abercrombie guys. She called herself Easy-Breezy.

Headline writers in the UK could have kissed her for that moniker, and British tabloids covered the newsstands with the scandal:

EASY-BREEZY SAYS "I WANT YOUR SEX!"

EASY-BREEZY SAYS "I DON'T KNOW HOW MANY LOVERS I'LL HAVE!"

BEDROOM DOOR WIDE OPEN—as his mother Shania insisted—Colton James looked at the articles with girlfriend Hayley on his homebuilt laptop and clicked through the links provided by the *Daily Mail* newspaper in the UK. As available as "Easy-Breezy" proclaimed to be in the articles they'd just read, the high school girl they knew didn't seem so wild. Others at Kingston were far wilder. As they read on the screen capture of the suddenly-deleted MySpace page, they saw that the reference to "I want your sex" was a joke Brianna had made about her father's George Michael CD collection. The "don't know how many lovers" comment so boldly touted on the front page of the paper was pulled out of a sappy post Brianna had made about not knowing how many boyfriends she'd have before she found the one she'd marry. She was only thirteen years old at the time.

"This isn't right, Colton," Hayley said.

Colton fixed his dark eyes on her. "I don't like Brianna, but yeah, it *isn't* right."

"I don't really know her," Hayley said. She didn't ever want people to think she was two-faced, a trait she considered among the worst a person could have. "I feel kind of sorry for her."

Colton nodded. "How can they say all that about her?"

"My dad says that there isn't anything the media loves better than a pretty killer. The media is dog-piling on her because she didn't act sad when the camera was watching."

"Yeah, but her behavior *is* kind of weird, to say the least," Colton said. "Given what's going on."

Hayley couldn't argue that, not much anyway. "Stupid, wrong, whatever," she finally said. "That doesn't mean that she killed Olivia."

Colton pushed a little. "She had that cut on her hand—remember? We saw it at school."

Hayley nodded. "But it was a small cut and the police didn't find much blood on her. If Olivia fought back, Brianna's injury would probably have been bigger and she would have been splattered with blood."

"Yeah, I guess so," Colton said, his mind now back to the first time he noticed the scars on his mother's palms. She'd lied to him that she'd fallen though a plate glass window, but he later found out they were from the time she'd been attacked in the Safeway parking lot while he was in his car seat watching everything, but not really seeing enough of it to understand what was going on.

At least never admitting to it.

As Hayley and Colton surfed the web, they discovered that most of the tabloids and webzines portrayed Brianna as intentionally hyping up the drama for a potential book or movie deal. Nobody had seen her or Drew since her dad and stepmother had returned to town, and until the pair surfaced, all the daily rags had was the same, tired footage that they kept replaying over and over.

The first was the Flip cam video that the *North Kitsap Herald* reporter took at the crime scene. The second was the surveillance footage from the Victoria's Secret shopping trip the afternoon after Olivia's murder. The last one was a grainy black-and-white make-out video taken by the surveillance camera in the elevator at the Silverdale Beach Hotel.

And then there was the *Inside Edition* piece. The reporter for the tabloid TV show had called it a "scoop," but in reality it was an ambush on Port Gamble's police chief.

Annie Garnett had taken a short walk to the General Store and back to clear her head when the *Inside Edition* cameraman and reporter—a young man with fake, tanned skin that made him look like a Cheeto with bushy eyebrows—scurried over to grab a few sound bites outside the police department.

"Isn't it true that Brianna Connors was doing yoga in the hall right after the murder?" he asked.

"I don't really want to get into that," Annie said, feeling very uncomfortable. She moved her large hands out of view.

The reporter cocked a caterpiller brow and went on. "Isn't it true that she's no longer cooperating in the investigation?"

Annie's unflappable composure sank a little more, though she hid it well. She was pissed off. Big-time. She wasn't about to lose her cool, however. Not then, not there with that twit from tabloid TV.

"It is true that Ms. Connors and Mr. Marcello have declined for now, but we're hoping we can schedule something soon," she said, stepping away.

"Wait a second! I have something to show you," the reporter said.

A second later, he thrust his cell phone in her face and played back a video.

"This will air tonight," he said.

The camera zeroed in on Olivia's parents as they sat on a sofa in some posh Seattle hotel. A floral arrangement of ice-blue hydrangeas and creamy-white gladiolas the size of a Mini Cooper provided the backdrop.

"Sources tell *Inside Edition*," the interviewer on the video said in a breathless voice, "that your daughter's murder might have been some kind of a game gone wrong."

Eager to make his point, Edward Grant nearly lunged at the camera to get closer to the lens. "Our daughter was slaughtered by a soulless girl and her boyfriend. I don't have any idea what they were doing that night, but I can tell you that Olivia was not a willing participant. This was no game gone wrong. No girl as smart as our Olivia plays a game to lose her life."

Mrs. Grant dabbed at her eyes when the interviewer turned to her.

"I just can't comment. I really couldn't. I'm not a judgmental person. I will say—and I hope this doesn't offend anyone because the people here have been rather kind—but I really do wish that the police would do something."

After ditching the reporter, Annie Garnett sighed. She felt upset and disappointed. Things were spiraling out of control. She wondered who told the TV reporter about the yoga. She didn't want that out. It was a piece of the puzzle—and an inflammatory one at that.

Once inside the safety of the station, Annie was greeted by Tatiana bearing licorice spice tea, the chief's favorite.

"I saw that through the window. You could use something to calm you down," she said.

Annie allowed a slight smile to cross her face. It was as fake a smile as she'd ever given.

"What I could really use now is a Xanax," she said.

Tatiana shook her head. "Just drink the tea. You're gonna need it." She held out a slip of paper.

"What's that?"

"Brianna's dad. He's mad, mad, mad. Says that Brianna ran away because of you."

"Ran away? What do you mean?"

"The father says that his daughter is missing. She's not returning his calls," Tatiana said, passing the slip of paper across the desk. "He's a real jerk too."

Annie nodded. That he was.

IF THERE COULD BE A SUBJECT that trumped Olivia's murder in the halls of Kingston High School as fodder for incessant gossip and *Criminal Minds*–type speculation, it was the sudden disappearance of Brianna Connors and Drew Marcello. One minute they were the focus of a police investigation for a murder and what they may or may not know about what happened Halloween night. The next, they'd morphed into the dreaded "persons of interest" category. And then, just as quickly, they were gone.

Beth Lee, Colton James, and Hayley and Taylor Ryan sat across from the library and tried to piece it all together.

"You run when you're guilty, right?" Beth said.

Colton unzipped his hoodie. "Or if you think you've been framed," he said.

"Guilty, I say," Beth repeated.

Taylor tapped the screen on her phone. "Neither one of them has posted anything on Facebook or Twitter for like sixteen hours."

"My guess is that they are dead," Beth said, testing the strength of her spiked hair by pressing her fingertips gently against each point. "Who can go without posting for sixteen hours?"

"Or sixteen minutes," Taylor said.

"Let's think about it a little," Hayley said, always approaching an issue or problem with logic. "Any number of things could have happened to them. Flight doesn't mean they went willingly."

"What are you getting at?" Beth asked.

"Maybe they were kidnapped by the real killer?" Colton asked.

"Possible, I guess," Hayley said, though she didn't think it was likely. Even so, she wanted to back up her boyfriend's theory.

"Like maybe they got in a car accident or something?" Taylor said, realizing that the minute she gave voice to the idea it was probably the lamest suggestion anyone could come up with.

"I'll stick with my original theory," Beth said. "You run because you're guilty."

LATER THAT DAY, the *Seattle Times* updated its website, moving the story of a police cadet who got drunk and rolled his car into a school playground from the top of the page to:

PORT GAMBLE COUPLE DODGES MURDER INVESTIGATION

Brianna Connors and Drew Marcello, the teenagers caught in the drama of an investigation surrounding the murder of Olivia Grant, a 16-year-old exchange student from London, have fled Port Gamble.

"I blame the media and I blame Annie Garnett, police chief, for the fact that my daughter has vanished," said Brianna's father, Brian Connors, a Seattle attorney. "This has been totally mishandled from the start."

Brian Connors was not only a braggart, a spotlight-seeker, and an egomaniac.

He was also right.

chapter 15

HAYLEY AND TAYLOR WERE CLEARING the dishes after dinner when another message from Text Creeper arrived on their phones like electronic slime:

CASE FILE #613-7H: SHE DESERVED WHAT SHE GOT.

If Text Creeper's first text had spooked Hayley and Taylor on Monday, this second message had them jumping out of their skin. Both girls knew they had to ignore it, but that was going to be far from easy.

"Nobody deserves to die like that! What does it mean?" Taylor asked as she turned off the stream of hot water that ran over the dishes in the sink.

Hayley shook her head. She didn't know. Who could?

Taylor reached for a paper towel. "Should we tell Mom and Dad?"

"Tell me what?" Kevin Ryan asked, popping his head into the kitchen. The call of the coffee pot had brought him back to the kitchen. It was a much-needed break from writing his latest book, *Killer Smile*, about a handsome serial killer from Iowa who charmed women into posing for a "classy" nude calendar before bludgeoning them to death. The real killer was neither charming nor handsome, but his publisher insisted that's what readers wanted to read.

"The tip-off, girls," he had told Hayley and Taylor when he had started the project that summer, "is that there is no such thing as a 'classy nude' calendar. If a photographer suggests that you or your friends should pose for one, report him to the police pronto. Don't even think about it. You'll save a life, for sure."

"It's about Olivia's murder," Hayley said, pouring soap into the sink.

"People are . . . saying stuff about what happened. We're all freaking out big-time," Taylor said. "Have you heard anything?"

Kevin dropped into a seat at the kitchen table. "I don't really have any inside info," he said. "You'll probably find out more on Twitter or Facebook."

The sisters knew that their father was probably spot-on in some ways, but they weren't really seeking specifics about the case. They were looking for reassurance.

"Do you think whoever killed Olivia might kill someone else?" Taylor asked. "Maybe another student at the high school?"

"Maybe that's what's happened to Brianna and Drew. Maybe they've been murdered?" Hayley added.

Kevin understood how fear enveloped people whenever a terrible crime occurred. A crime like what happened to Olivia was the scariest, most paranoia-inducing of all. At the moment, there was no telling if anyone else was in danger or not. Olivia's murder might have been random, which was potentially more terrifying than thinking that it had been premeditated.

The idea of a serial killer lurking around Kingston and Port Gamble hadn't really occurred to any of the Ryans until that moment. Kevin's first thought had been that some kid had gotten high and went berserk—a drug-addled killing. If not that, then maybe it was one of Brianna's father's clients? Someone who wasn't happy with his defense and sought revenge? Both scenarios had been in the news in the past couple of days.

Kevin looked at his watch. It was 12:45 p.m.

"Let me see what I can find out," he said. He knew that Annie Garnett would be in line at the Gamble Bay Coffee stand in exactly four minutes. Annie, who'd grown up with nothing that even closely resembled the consistency of a normal life, had forged her own with the regularity of a church chime. She ate lunch by the park, walked to the coffee place, and later strolled around the entire perimeter of the business district. She did that every single day, including weekends, at exactly the same time.

"Thanks, Dad," Hayley said.

STILL JOGGING EACH DAY—and still unable to shake off those last ten pounds—Kevin "ran into" Annie at the coffee stand that filled the spaces by the pumps of Port Gamble's defunct gas station.

She was there, getting her coffee, as he predicted.

The police chief smiled wearily when she saw him.

"Hey, Annie," he said, fishing for change in his jacket. "Surprised to see you here."

"I'm here every day at this time," she said. "Like you didn't know that."

Kevin shrugged and placed his order—a triple tall one Splenda latte. "I guess I did. Anyway, I wanted to get your take on the Grant case," he said.

She sipped her coffee. "Open investigation, Kev. You know I can't talk about it."

"My girls are scared. All the girls in town are. They think there's a crazed serial killer out there. I just wanted to, you know, put them at ease."

The police chief narrowed her gaze. "This isn't for a book, is it?"

Kevin shook his head, a little too vigorously. "No. I'm not that kind of crime writer. You know that."

She took off the annoying plastic lid and drank some more. "Right. Off the record?" she asked.

"You know you don't have to ask that," Kevin said.

"I was just burned by *Inside Edition*."

"I won't lie to you, Annie. I saw it. Just so you know, *everyone* gets burned by *Inside Edition*. But, yeah, this is only for me. I'm not working on anything. Besides if I ever betrayed your trust, Annie, you'd find ways to ticket me every single day for the rest of my life."

"You know me too well." Annie took a breath. The November air had chilled, and a white puff of vapor came from her bright red lips. "It's interesting you mention that people are scared there's a serial killer on the loose. My best guess is that this killer is not a stranger but someone much closer to the situation."

"Closer? Like Brianna? Drew?" he asked.

Annie looked around, surveying the town she loved so much. "I can say I've never seen anyone more disinterested in a slaying that happened in her very bedroom than this Brianna. She is *unbelievable*. It was almost as though she were mad at Olivia for getting slaughtered in her room. If you asked Brianna, it would have been much more convenient if Olivia had died downstairs, in say, the workout room, where she didn't need to go and could have someone hose out the place."

Kevin's interest piqued, thinking for a moment that if Olivia had been killed by her best friend, maybe there was a book in it after all.

"Maybe the kid was in shock?" he suggested.

Annie pulled Kevin away from the barista, who seemed to have pretty good hearing over the cloud of steam from the espresso machine.

"Possibly." She lowered her voice. "Hell, probably. I don't know. She was strange, and Drew wasn't much better. I don't want to put it lightly, because I'm not like that, but, honestly, someone made cold cuts out of a party guest and neither of them seemed to care much. Not about the girl or her parents or her friends. I've never seen anything like it in my life."

She stopped, realizing she'd probably said too much.

Kevin drank his latte. "I read somewhere that kids who play violent video games become desensitized and don't have a clue about the real thing or its impact on people."

"I don't buy that," Annie said. "I think a sociopath is a sociopath and no video game in the world can turn a normal person into a killer."

Annie's logic was reasonable. Kevin felt his theory was one he'd keep to himself from now on. His editor had suggested it once as a way to make a true crime story more "topical," and it was a flop back then too.

"What was Brianna like at the scene?" he asked.

Annie snapped her lid back on the paper cup. "Walk with me," she said. The pair started toward the big green water towers that welcomed people to the small business district. "That was even better. After she practically made out with her dumb-as-a-bag-of-rocks boyfriend on the front lawn, she proceeded to—and I'm not exaggerating—over-the-top whine about Olivia's murder."

As they reached the corner, Kevin went out on a limb and asked, "You think she's the killer, don't you?"

Annie didn't like the idea of rushing to name a suspect when the case was so new. It usually hindered focus, not strengthened it. "There wasn't enough blood on her to pin it on her, and we haven't found the murder weapon yet. But I think she's just about anything other than an innocent bystander. Really, Kevin, this is one messed-up girl."

They paused to watch people get on a transit bus, and Segway Guy, a Port Gamble resident nicknamed by the twins, followed in the vehicle's wake.

"Messed up enough to stab someone in the throat?" he asked.

"Not common for a girl, that's for sure," Annie said. "But it happens. Remember that case in Bremerton where the thirteen-year-old used an electric garden edger on the pervert next door?"

No one in Kitsap County could ever forget that case. "Smart girl, that thirteen-year-old," he said. "But that's not the case here."

Annie started across the street, turning to Kevin. "No, it isn't."

"So why the rage?" he asked, still keeping his voice low, even though there was no one near enough to hear.

Annie pulled her coat tighter as the wind kicked up off the bay. "Don't know, and when I find out, you won't be getting the scoop from me."

"Come on," Kevin said, only half-begging.

Annie shook her head, and her black hair swirled in the air. "You got me in a moment of weakness. Off-guard. No more. Like one of your books, this case is likely going to be a shocker. I want to keep my focus on finding out what happened before someone else does."

"Before someone kills again," he said.

She nodded and continued on. "That, too," she said.

WHILE DAD WAS TRYING TO DIG UP INFO on Olivia's murder, Hayley was at the Jameses' house next door hanging out with Colton again. Taylor took the opportunity to hit the books. Taylor's lame Family Life project was almost due, and in typical fashion she hadn't even started it yet.

Luckily, she knew Mr. Hayden was a style-over-substance sort of teacher. Bright colors and lots of sparkles always got his attention and a good grade. She pulled out her laptop and set up shop on the kitchen table. Faithful Hedda, the family's dachshund, found a warm spot on the heat duct and, being the greedy heat hog that she was, managed to settle herself completely atop it.

Grill marks, Taylor thought with a smile as she glanced at the hot-dog-shaped pet. Taylor ducked into her mom's closet for the family photos.

Being a full-time psychiatric nurse, mother, and wife left Valerie Ryan very little time to also be the family historian. Whatever family photos they had never seemed to make it into albums, which was fine by the Ryans who, for obvious reasons, preferred to live in the present. Instead, Taylor's mom kept photos in two Nike shoeboxes: one pre- and the other post-twins. Both sat unceremoniously on the top shelf of her clothes closet. No one had touched either box in years, not since the family had started taking their photos with digital cameras and smartphones.

Taylor slid the "post-twins" box off the shelf and dug down toward the bottom. Grabbing a fistful of photos, she sorted through them and set aside those she could use for her project. There was one of her dad carrying her and Hayley like a couple of footballs to the hospital nursery, and lots of them as tiny, pink babies. In several of the images, Taylor could see the small *T* and *H* her mom had written in Magic Marker on the backs of their wrists to help her know which was which.

As Taylor flipped through more photos, she saw herself growing up right before her eyes. There were school pictures of Taylor and her sister and even a couple of old letters mixed in with the photos. Taylor recognized one she had written from summer camp, the one and only time her parents had separated the sisters.

Mommy, I hate it here. I miss you. I miss Dad. I miss Hedda. Most of all I miss my sister. I have dreams every night that we're together, but when I wake up I'm all alone. The kid in the bunk above me wets the bed.

Taylor smiled as she carefully folded the letter and put it back into its rainbow sticker-covered envelope. The bed-wetter was Starla Larsen. Taylor had forgotten that little tidbit.

Could come in handy one day.

At the very bottom of the box, buried there like a tiny corpse in a coffin, Taylor found a single photograph marking the time just after the bus crash. It was a color snapshot of the twins wrapped in tubes and connected to a tangle of wires in the intensive care unit. On the wall behind them was a banner that read:

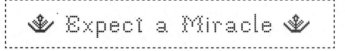

The crash and the month-long hospitalization was such a big, dark part of the Ryan family history. Taylor was sure it was the kind of thing that would tug at Mr. Hayden's heartstrings and get her a better grade. Now all she needed to do was find a few photos of her grandparents and parents as kids, scan everything, throw it into PowerPoint, and she was done.

"Better roll over if you want to cook evenly," Taylor told Hedda as she grabbed the small pile of "post-twins" pictures and the "pre-twins" box and padded down the hall toward the kitchen.

Hedda lifted her head briefly before going right back to sleep. Back at the kitchen table, Taylor lifted the top from the box.

The photographs on the first layer were familiar. She had seen them at her grandfather's memorial service. The first was a black-and-white photograph of her grandpa Chester Fitzpatrick standing in front of the McNeil Island Prison WELCOME sign.

Taylor grinned at the irony. *Who, really, wants to be welcomed to prison?*

Grandpa Chester had run the institution, and Taylor's mom grew up there. Beneath that photo were pictures of Valerie with her mom and dad at the prison, the guard towers looming above them. The rest were assorted vacation photos. In one, her mother was standing next to a slightly disturbing version of Mickey Mouse.

Taylor wondered, *just how old is that mouse anyway?*

While the shots on the first layer of memories in the box were interesting, they didn't advance her cause for Mr. Hayden's project. Taylor reached deep into the box and pulled out a manila envelope that had been folded in half.

The envelope's clasp, loose from overuse, fell off in her hand. Taylor fished out a small handful of newspaper clippings. She'd seen the first three before, online:

HOOD CANAL BRIDGE CRASH KILLS FIVE

A Port Gamble school bus being used by a Girl Scout Daisy Troop for an ill-fated picnic at Indian Island careened over the

Hood Canal Bridge yesterday afternoon, killing the driver and four girls, ages 5–7. Three children and an adult were airlifted to area hospitals.

Motorists on the scene indicated that the draw span had been retracted when the bus crashed in heavy rain and wind. State engineers say retracting the span is done to relieve pressure on the bridge.

"They were right in front of me," said Cindy Johnston of Bainbridge Island. "I was following them pretty closely because I could barely see. The rain was coming down so hard. In one second, the bus just disappeared."

Sustained winds of 50 mph, with gusts of 65 mph, were reported in the region by the National Weather Service.

The Washington State Department of Transportation and the State Patrol are investigating.

VICTIMS' NAMES RELEASED, TWO IN COMA

The names of the survivors of the Hood Canal Bridge bus accident were released this afternoon. Sandra Berkley, 30, and her daughter, Katelyn, 5, were thrown from the bus as it went off the bridge. Ms. Berkley suffered cracked ribs and abrasions. She and her daughter were treated and released from Harrison Medical Center, Bremerton.

The two other victims, 5-year-old twin girls Hayley and

Taylor Ryan, remain hospitalized. Their parents issued a statement yesterday.

"Our daughters are fighters. Please keep them in your prayers. Believe in miracles."

The parents indicated that the girls are still in a coma.

Visibly shaken, Adam Larsen, 34, spoke to reporters outside his home in historic Port Gamble.

"We are grieving for the families who have lost their children and for the bus driver's family too. This touches all of us here. I doubt many of us will ever get over it."

Larsen's daughter, Starla, also 5, was a member of the Daisy troop. She, however, did not go on the outing due to minor illness.

ELECTRICAL FAILURE LED TO FATAL HOOD CANAL CRASH

A spokesman for the Washington State Department of Transportation said today that the school bus crash killing five was a "tragic combination of the weather and an electrical fault that caused the span to open."

It had not been opened by the bridge tender, as previously reported.

Among the dead were Christina Lee, 7; Sarah Benton, 6; Violet Caswell, 5; and Emma Perkins, also 5. Also killed was bus driver Margie Jones, 29. Jones, according to the North Kitsap

School District records office, was an exemplary employee. She was completing her master's degree in education and was working as an activity bus driver. She'd planned to teach next fall.

"She wanted nothing more than to do something for kids," said Barry Jones, her husband of five years.

Three of the survivors remain hospitalized. One, a 30-year-old Port Gamble woman, has been released.

The next one was a new one, an article that hadn't been posted in any newspaper archive that she'd seen when she Googled the crash for the first time a few years ago:

BRIDGE TENDER CLEARED IN FATAL BUS CRASH

Timothy Robbinette, the 44-year-old bridge tender on duty the afternoon a school bus crashed killing four Port Gamble girls and the driver, was cleared when the Washington State Department of Transportation released its final report late last night.

"While there was concern that operator error or negligence might have been a factor in the accident, a full investigation has attributed the accident to a mechanical/electrical failure and not operator error, as had been suggested in the press."

When contacted by members of the media last night, Robinette, who has been on administrative leave, said he was "satisfied" about the panel's findings but indicated he would not be returning to work.

"Too many sad, bad memories there for me," he said.

As Taylor read, she noticed another clipping had been attached. It was a funeral notice:

ROBBINETTE, TIMOTHY

Husband and father Timothy Robbinette will be remembered at the Chimacum Lutheran Church on Saturday at 1 p.m. Robbinette, 44, died in an apparent gun accident at his home on Wednesday. Cake and coffee will follow the service.

Taylor checked the date on the article and the date of Timothy Robbinette's funeral, which was written in her mother's familiar handwriting. The events were four days apart.

Four days apart? What's all this about?

Taylor glanced over at Hedda, who was oblivious to all but the warmth of the heat coming from the furnace. In contrast, Taylor's heart rate was speeding up and she felt that sick feeling that came with anxiety.

Her parents, and especially her mother, Valerie, refused to talk about the bus crash. Whenever she or Hayley brought it up, their mom would change the subject. For the past few years, the twins had felt something wasn't quite right about what had happened that terrible day. One thing they'd never been told was facing Taylor right there on the page of a newspaper. Her parents had never said the police once thought the crash had been caused by a man named Timothy Robbinette.

Taylor's mind was still reeling when two yellowed pieces of paper stopped her cold. The first was an article from the *Daily Olympian*:

WARDEN'S DAUGHTER MISSING FOR TWO DAYS FOUND

Relief came today with the discovery of nine-year-old Valerie Fitzpatrick, the daughter of McNeil Island Prison Warden Chester Fitzpatrick. The girl, found alive and unharmed, had been missing for at least two days. She was discovered by her mother in a service area under the prison itself—a place that had been searched thoroughly when she first went missing. It is unclear how it was that young Valerie was not discovered during the earliest stage of the search.

"We are grateful for the volunteers, both inmates and staff, who helped in the search for our little girl," Warden Fitzpatrick wrote in a statement to the press. "It was a very difficult time for our family."

According to the statement, the girl disappeared from her bedroom in the warden's quarters outside the prison walls the night before last and somehow ended up inside the prison in the service corridor that provides steam, electricity, and passage for maintenance crews.

"Staff kids have been known to play in the area, which is off-limits. A review of making the location more secure is now underway," Fitzpatrick wrote.

McNeil Island houses 640 inmates, with 19 currently on death row.

Death row inmate Tony Ortega was scheduled for execution Friday. However, with the prison on lockdown, the governor stayed the execution. A new date will be set for the 20-year-old convicted of murdering his father and mother three years ago in Seattle.

A final piece of paper was included in the small stack. It was a letter from Savannah Osteen, dated back when the twins were babies, around the time of her videotaped research session:

Dear Mrs. Ryan:

First I want to apologize for the way things transpired after my last session with your beautiful and very bright girls. While I meant no harm, I know that my comments and persistence caused you a lot of pain. I should have taken a step back to better understand that you wanted some things in your family to remain private. My only defense is that I find your daughters and their ability to know things, dark things, quite remarkable. Even as I write that last sentence, I see how words cannot do justice to the magnitude of what you told me and what I witnessed.

I have called and left numerous messages on your answering machine. Per your request, I will not try to contact your husband again. I want you to know that I will not share the contents of the video tape with anyone. Nor will I disclose what I know about your daughters and what they are capable of. You have my word on it. I am not a mother, though I hope to be one day. I hope that when and if I am blessed with a child, I will be as loving and strong an advocate for my child as you have been for Hayley and Taylor.

Sincerely,
Savannah Osteen,
Researcher, University of Washington,
Linguistics Laboratories
Seattle, WA

What? Taylor could barely breathe. She stuffed the papers back into the manila envelope and stared absently at her laptop screen, wondering when Hayley would come home. Taylor wasn't sure what to think. She knew only one thing to be true: Mr. Hayden's idiotic report had just made her life much more interesting. And a little scary.

HAYLEY RYAN AND COLTON JAMES were right next door working on their AP math assignment in the cozy cream-and-blue kitchen of house number 17. Despite everything going on in Port Gamble and the unsolved murder that Hayley felt she and her sister could solve somehow, life was mercilessly still marching steadily forward—and that included homework. The couple settled on some Death Cab for Cutie as background noise and dug in. For a snack, Colton's mom, Shania, had set out a plate of homemade Fig Newtons, which Hayley actually thought were pretty good. No small feat, considering that the store-bought version seemed like pastry wrapped around a disgusting brown jam.

"Who makes these from scratch?" she asked starting on another of the square cookies.

Colton grinned. "My mom does. You ought to try her homemade Oreos sometime."

"Why not just buy them?" Hayley asked, flicking a crumb off of her boyfriend's lightly stubbled chin.

"When you're agoraphobic like Mom, your options are limited. You can't order everything online or through catalogs," he said. "If I wanted something and if Dad wasn't around, Mom would make it from scratch. The first time she made Fig Newtons she used orange marmalade because it's all we had in the house. If you think real Fig Newtons are bad, you should have tasted those."

In midbite, Hayley sprang to her feet. The hairs on the back of her neck were standing straight up, and her body tensed as if it were listening carefully. And responding.

"I gotta go. I just thought of something," she lied and started for the door.

"What about our homework?" he asked, indicating the work they'd been doing.

"Later," she said. "I'll come back."

TAYLOR HEARD THE FRONT DOOR SLAM SHUT. Her heart was in her throat. Hurried footsteps were coming toward her.

"Taylor! I got your message. What's wrong?"

She looked up. It was her sister, looking frantic.

"You scared the crap out of me," Taylor said. "And I hate to break it to you, but I didn't text you. I was just thinking about you. How did you know . . . ?"

Hayley shook her head. "I just knew. You needed me here fast," she said. "I knew it, even without a text. I ran from next door."

Taylor knew that Hayley was telling the truth. In some peculiar, subconscious way, she had indeed sent a message and it had been flagged urgent. Like the night Olivia Grant died, she and her sister had talked to each other without words.

Taylor pulled the articles and the letter from Savannah out of the worn manila envelope and held them out for her sister to see.

Hayley's blue eyes widened as she scanned each one.

"What does all this mean?" Hayley asked.

Taylor shook her head. She wasn't really sure. She felt hurt and betrayed by their mother.

"It means there's no doubt that Mom and Dad, but mostly Mom, has lied to us about our past," she said.

"And hers," Hayley said.

Taylor nodded and added, "Yeah. And do you know what else it means?"

"It means we have to confront her," Hayley said.

Taylor refolded the articles into a neat bundle. "Yeah," she said, "and you know I hate confrontation."

"That's all right," Hayley said, managing a brave smile. "I don't mind it. And this confrontation *needs* to happen."

chapter 16

ANYONE WHO OBSERVED STARLA LARSEN over a period of time knew that she was no quitter. She'd fought too hard to be the youngest cheerleader in the history of the Kingston Buccaneers, and having her mother and brother ruin everything by kinda, sorta causing the death of her former BFF, Katelyn Berkley, was not going to knock her off the top of the Kingston High social pyramid. That would be super humiliating.

Starla used the summer to lay low and keep her head held high at the same time. She even broke up with her BMW-driving boyfriend, Cameron Corelli. She'd planned on taking Driver's Ed with Hayley, Taylor, Colton, and Beth, but Port Gamble's disgraced It Girl backed out at the last minute. Her brother, Teagan, was still being evaluated by psychiatrists, and her mom was doing community service by going to schools and speaking about the dangers of the Internet and how cyberbullying had to be stopped. Kingston High was on the list of Mindee Larsen's tour of shame, but Starla figured she'd do just about anything not to have her mom come and talk there. That would be the absolute worst. Starla knew a senior, a total marching band dork (tuba!) who she could easily persuade to phone in a bomb threat the morning of her mom's school appearance.

Certainly, her brother's and mom's involvement with Katelyn's death had knocked Super Starla down a bit, but she was far from finished. She thought of how Kim Kardashian married that what's-his-name jock for five minutes, looked all tacky for breaking up with him, but was able to go on TV, tear up a little, and still keep all the cool wedding gifts. If Kim could hold her head up high, then so could she. Besides, when she made it big, Starla would be able to look Anderson Cooper in the face and tell him the backstory that made her pre-Hollywood misadventures seem like the boring middle part of a YA novel:

ANDERSON: *You've had some challenges at home, haven't you?*

STARLA: *That's putting it mildly, Anderson. Basically, my mom and brother killed the girl next door—my bestie all the way back through grade school. It was devastating, for sure. I've dedicated my new CD in her memory.*

ANDERSON: *That's great, Starla, but isn't it true that you were involved with some of the cyberbullying aimed at your friend, Katelyn Berkley, which ultimately led to her death?*

STARLA: *I'm a little surprised, Anderson. This type of questioning seems more Maury or* Inside E *than I'd ever have expected from you. I'm the victim here, but I won't be victimized anymore. I'm for empowerment. My first single, "I'm the Best Best (And You're Not Not)," is about rising above it all.*

"Starla?"

Starla snapped back into the moment and looked up as her mother breezed into the living room. Dressed in a headband-wide skirt and six-inch spiked heels that made the floorboards of house number 22 look like they'd been mauled by woodpeckers, Mindee Larsen smelled of permanent solution and her signature perfume, Poison. She'd just come home from Shear Elegance.

"What's for dinner?" Starla said.

"Would it kill you to help out around here? I did fourteen heads today."

"I still hate you for what you did to me," Starla said, making a face and enjoying punishing her mom for the umpteenth time.

Starla got up from in front of the TV and went to the freezer. She opened it for a flash, and then slammed it hard, rattling its contents, before turning her gaze and glaring at her mother.

"There's nothing to eat in this house!"

"I bought two hundred dollars worth of groceries yesterday, honey. The freezer and the refrigerator are full."

"I don't like any of that stuff," Starla sniffed. "I want take-out."

Mindee sighed. "Honey, I'm so tired."

"Teagan is being evaluated by a team of shrinks. Your fault!"

Mindee picked up her purse and started for the door. "Chinese or pizza?" she asked.

Starla smiled. "Chinese, but not from Hot Wok. I want Mandarin Garden."

Mandarin Garden was another ten miles away in Silverdale, but Mindee didn't see that she had much choice. Starla relished her role as the consummate button-pusher, and Katelyn's tragic death had given Starla the upper hand. Mindee felt so guilty over "ruining her daughter's life" that she'd do anything for her—and Starla knew it.

Mindee had made her bed, so to speak, and her daughter, Starla, liked to keep the sheets up tight to her neck. So tight, that she couldn't move unless Starla said so.

As Starla waited for her food to arrive she decided to call an old friend.

Just because she could. Dropping a bomb made her feel so much better.

BETH LEE, A COMPULSIVE TV WATCHER, couldn't find a single thing on as she sat on the couch facing a dark TV screen. No QVC. No Food Network. Not even that channel where people make over their living room with a designer who "reveals the décor in you."

If it was so totally you, Beth would snicker to herself, *then why did your house look like Goodwill was your decorator?*

Nothing could take her mind off her troubles right then. She considered getting out the sketchbook and drawing, but she knew there wasn't enough black pencil in the world to fit her mood. Her stomach was knotted like one of those nets her father used to take shrimping on Hood Canal.

Beth's phone broke the spell of her pity party. She looked at the screen and couldn't believe her eyes.

What does she *want? Must be a butt dial.*

"Hey, Starla," Beth said without emotion.

"Lizzie-B-e-e!"

No one had called Beth that since first grade. It was the kind of nickname that other people thought was cute but Beth would rather forget. The way Starla Larsen dragged out the last syllable made it even more cringeworthy.

"What's up?" she asked.

"I heard some really disturbing news and I just had to call to give you my support," Starla said.

"What did you hear?" Beth asked, now wishing she hadn't answered the phone.

Starla hesitated a little, as if conflicted about what she was going to say.

"I heard that they are questioning you about the murder of Olivia Grant."

Beth's heart fell like someone had yanked it out and bungee-corded it off the Tacoma Narrows Bridge. She didn't say anything. She almost couldn't breathe.

"You know, *your* exchange student," Starla said.

Not wanting to give Starla the satisfaction of riling her up, Beth answered casually, "I don't know what you're talking about."

Beth was irritated and angry at the same time. Starla was obviously feigning concern and was fishing for more information. The last time

Starla called her was in sixth grade when she was doing a book report on China and wanted to know the length of the Great Wall.

"You know, in miles," Starla had said.

"Sorry," Beth had answered, though she wasn't sorry at all. "I don't know how deep the Grand Canyon is either."

To which Starla had famously replied, "Why would I ever ask that? That's in America. Don't you just know about the Great Wall? Aren't you Chinese?"

But that was then. This was now. This was about a murder investigation.

Starla went in for the kill. "I heard that you're the prime suspect because you had a fight with Olivia the night of the party and the police have evidence against you."

"Who told you this bit of news?" Beth asked, doing her best to remain cool, which wasn't easy.

"A friend," Starla said. "Let's just leave it at that. You don't have to get all over me because I just called to *help*. Circumstances beyond my control have pushed me in the direction of the juvenile justice system and, well, I just think that if you're in trouble you need to know that I'm here for you."

"Thank you, Starla. I really appreciate your thoughtlessness. I mean *thoughtfulness*."

Beth didn't even wait for Starla to answer. She cut the call short and hung up.

A friend? Beth had told only one person that she thought she was in trouble. Why did Taylor tell Starla, the girl who wanted nothing more than to be the center of attention, all day, and every day?

KEVIN RYAN ON DEADLINE was not a pretty sight. He looked more like the criminals he was writing about than the purveyor of their sordid stories. When he was racing to the finish, Kevin didn't shave and he didn't shower until noon. Hygiene could wait during the crunch of getting a book off to his New York publisher. He even wore the same ratty Levi's for three days (at least that's what he'd admit to—his daughters thought it was closer to five).

As he tapped away on his keyboard, he heard a pounding at the front door that came with the fury of a WWF wrestler. He turned and looked out the window. He had been expecting a FedEx with some jail mug shots from a county so small and backwards it didn't have a scanner. No familiar delivery truck, but still the very persistent and bruising knock.

"Taylor, can you get that?" he called out.

No answer. She probably had her headphones on.

Kevin sighed, saved his file, and scooted down the hallway. En route to the door, he noted that the chronically pathetic Boston fern on the entry table looked like it needed water or a quick trip to the compost pile. He'd opt for water, if he'd only remember to do it.

He swung open the door to a fuming, looking-for-trouble Beth Lee.

"Hi, Beth," he said, immediately noticing her puffy, red eyes.

Barely making eye contact, Beth asked, "Hey, Mr. Ryan. Is Taylor here? I need to talk to her . . . *now*."

Kevin had known Beth since she was a baby. While Beth wasn't on the bus the day of the crash, her sister, Christina, had been, and the tragedy had brought the two families close together.

"You okay?" he asked, knowing that she wasn't okay at all. He opened the door wider.

She looked up at him and shook her head. "No, I'm not. I'm really, really upset."

"About Olivia?" he asked.

Beth turned her gaze downward. "No. I mean, yes, about Olivia, but mostly about Taylor."

Upset about Taylor? He didn't even want to ask.

"She's in her room. Go on up."

Beth pushed past him, her familiar Doc Martens hitting the floorboards hard. She disappeared up the stairs.

Kevin shut the door wondering how he was going to survive teenage drama with all the regular drama that seemed to permeate Port Gamble like a thick fog.

A second later, Beth Lee appeared in Taylor's doorway.

"Hey," Taylor said, looking up from her laptop. She pulled off her earbuds. "I didn't know you were coming over."

"I can't believe you told Starla," Beth said, still in the doorway.

Taylor cocked her head a little. "Told her what?"

Beth had told herself that she was going to say what was on her mind and then leave. She was not going to cry. She hated crying in front of anyone. And yet, she could feel the tightness of her throat, throttling her, trying to force her to do so.

She fought it hard.

"You know damn well what you told her. I thought we were friends and that I could trust you. I feel bad enough about Olivia and everything and I didn't need you of all people to make things worse."

Taylor got off her bed. "I don't know what you're talking about. Really."

Beth held out her hand, keeping Taylor at arm's length.

"You know something?" she said, her eyes now brimming with tears. "After Christina died, I felt like you were my family. Your mom, your dad, but mostly you and your sister *were* my family. I knew I couldn't ever match the kind of closeness that you and Hayley have. I get that. I understand the whole twin thing. But you made me feel like I was your sister."

"You are like a sister to us, to *me*," Taylor said, confused.

Beth crossed her arms. "That's almost funny. Because as much as I know you have complained to me about Hayley and Colton and everything, I've never once said anything to either one of them. I figured you needed a sounding board, separate from Hayley."

"I do, and you are it," Taylor said.

"Part of me was a little bit glad that you felt left out. I've always felt a little left out. Now I know that when I'm really scared, when I really need someone to support me, you aren't that person. You told Starla something I wanted to keep between us."

"I never told her anything," Taylor said.

Beth was shaking she was so mad, so hurt. "You know what really bites, Taylor? You can look right at me and lie."

Taylor, now trembling, shook her head. "I'm not. I swear it."

Beth refused to waver.

"Whatever," she said. "I don't know if I can forgive you. I'm going through lots of stuff right now. And I guess I'm going to have to do it alone. Thanks for nothing, Taylor."

"I didn't tell Starla anything," Taylor repeated. "Sit down. Let's talk about this. There has to be some other explanation."

"I'm not talking. I'm not staying."

"Please," Taylor said, now almost ready to cry herself.

Beth shook her head. "Here," she said, pulling a frayed bracelet from her wrist. Her hand trembled a little as she held it out to Taylor.

Taylor knew what it was and what it meant immediately. She, Hayley, and Beth had made matching friendship bracelets out of embroidery floss and seed beads. They'd promised never to take them off. Hayley's and Taylor's fell off a month or two after they'd made them. Not Beth's. Beth had worn hers every day since seventh grade. Until today.

"I don't want that," Taylor said.

"Neither do I." Beth dropped the bracelet on the bedroom floor. She turned around and ran down the stairs.

The front door slammed so hard it rattled the dishes in the china hutch. Kevin looked up from his computer screen. A second later,

Taylor's door slammed shut. Kevin knew that it wasn't his place to intercede. Teenage girls take no prisoners. No dad ever wanted to be caught in the middle.

The place in the middle was filled with quicksand.

BACK IN HER OWN BEDROOM, Beth Lee pulled down the window shades and ignored the texts from Taylor, a series of which had started to bombard her as she walked home from the Ryans:

> **TAYLOR:** WHAT JUST HAPPENED?
>
> **TAYLOR:** I DIDN'T TELL HER!
>
> **TAYLOR:** WE ARE BFFS.
>
> **TAYLOR:** TALK TO ME.

Beth flopped on her bed and buried her face in her favorite squishy pillow. She wanted to shut out everything that had to do with Olivia Grant just then, but she couldn't. She felt such guilt, such deep shame, over what she had said to Olivia the day she died. Trying to make it go away only served to push it more in the forefront of her thoughts. It ran over and over in her mind even as she desperately sought to erase it forever. Right after she had snapped the Polaroid, before she opened the door for Drew, Beth had begged Olivia not to go to the party without her.

"Don't be so bloody needy, Beth," Olivia had said, running her fingers through her long red hair. "You're so intense about everything. Everything is so important. I mean, costume shopping with you was fun, but now I need to get out of here."

"Don't go! Let's just stay here and have our own Halloween party," Beth had thrown out in desperation.

"Are you kidding? That's crazy. I wish I'd been assigned to another family. Cheers," she said and slipped out the door.

At the time, Beth had considered jamming out Olivia's eyes with the chopsticks in her hair, but the idea was only a thought, not a plan. As the front door closed, in an undertone so very low, Beth let out her final thought: "I wish you would drop dead."

The memory sent a pool of acid to her stomach, and Beth fought the urge to throw up. Saying something so ugly to another person wasn't who Beth was or wanted to be.

Yet she'd done it once before. She hated thinking about it, but that horrible memory came back so, so clearly.

The night before the Daisies' crash a decade before, her sister, Christina, refused to let her use the periwinkle-blue crayon. Beth had wanted it for some flowers she was drawing, but Christina was using it to color a Disney princess and refused to hand it over.

"It's the wrong blue," Beth had said, trying to give her sister a better color.

"No," Christina had said firmly. "Mine. *You* use another."

Beth had shoved the box from the tabletop to the floor. A rainbow of crayons scattered. She pushed back from the kitchen table and started for her room.

"I wish you were dead," she had said, stomping away. "If you were dead I'd use any color I want any time I want. You'd never boss me around again. You're such a brat!"

"You're mean!" Christina had cried.

By the middle of the next day, rain pouring down, wind howling across the Hood Canal Bridge, Christina and four others had perished in the choppy, cold water. For two years the Disney princess coloring book page hung on the Lee refrigerator. It was the last thing that Christina Lee had made.

Every day Beth had looked at it and wanted to tear it into confetti and flush it down the toilet, because she'd never get a chance to unsay the awful thing she'd said.

Now, Beth had done it again. She had wished Olivia Grant dead. And she was.

Beth rolled onto her back and looked at the web of tiny cracks in the plaster ceiling. She didn't believe in the supernatural, but she did believe in coincidence and karma. Two people were dead, and Beth tossed and turned on her bed wondering, *Did I have something to do with it?*

She got up and went for her sketching supplies. She fished through the pile and found just the right pencil. She drew water, sky, and an island in the center of it all. Her movement across the page was fast and furious. Somewhere between art and therapy, a picture emerged.

All in periwinkle blue.

Christina, I miss you. If Olivia is with you, tell her I'm sorry. I didn't mean it.

chapter 17

IT WAS LIKELY ONE OF THE SADDEST homecomings ever. The British Airways flight from Seattle to London carried the entire Grant family home. Edward and Winnie were ensconced in business class, while their daughter was stacked among the luggage in the cargo hold. The dead sixteen-year-old's body, released from the Kitsap County morgue the day before its departure home for burial, had been sealed in a wooden box and then in a box marked with red and black biohazard stickers and a notation that the coffin contained human remains. Down in the belly of the 747, the air was cold and the sound of the aircraft was nearly deafening. It was no place for the living. And aside from the animals being shipped overseas, it wasn't.

Inside the passenger section of the aircraft, Edward and Winnie tried to pass the time watching movies, but neither could focus on anything. Edward, in particular, was having a hard time of it. He wondered over and over if there was something he could have done that would have changed what happened to his only child. If he'd let her go to Malta with friends the previous summer, maybe she would have met a boy. Maybe she would have never come home, and while that would have been far less than ideal, it would have been better than going to America and being killed. Everything would have been different. The ramblings of his mind were ludicrous and he knew it, but he'd lost his baby and the hurt of that loss was deeper than he could have imagined.

People had tried to make Edward feel better. They told him that time heals all wounds. Even those who had lost a child of their own offered words of comfort. But what was meant as a gesture of support came across as glib. Edward Grant was coming to the realization that there was no loss greater than the loss of one's child. And even with all his money, status, and power, there was not a single thing he could do about it.

If Olivia in her shipping-crate coffin could have commented on her current accommodations, she would have been mortified that she was now considered a biohazard. It seemed like a mean designation to put on a girl. She also might have taken some delight in her traveling companions in cargo. Olivia's body was stored next to a series of crates containing four miniature poodles and a golden retriever. Olivia loved animals. She really did. She also would have told her father that she loved him if she had had one more chance. Winnie, not so much.

Just because she was dead didn't mean she had to lie.

IN THE DAYS AFTER HER DEATH viewership of Olivia Grant's YouTube videos went up exponentially. She had posted them under the name Cher Boynton for her friends back in London, and by the Thursday after her murder they were making the rounds of the Facebook and Twitter accounts of Kingston High students faster than the Missoni line at Target had sold out.

Hayley and Taylor kept track on their phones during the break between first and second period. Brianna and Drew were now officially MIA and APB'd and if anyone had any real leads as to who might have killed Olivia and why, they weren't talking. The twins hoped the videos would shed some light on who might have wanted Olivia dead. While lots of people had the opportunity at the party, the girls had no idea who might have had a motive. Their dad's latte stand chat with Police Chief Annie Garnett didn't get them any closer to finding out, either. With what one blogger was calling "ice-cold lovebirds" gone, suspicion and worry focused on Brianna and Drew—big-time.

"This is so Brianna," Hayley said. "Olivia gets murdered and Brianna steals the spotlight from her."

"Maybe she's been kidnapped?" Taylor said, scrolling through the video, and only momentarily being distracted by a clip featuring four hundred Filipino kids singing a Kesha song.

"Maybe she's dead?"

"Then she'd really get some attention, wouldn't she?"

"Yeah, but not of the type she could brag or whine about," Hayley said.

Taylor clicked Play on the video. Olivia waited for a musical interlude (a snippet of a Jessie J song) before she started talking. She moved her fingertips through her long cinnamon hair and spoke.

"Hello, kitties," she said, her eyes fixed on the lens of her webcam. "I've been immersing myself in so-called American culture in the most miserable place on the planet. All right, maybe not as miserable as Birmingham, but close enough."

She caught herself in the reflection of the computer screen and paused long enough to adjust her hair again before carrying on with her video blog. Her face went from interested to dour as she composed her thoughts.

"Nothing but rain and wind. I haven't felt warm in three days. No kidding. The bedroom, which I call DSB for 'dead sister's bedroom,' is a freezer. Now I'd like to update you on the people I've met here. First of all, there's Beth, whom I consider to be a nice but confused girl. She seems to want to fit in so badly she'll be whatever anyone wants her to be. I like her. At least, I like some of her divergent personalities, but sometimes she tries too hard. There's also Beth's friends who keep coming 'round: the Ryan twins, Hayley and Taylor. Beth can't seem to tell them apart, but it's obvious to me. Hayley has a boyfriend, Colton, who is pretty cute, and Taylor has no one. Taylor is always fussing around like she's mad at her sister, and her sister is always trying to appease her. They act all close and everything, but I'd bet that they'd take each other out if they were locked in the same room. Colton is part American Indian, and he's been nice to me. *Really* nice, if you know what I mean. I like him. The good news is I have a new best friend. Her name is Brianna, and she's exactly the sort of girl you'd expect me to hang with. She's popular, fun, and so like moi. I've got to run, but I'll be reporting more when I can. Beth's mom is fixing some kind of hideous dumpling for lunch, and I promised to help. More later."

"Wow," Taylor said. "She's mean. At least Colton got a nice shout-out."

Hayley shook her head and glowered. "Yeah, a little too nice, if you ask me."

Taylor clicked on Olivia's second video. Like the first, it was filmed in Christina Lee's old bedroom. One of Beth's drawings, a dark and brooding piece with a ghostly figure in a bramble forest, filled the background.

"Hello, kitties, it's me, Olivia. I'm a little down today. I had to spend the day with Beth, her mother, and those Ryan twins at the Silverdale Mall."

She held up a pale orange, scoop-necked top. "I got this top, which I think is brilliant, from the Gap. Love it? I do. We had lunch at the Red Robin restaurant, and I had the worst thing ever. Something called a Banzai Burger, which is a Japanese take on a hamburger, America's national dish. They make fun of British cooking all the time in America, but at least we've never come up with an abomination combination like hamburger, teriyaki, and pineapple. I can almost feel it rising up from my stomach to my throat right now. Also on the down side, things have been getting a little weird with my new best friend, Brianna. Her boyfriend, I fear, isn't all that he's cracked up to be. I heard him talking to another girl on the phone the other day. He definitely thinks he's a player, though in a kind of common, dull sort of way. I think I'm in the middle of something. Of course, I like to be where all the excitement is. Except not like this. Just too much drama for me. Sending kisses across the pond."

"Drew *is* a player, if you ask me," Hayley said.

"Maybe last year," Taylor said. "This year he seems to have settled down. Getting Brianna was definitely a level above the girls he'd dated before."

"Two levels," Hayley said, thinking. "Remember Jennie O'Hara?"

"'Jennie the Skank?' Yeah, I remember her. The reality was she wasn't a skank, just the victim of trashy taste. She's going to a school in Gig Harbor now. We're Facebook friends."

Hayley didn't know any of that. Taylor had her own life too.

Taylor waited for the next video to load.

"Olivia looks different in that video we just watched," Taylor said.

"How?" Hayley asked.

"A little scared. Did you see how her eyes kept straying from the camera lens?"

"I guess so," Hayley said. "I thought maybe she was annoyed by someone else in the room."

Taylor shrugged. "Maybe. Let's watch the next one."

Finally, for the third time, Olivia Grant took to her computer video cam. It was a different kind of Olivia this time, quite a bit less focused, almost frazzled. She didn't adjust her hair. She didn't pause for a musical interlude. She just started talking.

"Hello, kitties, Olivia here. Just a few words about Kingston High School. Not sure why they call it Kingston High. There's nothing high about it. Don't get me wrong. I think the school itself is pretty decent, but the students seem to spend half their time talking about the football game and what Katy Perry song they like the best. Between us, they all seem the same to me. The classes aren't challenging at all. I'm surprised how much these kids don't know about the world. I was talking about the euro the other day, and one girl said her brother drove a Euro and had nothing but problems with it. No joke! It was all I could do to stop myself from laughing right in her dull face. In case you don't get the reference, she thought the euro was a car! I'll bet she thinks Greece is a musical. I'm getting really close with someone, but for now it has to be a secret. Not my choice, but I guess if I actually lived here I'd be more wary of any repercussions."

Taylor set down her phone and met her sister's gaze.

"Wow," she said.

"Yeah, wow," Hayley said. "Olivia seemed so nice, so classy."

"It was that accent of hers," Taylor said. "The accent made her seem regal."

"Did she always talk that way?"

"With the accent? Yeah. Trashing everyone? Probably."

"I wonder who she pissed off. Because someone must have been pretty mad to do what they did to her that night."

Taylor agreed. "Yeah. And who was she getting close to?"

"No idea," Hayley said. "But it sounds like whoever it was had a reason for nobody finding out."

Taylor looked back at the cell phone screen, frozen on Olivia's face. Behind her in Christina's bedroom was a bulletin board with a series of photos pinned neatly along the edge. Even in the minuscule format of her cell phone she could easily make out a shot of Olivia and Drew. She pointed it out to her sister.

"That's weird," Hayley said. "When was that taken?"

"I don't know," Taylor answered. "I've never seen it in my life."

HE LOOKED OUT THE WINDOW as the sun set over the Olympic Mountains, burnishing the overcast sky with a bloody red hue, and considered something that had never entered his mind before. He thought about just how easy killing had become. On purpose or by accident, it didn't really matter. It was easy.

Murder, he'd come to know, was not about what he got from the act—not the act itself—but the way it made him feel. He was out of breath. He was sweaty. He had a layer of grime that coated all of his skin. His hands were sore and there was a tiny gash over his eye. She'd been a fighter. His dark eyes followed the trail of starlings as they began to land on the clothesline of the neighbor's house. When he was a boy, he used to shoot birds with a slingshot and a BB gun. He remembered how their heaving bodies felt when he picked them up from the ground. Breathing hard. Trying to survive. Looking up at him with tiny, but very alert, black eyes until he crushed them in his bare hands.

Power. A taste of power. The first bite. The birds had been the beginning of what he was going to become. His family knew it. Friends could see it too.

His first human victim was like one of those birds. She was already halfway down for the count when he finished her off.

He reached for his phone and prepared to text a message.

chapter 18

IT WAS EARLY SATURDAY MORNING. Cruelly early. Taylor Ryan took her mother's car and drove to the North Kitsap School District pool in Poulsbo. It was just after six. She punched the keypad code used by the swim team and went inside. Chlorine and steam wafted through the air. The familiar smell was almost soothing. She liked how quiet the pool was when no one else was around—a refuge, a place to think. At that hour there were no pesky Kitsap Water Blossoms, the local synchronized swimming team, to tell her that she and her sister would be the ultimate addition to their team.

"You look alike. You swim. You even move the same. We can gel your hair in identical swirls. We, like, totally could use you on the team," said Crystal Brennan, the team captain, who apparently didn't know the only thing worse than synchronized swimming was, well, *nothing* could be worse.

As Taylor undressed in the locker room, she caught her reflection in the mirror. She thought about herself and Hayley. Where everyone else saw similarities between them, Taylor could see nothing but the differences.

A gazillion of them.

She knew what only identical twins knew with any genuine certainty: there was no such thing as "exactly alike." Sure, Taylor and Hayley were genetic copies. That was a medical fact. They were the kind of twins that occurs in about one out of a hundred births. Twins with the same genes in the same sequence. As disgusting as the girls thought because it went back to their conception and the truly icky idea of their parents having sex, Hayley and Taylor were from the same egg and the same sperm.

Identical. Copies. That's what the Ryan sisters were to the untrained eye of a singleton.

Thankfully, their differences, while many, were not of the kind that would have one be known as the "fat twin" or the "twin with the ugly birthmark" or the "twin with a peculiar left nostril." Those were distinctions of other twin girls they'd known over the years, mostly through school and, when they were very young, through the Mothers of Multiples group that Valerie had joined in order to get good deals on double-castoffs of questionably adorable matchy-matchy clothing, highchairs, and tandem strollers.

Taylor and Hayley were the same but different.

In the scattershot sunny days of a Puget Sound summer, the bridges of both of their noses freckled and faded when fall came with its curtain pull of sunlight. For some reason, however, Taylor's freckles didn't fade to the same extent that Hayley's did. There were seven stubborn specs of pigment that ran over her nose in what she was sure was the shape of the Aries constellation, which unfortunately was not her zodiac sign.

Taylor wrinkled her nose, making the spots disappear in the crinkles of the nasal crunch. *Now you see them; now you don't.*

Her eyes still on the slightly foggy mirror, Taylor twisted her hair into a loose ponytail with a big black rubber band. Her hair, like her sister's, was blond, thick, and sun-streaked—the kind of hair every girl in school coveted. One time, sick of their sameness, Taylor dyed her hair red with cherry Kool-Aid. That fit of rebellion looked terrible in seventh grade, but everyone had to admit that she smelled wonderful.

"Like the biggest cough drop ever," Beth Lee had said.

And yet Taylor's hair was different in that its natural part was on the left side, with Hayley's on the right. As a mirror twin, logic would have Taylor left-handed and Hayley right-handed, but in that way they confounded twin experts. Both girls were right-handed. One thing dissimilar about them was that Taylor's neck and shoulder were marked by a series of three tiny scars. She rolled her shoulder and turned her neck to take a full accounting of them in the mirror. *Still there.* Most people probably assumed the scars had come from an injury pertaining to the bus accident, but the truth was far more sinister. It was somewhere near the top of the list of things that the family didn't like to revisit, talk about, or even admit had once occurred.

As she finished putting on her team suit—a burgundy one-piece with two yellow stripes down each side that made the girls look more like a half-naked road crew than a fiercely competitive swim team—Taylor Ryan considered something that she'd never really admitted to herself. She was jealous of Hayley. It was so stupid, so completely dumb of her to feel that way, and she knew it. It wasn't her twin's beauty—Starla was the most beautiful girl in town. It wasn't that Hayley was adventurous when Taylor was a little cautious. Beth Lee was the girl who would do just about anything and had the attitude that came with that.

It felt dumb, but Taylor couldn't help but envy Hayley for having Colton. Taylor had had a few boyfriends, or rather a few dates herself, but they didn't go anywhere. She didn't seem to mind. Whenever Beth complained about some boy, Taylor considered herself a little lucky not to be caught up in some idiotic drama in which having a boy "like" you was more important than anything else. More essential than your grades being in the top tier of your high school. Or the fact that you held a diving record for your district. Or maybe even that you were a good listener, kind to people, genuinely so and not because it was something that you could add to your college entrance applications. All of those things were Taylor Ryan. Her sister was some of those things too. But Hayley didn't hold a diving record, and she had been too busy the past year dating Colton James to help out at the food bank or call times at the Special Olympics Games held every year south of Tacoma at Joint Base Lewis-McChord.

Taylor climbed up on the diving board and put her feet in perfect position. Her painted toenails looked like a row of bluebirds on a wire. She took a deep breath, bounced on the board, and flew toward the glassy surface of a pool that had been quiet all night.

As Taylor hit the water, Olivia Grant suddenly commanded the forefront of her thoughts.

Olivia, who did this to you?

Olivia, talk to me.

Olivia, I can help find your killer.

She kicked her legs and glided over the bottom of the pool, holding her breath and waiting for something to come. It was the "hope and focus" part of how she and her sister did whatever it was they did. Of the two, Taylor could outlast her sister underwater. She'd proven that in the bathtub at home and in the pool as a member of the Kingston swim team. Her record going without air was the entire length of Demi Lovato's "Skyscraper," a song she liked more for the positive message than its singer's performance.

She stayed calm, allowing the water to hold her as she moved through her lane.

And as she knew they would, with her goggled eyes wide open, letters came at her like a swarm of bees.

Atone.

Buffy.

Kinin.

Taylor held on to the first two words, convinced her observation was correct. But the last one? It didn't seem like a real word. Maybe it was a name? Buffy Kinin? No one at Kingston had that name. Atone for what?

Taylor held the words in her thoughts.

Atone Buffy Kinin.

Gasping for breath, Taylor shot through the water's surface and pulled herself up and out of the pool. Tracking water all over the pool deck, she hurried back to the locker room. The warmth of her body instantly fogged the mirror. The teenager wrote the phrase with her index finger. Her eyes reflected in the two *F*s staring back at her.

She didn't need a Scrabble board to mentally unscramble the letters:

KNIFE BY FOUNTAIN

Taylor didn't even bother to shower. She didn't care if the chlorine turned her hair green. She hastily dried off and dressed. There was no doubt about what knife and what fountain. Grabbing her duffel bag, she sat on the bench and retrieved her phone. A second later, she logged on to the Crime Stoppers website. It guaranteed anonymity and was the only way she could think of to tell Annie Garnett without having to answer a bunch of questions for which she really didn't have answers.

> Please tell Chief Garnett that the kitchen knife used to kill
> Olivia Grant on Halloween night is in the bushes by that
> tacky fountain in front of the Connors house.

Before she pushed the **send** button, she deleted the word *tacky*. She wanted to stick to the facts.

Just like a cop.

LUCKILY FOR ANNIE GARNETT, finding the murder weapon only took twenty minutes and two antacids to calm her roiling stomach. After receiving the tip from the Crime Stoppers site about its whereabouts, a Kitsap County Sheriff's deputy, crime scene tech, and the police chief herself made fast work of the search in front of the Connorses' house, converging there after meeting at her office in Port Gamble. They recovered a knife from the lush green folds of landscaping, adjacent to the imported Italian fountain of three cherubs.

"Right there," the deputy said, pointing with the shiny tip of his black boot. He aimed the beam of his Maglite. Glinting under the edge of a spindly branch of a sprawling juniper was the elongated and bloody edge of an expensive butcher knife.

"I'll bag and tag it," he said.

"How could we have missed it?" Annie said, knowing that the media would bash the police for the rookie mistake. Searching a crime scene twice or even many more times wasn't unusual, but missing something as crucial as the probable murder weapon was a big blunder—the kind of mistake that would call into question whether or not it had been collected properly. The crime scene, after all, had been abandoned. She'd added that error to the growing list of screw-ups that would give any defense lawyer ammunition against the prosecution. The evidence had been trampled, contaminated, compromised.

All of those adjectives would surely be hurled at her if the case got to court.

chapter 19

THEY'D BEEN DRIVING FOR HOURS, first across the Hood Canal Bridge and then onto the back roads along the tree-shrouded edges of the inland waterway that was America's answer to a Norwegian fjord. Drew Marcello had ditched his tricked-out black Honda Civic for his mother's old commuter car, a burnt-orange Accent, a vehicle he considered a complete dorkmobile. But he was willing to drive it, as he was all but certain that no one would ever be looking for that car. His mom would never, ever turn him in. Of that he was certain.

"You want me to tell Dad?" he had said, a threat implicit in his tone.

Marsha Marcello didn't need to ask what her son was getting at. She fished her key ring out of her purse and pulled off the key.

She looked over at Brianna, who was standing next to Drew's car. Brianna's stare was ice. Green ice.

"I suppose you need some money too," Marsha said. She held out four twenties and a ten. "That's all the cash I have."

Drew snatched the money from her fingers. "Wow, you're really coming through for me now, Mom. 'Bout time."

Marsha, a spiny woman with small birdlike eyes, couldn't resist a jab back at her son. They'd played a kind of mean version of verbal ping-pong for years. It wasn't so much as a game between them, either. It was the way they related to each other.

"Which one of you killed Olivia, Drew?" she asked, her tone pointed and hurtful.

Drew shook his head and started walking toward the garage. He waved for Brianna to get behind the wheel and follow him there. Under his arm he carried a dark-blue plastic tarp—one of two he'd purchased at the Home Depot in Silverdale.

"Talk to me," Marsha called out, but her son kept going. She hurried toward Drew, her arm on his shoulder to stop him from going a step further. Drew turned around and gave her a little push, which sent her onto the soaking wet grass. She looked up, disbelieving what was happening.

What had happened.

Drew's eyes were fixed, dark, swimming in anger.

Marsha stretched out her hand to have Drew help her up, but the teenager ignored her. He hadn't meant to cause her to fall, but he kind of liked seeing her there on the muddy lawn.

"If the girl did it, you need to turn her in. That's the right thing to do," she said.

"Really, Mom? You're going to give me tips on morality?"

"I want the best for you," she said.

Drew's impulse was to laugh out loud, and that's exactly what he did.

"You were never, ever there for me," he said. "You don't know what the best for me is. You don't even know who I am. All you've ever cared about is yourself. I'd tell Dad everything I know, but I don't want to hurt him like you have."

The clouds opened, and Marsha looked up at the sky, cowering from the onslaught of rain. She looked small, helpless, and afraid. Seeing that, Drew felt a surge of power and it felt good. It was the way it should be. He was cutting ties. With his mother. With his school. With his old life. It felt good to be him just then.

There was no uncertainty anymore.

"Thanks for that," Brianna said as they pulled the blue tarp first over the hood, then the rest of Drew's car.

"For what?" he asked.

Brianna got into the passenger seat of the golf cart-sized Accent. "For defending me," she said. "The whole world hates me right now."

Drew looked right at her and put his hand on her knee. "I don't, Bree," he said.

She smiled, leaned over and kissed him. "I know."

"I'll figure out a way to take care of everything," he said. "That's what I do. For now, let's drive and get the hell out of Kingston. We need us some downtime."

"Your mom just had some downtime," Brianna said grinning as she watched Marsha Marcello scramble back toward the house, her backside all covered in mud. "You really don't think she'll turn us in?"

Drew smiled. "Not if she wants to keep her job and her marriage," he said.

"You'll have to fill me in sometime," Brianna said, trying to snuggle next to the window. "Right now, I'm beat. I'm going to try to sleep. Can you turn the seat warmers on?"

"Sorry, Bree. No seat warmers in this piece-of-crap car."

He reached into the backseat and pulled out a blanket with the Buccaneers logo. "Use this. Mom bought it from the Kingston Athletic Boosters two years ago. Never came to any of my games. She was always about acting like an interested parent to other parents who actually cared about their kids."

"Nice," Brianna said, drifting off to sleep. "Sounds familiar."

An hour later, Drew pulled the orange compact car over to the side of a soggy logging road not far from Brinnon. He looked down at his phone.

"Damn," he said, his eyes fixed on the tiny screen. "Reception sucks out here. I need to check my messages to see what's up."

Brianna stirred and opened her eyes. "What's up is that people are so judgy and they think we're garbage," she said, also pissed off that she couldn't use her phone to text, log on to Facebook, or tweet about whatever it was that was on her mind. Instead, she pulled out a copy of *Lucky* magazine and a can of Pringles they'd picked up at a convenience store. She twisted her long reddish-blond hair on top of her head and then let it fall over her shoulders.

He opened the car door and went up an incline above the roadway. Brianna glanced up from the article that detailed how a girl could buy designer clothes at a fraction of the price. She wasn't sure how long she was going to be on the run with Drew, but she put a sticker on the page just in case she had to learn to make do. She glanced up at Drew, who must have managed to get reception and was talking and waving his arms in the air wildly.

"Talk with your mouth, not your hands," she wanted to say.

A minute later, he got back into the car.

"Who was that?" she asked.

"Nobody," he said.

"You looked pissed," she said.

"Just listening to voice messages."

"Really? From down here in this crappy car it looked like you were fighting with someone, Drew."

"Things aren't always as they seem," he said, turning the ignition and putting the car in gear.

Brianna nodded. "Yeah. I get that. That's why everyone is saying I'm a cold-blooded killer. And I'm not. *We're* not."

She'd added his name into the mix, even though the TV and newspaper coverage had really focused its hate lasers on her.

"We gotta figure out what we're going to do," he said.

"When you say *we*, I guess you're making me come up with it. You haven't had a good idea since the ninth grade," she said, only half teasing.

Drew glanced at her. "I think we should go back."

"Like that's going to help me? They'll put me in jail. I'll have to rot there with a bunch of women who will want to pet my hair. No thanks."

"No," he said. "I know a place. I think we can hide in plain sight until your dad fixes everything. If we keep running, they'll find us. Or even worse, some creep will pull a gun thinking he's destined for *America's Most Wanted* type fame."

Brianna nodded. "I guess. But where? Where are we gonna go?"

Drew leaned closer and tried to kiss her, but this time she pulled away. "I think I know a place where no one will find us until this mess blows over."

She turned her attention and started to type on her phone's keyboard.

Drew reached over and put his hand on hers.

"We can't use our phones anymore," he said.

"I want to text my mom."

Drew nodded. "I know, but you can't. From now on, we have to stop texting, calling, Facebooking." He pointed to a cell tower they whizzed past along the roadside. It had been painted green and outfitted with branches so fake they looked like throwbacks to the seventies, when synthetic trees were in their beginnings. "Everything we do can be tracked off those towers. They will find us."

"I can't live without my phone," Brianna said, in a statement that was true for just about everyone she knew.

"We have to," he said. He handed over his phone. "Take out my SIM card and then remove yours."

"That seems extreme," Brianna said. "What if I only read my feed? I'm actually getting some support from a few friends at Kingston."

He looked at her. "You can't read it. The towers are collecting every little click. Even when your phone is off they can track us."

Reluctantly, Brianna pried open the back of her phone with her fingernail, and pulled out the battery and the delicate SIM card underneath. She repeated the procedure with Drew's phone. She handed both cards over to Drew, who stuck them gently into his jacket pocket.

"I'm not letting anything happen to us," he said. "I'm not taking any chances."

The sky had darkened by then, and Brianna turned on the radio to try to find some decent music. She looked out the window as the rain streaked the glass. She made a face. Driving without texting was *so* boring.

chapter 20

HAYLEY WOKE UP IN THE MIDDLE OF THE NIGHT, just past 1 a.m. The movie she and Colton had seen was about a town full of possessed teenagers, and while it was scary, *Little Town Dripped in Blood* wasn't the cause of her insomnia. Something else was. Her heart was racing. She wasn't thirsty, but she knew that she needed a big glass of water. Water fueled the gift she shared with her sister. Somehow the fluid made the messages flow in the way electric current passes through water.

She threw a robe over her nightgown and quietly went downstairs to fill a glass from the tap. Hedda, who didn't like to be alone for even a second, followed her. After she drank, Hayley carried the dog to the overstuffed sofa that her mother always said was too big for the living room. The night was still. She could hear her father's light snoring from her parents' bedroom. The clock ticked. An animal rattled the Jameses' trash cans left out on the street for pick-up later that morning.

Hayley sank into the cushions and waited. It was 1:23 a.m. and for some strange reason that particular time always seemed to hold a little power for her. Hayley softly closed her eyes.

"Hedda," she said, petting the dachshund's wiry coat. "I wish you could talk to me. I know you feel things too. Unfortunately for us," she continued, "this doesn't work that way."

With that, she waited. The waiting felt a bit like sitting on the shore and staring out to the flat line of the horizon, squinting hard for the mast of a ship, or maybe the dorsal fin of an orca, something, anything. Just a hint that something lay just beneath the murky surface.

Her eyelids fluttered as she held on to the dog, thinking, concentrating, hoping for relief from whatever it was that was keeping her awake.

The first image was unmistakable. The low-slung expanse of the concrete ribbon that traverses the Hood Canal channel, the floating bridge, *her* bridge, came into view. Hayley held the image a second, scanning for something new, something recognizable, but it was empty. Just the bridge. No cars. A second later, she saw the back of a school bus. The Olympic Mountains were in the scene, so Hayley knew the bus was headed west, away from Port Gamble. On the back of the yellow bus were the words north kitsap school district. The bus was small, a short bus, and in that moment Hayley knew it was going toward Indian Island and that Girl Scout Daisy Troop picnic. She was seeing that fateful day more than ten years prior.

Hedda squirmed in her arms, but she held the dog tightly. She could feel her anxiety escalating, almost choking her as she braced herself for whatever was next.

Suddenly, the scene changed. The flash of a man's face came into fleeting view. It was a face that was unfamiliar to her. He had dark hair, dark eyes, and a swarthy complexion. He was average in height, maybe a little stocky in build. She couldn't quite grab how old he was. Then, like a slide show on its fastest speed, another man—this one older with sandy hair and light eyes, holding a folder or an envelope—appeared. Hayley felt a flash of terror.

He shoved the envelope at the first man who took a step backward, nodding unhappily. Hayley's heart rate, already fast, had started to accelerate more. Even in the midst of the images coming from behind her shut eyes, she could feel the dampness spread across her brow. It was the kind of moisture that came with rigorous physical activity—or fear.

The scene changed to an office with a view of the water from both sides. A nameplate flashed, but it was too fast and Hayley couldn't make out what it said, except for the first letter, *T*. She strained to look closer. It might have been a *J*. The swarthy man, wearing a different shirt than in the first image, took some pills from his desk drawer. He returned his nervous gaze to the bridge as a storm moved in.

Hayley wondered if the man was worried about the weather just then.

The phone on the edge of his desk rang, and the man picked it up. He held it to his ear and nodded.

As Hayley watched the scene, she saw the man press a button and then put his face in his hands. He started to shake.

Is he crying? What is he crying about?

The next image came from above, like a bird rising over the water and the bridge. Hayley could see the bridge sliding open amid a storm that was a mix of an angry wind with a fury of raindrops splashing the bridge deck. The infrastructure rumbled as it slowly opened.

Hayley watched the short school bus approach. But it wasn't just any bus. It was *the* bus. She wanted to scream just then at the driver, a young woman with a big smile and the longest braided ponytail she and her sister had ever seen. She remembered her as Ms. Margie the driver.

"Girls!" Margie called out as she swiveled slightly to face the passengers in the bus. Her eyes were filled with terror. "Brace yourselves behind the seatback in front of you. I don't think I can stop in time!"

Margie was screaming, then, in the chaos of the moment, she simply stopped. Hayley watched as Katelyn and her mom were thrown out of the bus and onto the roadway from the open emergency door in the back of the bus.

The images went black. Then red. Then yellow. Then black again.

The bus was on its side, slipping in the water like a summer day into night, slowly, evenly. Quietly. The screams had stopped. Switched off. Suddenly. The lid over Hayley's head seemed made of lead. It was gray, heavy, and impenetrable. She reached up through the cold water of Puget Sound and pushed at it, but it stayed out of reach of her flailing fingertips. Her tiny, five-year-old fingertips. A stab of white light passed over her. She looked for her sister, but she wasn't there.

She was in the water.

Both of them were in the water.

Words came, not from her mouth but from her brain.

"Help us. Get me and my sister out of here."

As a hand touched her shoulder, she saw another figure in the murk.

Is it Taylor? Where is she?

The saltwater gnawed at her eyes, but she refused to shut them. She was sinking, falling, into a swirl of silt as the wheels of the short yellow bus continued to spin.

She glimpsed a man's face, but she couldn't see who it was.

A beat later, Hayley watched four daisies, their cheerful yellow-and-white forms, floating against the dark waters of Hood Canal. Inside the center of each blossom she could easily make out the faces of the girls on the bus: Christina, Sarah, Violet, and Emma.

Hayley opened her eyes and tried to catch her breath. Hedda was shivering in her arms. She felt sick to her stomach, her throat tired and tight like she'd been screaming. She touched her throat. It felt hot and achy.

"It's okay, baby," Hayley said, stroking Hedda as the dog burrowed into her lap, shivering, shaking. "Everything is okay. I'm all right. We survived. Good girl," she said.

When she finally looked up, her sister was standing in front of her.

"You look like crap. What is it?" Taylor asked, finding a spot next to Hayley and Hedda.

"What happened to us . . ." Hayley said, her voice fading a little.

"What? What are you talking about? What did you see?"

Hayley's heart was pounding like a carpenter's hammer at the end of the day when that last nail just wouldn't go in straight. It was as if everything she'd ever believed was some big, fat lie. It was like finding out that the world wasn't what it was supposed to be. That people weren't as they seemed. History was wrong.

"The day our bus was on the bridge," Hayley said. "That's what I saw."

Taylor tilted her head, her eyes sharpened onto her sister's. "I knew it. I felt the weirdest feeling about you. I didn't know what it was. Talk to me."

Hayley swallowed, but it hurt. She took her time in answering, not because she didn't want to tell her sister every single detail. She simply didn't know where to begin. She wasn't exactly sure *what* she'd seen. The images had come at her faster than fast-forwarding through commercials on a favorite TV show. There was no pause. No way to go back and replay the images. She looked up at the mantel clock. She had been on the sofa for more than an hour. It seemed like two minutes.

"That day on the bridge, Taylor," she said, "wasn't an accident. I think what happened to our bus was on purpose."

Taylor leaned forward, her hand stroking the bump on the top of Hedda's head. "On purpose? That's stupid. There was a big investigation. We saw the clippings."

"I know," Hayley said. "Electrical or mechanical failure."

"Right. That was an accident. That's why the state settled. It was the equipment's fault. Equipment they designed and built."

Hayley shook her head and held their dog a little closer. Hedda continued to dog-purr. "The person I saw was responsible for the electrical failure. He waited for our bus."

"That bridge doesn't open like a mousetrap, Hayley. It takes fifteen minutes to get it open. We've been stuck there waiting, and it's never a short wait. You know that."

Hayley shook her head and got up. "Look, I know what I saw. Some evil-looking guy called the bridge operator and told him we were coming. The operator didn't want to open it. I'm sure of that. The skeeze made him do it."

"Made him kill four girls and a bus driver?"

"That's what I'm saying."

"Why would anyone do that?"

"He was threatened with something. I don't know. The evil guy had something in an envelope and showed it to him. When he saw whatever it was, he didn't seem to have a choice."

"Who are they? So they're both to blame?"

"I guess they are. But I think the one who opened the bridge really didn't want to. The other man made him do it. I think he was being blackmailed."

Hayley thought for a moment.

"It would have to be pretty awful information to make someone do something that terrible. I can't even think of what it could be. But I think I know who it was."

Taylor waited. "Who?"

Hayley retrieved the name she'd seen on the news clippings Taylor had pulled out for her stupid class project. "Timothy Robinette. The man who was investigated and then, you saw the clipping, died four days later."

Taylor nodded. "Right after a hunting accident or something."

"That was no accident."

"And neither was the bridge opening."

"That's what I'm saying."

IT WAS AS DARK AS STARBUCKS over-roasted coffee when Drew Marcello maneuvered his mom's half-pint car up the rutted driveway of house number 7734, a dingy gray-and-white clapboard two-story on the edge of Port Gamble. It wasn't considered the town's haunted house—that was reserved for the 1888-built Walker-Ames House—but it was a decent stand-in. One of the front windows had been shattered and repaired with a big piece of plywood. A barren maple tree, with the remnants of a tire swing, framed the empty space of the backyard with its jagged scaffolding of black branches.

"We're staying here?" Brianna Connors said from the passenger's seat.

Drew looked over at Brianna and grinned.

"Told you, Bree, hide in plain sight and no one will ever find us."

Brianna wasn't convinced. "I'd rather go home," she said.

Drew parked the car behind a woodpile. "Then I guess you're saying you'd rather be arrested for something you didn't do."

Brianna was tired, and her neck hurt like it had been twisted around *Exorcist*-style. The day had been an excruciatingly long one. She was ready for bed. There was no way she could sleep in that silly little car. That much she knew.

"I guess I kind of expected something better than Port Gamble, for sure. Who lives here?"

Drew got out and opened her car door. "No one. It's as empty as a tomb. My buddies and I used to come here and get baked when we cut class."

Brianna lingered in the seat.

"Come on," he said. "It'll be fun."

"None of this has been fun so far," she said, stepping onto the mud and gravel path to the door. "I wish none of this ever happened. I want to feel sorry about Olivia, but she's dead and there's no way she's going to benefit from my grief. I think I feel sorrier about me. In a week's time the forces of the universe have conspired to ruin my life."

Drew put his arms around her. "We'll get it back on track. Once *Mannie* Garnett catches whoever killed Olivia, the heat will die down."

"Don't call the police chief that," Brianna snapped, pulling away in an uncharacteristic moment of kindness. "She's pretty nice. She's just doing her job. How are we going to get inside?"

Drew held up a key. "With *this*."

Brianna regarded the tarnished key, one that had been hanging on his key ring the whole time. She'd never noticed it before.

"Where'd that come from?" she asked.

"Come on," he said, leading her to the door. "I told you this was my hangout with my boys."

He twisted the lock and opened the old paneled door, sending the sound of its squeaking hinges through the night air.

"We won't be here long," he said. "I'll get you out of here. Promise."

Brianna was tired and she had no phone, no connection to the world. She doubted the house had a TV. She was totally and unnervingly unplugged.

"How long?"

"Only long enough." He put his fingers to his lips. "We have to be quiet. Quiet as mice."

SUNDAY MORNING, ALL OF THE LOCAL NEWSCASTS led with the story of Brianna Connors and Drew Marcello sightings—as everyone tried to find the pair of renegade, murderous teens that the media was now calling "Brianna and Clyde" after the famous outlaw duo from the 1930s. A woman at a gas station in Portland, a couple hundred miles south of Port Gamble, insisted she was absolutely sure she'd seen them the week before.

"Yeah," she said, tapping her fingertip on a photo of the pair printed from the "Find Bree & Drew" Facebook page that had two hundred "fans" since its launch the previous day. "Those are the ones I saw here yesterday. That girl from TV, the one with the thongs, was buying cigarettes, and her boyfriend was hanging around waiting to use the bathroom. I wanted to say something to the girl about smoking being bad for you, but for some reason, I didn't. Looking back now, I guess I didn't want her to go off on me. She just looked so cold. So evil. No telling what she would have done. I think I'm lucky to be alive."

chapter 21

WHAT WAS IT THAT SHE WAS MISSING? Taylor returned to her parents' bedroom closet and pulled out one of the Nike shoe boxes that held bits and pieces of her life, her sister's, and, of course, their parents'. With her dad working on his book, her mom reading the Sunday edition of the *Kitsap Sun*, and her sister standing guard in the hallway, Taylor fanned the contents out on the bed.

She returned to the letter that had been sent from the University of Washington in Seattle. The name typed above the university's printed return address was S. OSTEEN.

Savannah Osteen was the linguistics researcher who had videotaped the girls when they were infants. Savannah was conducting a study about the secret language twins purportedly share when something very unexpected occurred. The Ryan twins had spelled out a message in alphabet pasta on their highchair trays. It was a warning to Savannah that her sister, Serena, was in grave danger:

TELL SERENA NOT TO GO

The camera had caught it all on tape—including the twins' mom, Valerie, who clearly saw the message and then inexplicably wiped the trays clean.

The video that Savannah had recorded was what had gotten reporter Moira Windsor all riled up and ready to expose Hayley and Taylor's "gift" the night that she died in the waters of Paradise Bay.

The night that Colton's mom ran her into the bay and killed her.

Taylor looked over at Hayley, who was standing in the doorway, ping-ponging between watching her sister and the hallway.

"Let's ask Dad if we can borrow the car," she said.

"You want to go back to Savannah's?"

"Yup."

WHEN HAYLEY AND TAYLOR PULLED INTO the tree-shrouded driveway leading to Savannah Osteen's cabin, it was apparent that something beyond terrible had occurred. The first indication was the driveway itself. It had been deeply rutted by several large vehicles. Hayley had to maneuver along the outer edge of the driveway, hoping that the winter-tough sword ferns and vine maples didn't scratch the paint on their dad's car.

As they drew closer, the twins almost stopped breathing. The log cabin that the former researcher from the University of Washington had lovingly restored and made her home had been obliterated. In its place was a pile of burned-out rubble and charred logs, a portion of which resembled the remains of a mammoth campfire. The only survivor, the only real proof that a house had once been there, was the river rock chimney and fireplace that stood abandoned, reaching toward the drizzly sky.

Yellow police tape wrapped around the charred remains of Savannah's house. A red-and-white sign hung from a shriveled cedar tree:

DANGER! CRIME SCENE! DO NOT ENTER!
Contact Kitsap County Sheriff or Fire Marshal
with any information.

Hayley looked at Taylor, but said nothing. There was nothing that could be said. Not really. What had happened was clear. An enormous fire had consumed everything in one big, hot, flaming gulp.

A woman in gray sweatpants and a navy-blue down vest was picking up bits and pieces of debris that had been blown from the house by the fury of the fire hoses. She had a large plastic bag slung over her sagging shoulder and a ski pole at the ready.

The twins, stunned by the sight, jumped out of the car.

"What's going on here?" Taylor called over to the woman.

The scavenger paused mid-stab at the ground and leaned on her pole, looking over at the girls. "You related to the lady that lived here? I'm not taking anything of value. Just bits of metal that'll rust out here in the elements anyway."

"No, we're not," Hayley said.

"We know her, though," Taylor added. "Where is she?"

The woman shifted her weight and aimed the grimy tip of her pole in the direction of the cabin.

"There," she said. "They found her there."

"Is she at the hospital?" Hayley asked, sensing that the question was going to bring only grief.

The woman, who seemed standoffish at first, now softened a little. "She was practically a briquette, dear. Deader than a doornail. You said you knew her?"

A plane from the little airport next door buzzed overhead.

Taylor nodded. "Yeah, we did."

The kind look she had disappeared. "You must not have known her well. She was a cooker."

"A cooker?" asked Hayley, totally confused.

"Meth," she said. "You girls aren't here to get that crap, are you? Because if that's what you're up to, I just want to warn you that you'll end up looking like trash. You know, with the yellow candy-corn teeth of a user."

Taylor shook her head, a little insulted that the stranger suggested they were druggies. She and her sister were far smarter than that. So was Savannah Osteen. They knew from their first encounter with her last winter that she was a greenie. She raised pheasants just to release them in the wild. It was beyond belief that she was a drug dealer. While Savannah had had problems with substance abuse in the past, Taylor doubted it had changed the pure goodness that was still inside of her. The Savannah she knew would never hurt anyone.

"No," she said, firmly. "Never. And for your information, Savannah wasn't a 'cooker' either."

The woman in the vest shrugged a little and backed off. "I'm telling you what I know. Why are you here, then?"

"We wanted to ask her something . . ." Taylor said, trying not to betray any emotion as she scanned the blackened space beyond the picker.

Hayley added to her sister's story. "About the pheasants. My sister and I were going to raise them this year. Savannah was going to help us."

"If you knew her so well, why didn't you know about the fire? It was on the news. Twice, I think," the picker said.

They ignored her and moved toward where the front door had once stood. They thought about the night they'd come to this very spot with Shania and Colton. How they had seen the tape that threatened to expose their gift. How Savannah had seemed genuinely concerned about them. Her letter was proof of that. And now she was dead under suspicious circumstances. Though they didn't know Savannah Osteen well, both girls felt grief seize them. They didn't cry. They simply stood silently mourning her death.

And maybe, just a little, mourning the opportunity to find out more about themselves.

The picker moved on, and the girls got into the car. Hayley put it in gear and drove back to the main road. Taylor kept her eyes on the scorched earth that had been Savannah's home and had become her grave. As the property receded from Taylor's view, her mind wandered to another grave—a much, much older one—in the Port Gamble Cemetery. It was marked with a small, faded plaque:

PETER O'MALLEY, 15,
was interred in the sea on April 22, 1792.
He is now in God's hands.
May he rest in eternal peace.

According to the legend, passed down from generation to generation in Port Gamble, young Peter had died from cholera and his wasted body had been buried in what was later named Port Gamble Bay inside a salt-cod-crate coffin. The coffin had washed up on shore, and was forced open by three curious S'Klallam Indian boys, who found nothing inside except a silver crucifix, a swarm of flies, and a horrible odor of death. Soon after, the story went, the oyster beds died and the seabirds refused to nest there. People were certain the site was cursed. They called the place Memalucet, which means "empty box." Those with darker minds called it Empty Coffin. Decades later, Port Gamble was founded there.

If only Port Gamble had fewer full coffins, Taylor thought darkly, *and more* empty *ones.*

Hayley's voice brought Taylor back to the present. "Someone killed Savannah because of us," Hayley said, her eyes fastened to the rearview mirror.

"Yeah," Taylor said in the softest voice. "I know. I don't care how weirded out Mom is about us and the crash. She knows about our connection. She saw our message to Savannah before Savannah's sister died," Taylor said. "We have to get her to talk to us. We're her daughters. She owes it to us."

Hayley understood her sister's feelings completely. Yet, she also felt sorry for her mother. There must be a reason she didn't want to talk about any of it. The reason had to be big.

IT WASN'T EVERY NIGHT, but several times a week Valerie Ryan somehow managed to serve dinner at the table, with the entire family at the same time. Sometimes she served take-out, and occasionally dinner was something she'd tossed together in the Crock-Pot before heading off to work at the hospital. Kevin cooked, too, but his idea of a meal was meat of some kind. No side dishes. No vegetable option.

It was pizza that night—vegetarian "with meat" and a Caesar salad. Taylor's would be served without croutons, which she called "dead bread."

"How was your day?" Valerie asked no one in particular. It was just a question tossed out into the open. Chicken scratch tossed in the yard.

Kevin answered. "Fair. Having a hard time with the apprehension scene. Tough to make it exciting for the reader when the killer just basically turns himself in."

She nodded. "I see your point." She turned toward the girls. "Hayley?"

"Mine sucked."

Taylor jumped in. "Mine, too."

Valerie stopped eating, her eyes full of concern. "Why, what happened?"

Taylor put down her fork and stayed riveted to her mother. "We found out that a friend of ours died."

"Oh no," Valerie said, looking at Kevin with concern, red flag up. "Was it another kid from school?"

Taylor shook her head. "No. I said a friend of *ours*. Yours, mine, Dad's, Hayley's. All of us."

"Really? Who?" Valerie asked.

"Yeah, Taylor, who died?" Kevin repeated.

"Savannah," she said, waiting for a reaction from her parents. None came.

"We don't know anyone named Savannah," Valerie said carefully, searching her daughters' and husband's eyes. She scooted to the edge of her seat, as if readying herself to make a hasty escape.

"Savannah Osteen," Hayley said.

Valerie glanced at Kevin nervously.

"Isn't that the name of the researcher from years ago, Val?" Kevin asked. "Wasn't she the one who came out here when the girls were little?"

"I think so," Valerie said, turning her eyes down to her suddenly very interesting plate.

Both girls felt sick to their stomachs. Their mother knew full well who Savannah Osteen was, and they knew it. The proof was only inches away. Yet there, at the dinner table, Valerie tried to play dumb.

"What happened to Savannah?" Kevin asked.

"Well, her house blew up and she died. Allegedly, she was manufacturing methamphetamine," Hayley said.

"I remember her now, Kevin," Valerie said tentatively and pushed her croutons underneath some greens. "Didn't Savannah get fired from the university for using drugs or something along those lines?"

"Mom," Hayley said, her voice getting louder and firmer, "Savannah didn't get fired for that, and you know it. What's wrong with you? Why don't you just admit you know all about Savannah and me and Taylor?"

Valerie pushed back from the table and stood. "I don't know what you're talking about."

Hayley stood. "Really, Mom? You're really going to be that way?" She reached under her place mat and pulled out Savannah's letter.

"I'm talking about this, Mom! This letter!" She held it out, but Valerie didn't take it. Instead, Valerie looked first at Kevin and then back at the girls. The room was still, tense, and filled with the hurt of a million lies.

Seeing that she was adrift without one bit of support, Valerie turned back to Hayley. She took the letter. "Don't you ever speak to me like that again, Hayley. It is rude and disrespectful. And I don't appreciate you going through my things either."

Hayley loved her mother with every fiber of her being, but she didn't think love meant burying family secrets—certainly not ones as big as this. "It's rude and disrespectful, Mom, to lie to your kids."

Taylor's mouth fell open in disbelief.

Valerie shot Kevin a look that was a request for a lifeline, if ever there was one. "Kevin, are you going to let them talk to me like that?"

Kevin lasered his eyes on his wife, and then he turned to his daughters. "Girls," he said as sternly as he could, "apologize to your mother."

Taylor finally spoke up, though her voice squeaked in apprehension. "We have questions, Dad, and she won't answer us."

On that note, Valerie turned, her feet hitting the floorboards harder with each step away from the kitchen. Her bedroom door shut. It wasn't a slam, but it was close. It meant: *You've hurt me. You've made me angry. Do not ever push me where I don't want to go.*

"She won't ever talk about it," Hayley said, her eyes now back on her father's.

Kevin's thoughts wandered back to the strange e-mail he received from the newspaper reporter last year. It was about Savannah, and he and Val had fought when he brought it up. She hadn't shared what happened then, and she clearly wasn't going to now. Kevin picked up his plate. Dinner was over. "I don't know exactly what this is all about. Maybe, honey, she can't. Don't you get that? Don't you both understand that some things are just too painful to relive?"

"We're her daughters," Hayley said. "We need to know."

"We have a *right* to know," Taylor added.

"She'll tell you when she's ready," he said, putting some dishes in the sink. His face was red. It was possible he was even more in the dark about what had just transpired than his kids.

"You cannot push your mom. You know that."

Taylor got up and stood in the kitchen doorway. She didn't want her dad to leave, too. This was all too important. He had to listen.

"Dad," she said, "someone set up Savannah. Someone killed her."

Kevin, who clearly had had enough of the confrontation, wasn't sure he heard Taylor correctly. "What do you mean? Did the sheriff tell you that?" he asked.

By then, Hayley was standing next to her sister in the doorway. They were like bookends, making the space completely impassable. Kevin Ryan, who had faced off with serial killers, had never met a force with as much determination as his girls right then. They were going to get the last word, no matter what.

"No," she said. "Not really. But we know it's true."

"How do you know?" he asked.

Taylor's eyes fastened onto her father's. With a final sigh, she said simply, "Ask Mom."

chapter 22

WITH SOFT ROCK HITS PLAYING from the radio on the credenza behind her desk Monday morning, Annie drank the last of her coffee and opened the file of cell phone records for the principals in the Grant murder case: Beth, Olivia, Drew, and Brianna. It had been exactly a week since the girl in the bloodied white slip was found at the Connorses'. In a week's time, the world had churned and turned like a paint mixer. Everything had changed. Almost everyone regarded Katelyn's death as a fluke. But with a second teen death in less than a year, the fluke was starting to look like a pattern. People no longer talked about the charm of Port Gamble, but rather its creepy underlying vibe.

Office administrator Tatiana Jones pointed out a trending tweet when she got in:

Port Gamble is to die for #suckycityslogans

"Licorice tea time?"

Annie shook her head. "Lobotomy time. This thing is a mess. With Brianna and Drew missing and the Brits slinging mud from London by the hour, this whole thing is spinning out of control."

"You'll sort it out," Tatiana said.

"I hope so. In this whole circus, everyone is forgetting about the murder of an innocent girl."

Tatiana left, and Annie reviewed the phone records. Nothing out of the ordinary stood out from Beth's list of calls. Even so, Annie couldn't help but think that Kim Lee might need to look for a provider with a better text-messaging plan. Beth had texted more than two thousand times in the past month.

Who has that much to say? Annie wondered.

Olivia's calls were mostly to Port Gamble kids and to a few phones back home in the United Kingdom. Most of those were to her father and to friends. Or so Annie assumed.

The day she died, Olivia had made six calls to Brianna and one to Drew. That seemed to match what Beth and Brianna had said about the change in plans for the party.

Right after Olivia's final call, Beth had sent a text to Hayley and Taylor.

Brianna's calls were consistently to Drew, Olivia, and her mother, and several dozen other numbers, all of which would have to be checked out. Though they had texted and talked throughout the weeks and days before Halloween, the most relevant call from Brianna to Drew was placed just after 1:23 a.m., which supported her story that he was not at the Connorses' house when she found Olivia. Then she called her mother, the first of fifteen calls to Brandy Connors Baker all starting at 1:24 a.m. By the time Brianna called 911, Drew was already there, purportedly watching TV.

Annie cursed her bad vision, and fumbled for her reading glasses, something she hated to wear because they made her look like a manly Sarah Palin. Or maybe Tina Fey.

As she continued to pore over the printout, Annie paused and did a double-take.

What the . . . ?

She reached over and turned off the radio, silencing the uber-annoying John Mayer, who was still waiting on the world to change. One of the phone numbers that appeared on Drew Marcello's log of Halloween night calls seemed completely out of place. It was to one of the same numbers on his girlfriend's call log.

Drew had dialed that number forty-eight times the week prior to the murder and four times that night.

What in the world? Something's wrong here, she thought.

Just then, the phone rang with the news that the knife found at the Connors house was indeed the murder weapon. The full report was being faxed over from the Olympia lab.

Annie leaned heavily back in her chair. The pieces of the puzzle were starting to fit together. Annie had initially thought that the crime had not been premeditated, but the phone records gave her reason to suspect otherwise. The killer may have planned what happened.

On the other hand, the Zodiac Killer brought a gun. The Night Stalker his own knife. Ted Bundy brought an entire kit of tools that he used in the commission of his unspeakable crimes. Serial killers, like Boy Scouts, come prepared.

If the kitchen knife they found had killed Olivia Grant, then it was possible the attacker *didn't* plan her death after all. *And if her killer was a novice*, Annie thought, *and just grabbed the first weapon available, he or she surely made some mistakes.* She hoped that the murderer's fingerprints and DNA would be on the knife.

If so, case closed.

Annie stood by the fax machine, impatient for the report to spit out. While she waited, she placed a call to Brianna's cell phone four times. Each time it went to voice mail.

While screening a police chief's calls in the middle of an investigation seemed well within character for a girl like Brianna, there was one more likely explanation for why the calls went directly to voice mail.

Like her former best friend, Olivia Grant, Brianna Connors's phone was dead.

THE ONE BRIGHT SPOT IN THE WORST WEEK ever came in the form of the report from Olympia's crime lab. As Annie read through it, she allowed a faint smile to cross her lips. The spot on the kimono that Beth Lee wore at the time of the party turned out to be plum wine, not blood. That, along with pegging the time of Olivia's death after Beth and her friends had left the party, put her just where Annie expected she'd be—in the clear. The lab's latest report also indicated that the necktie found in Olivia's mouth had a black fiber on it, which didn't match anything Beth was wearing. There was no DNA or other evidence that directly connected Beth to the murder.

Annie had always liked Beth, her spirit, and the way in which the girl tried to be different. Annie could relate to that, though on a different level. Annie knew that when Beth found her true self, she'd be unstoppable. All the girls who marginalized her would beg to be part of her inner circle.

The police chief swiveled away from her computer, picked up the phone, and dialed Kim Lee's direct line at the mill office. She'd been through enough with the loss of one daughter, her husband, and the foreign-exchange student who'd been living with them until that bloody Halloween night. As tragic as the past ten years had been, Annie was glad it was not going to get any worse. Kim wouldn't have to add "mother of a murderer" to her misery index.

"Kim, Annie here," she said.

A small beat passed before Kim spoke. "Yes, this is Kim. Is everything all right?"

"Yes, it is. I just wanted you to know—"

Kim cut Annie off. "Beth is a good girl. She couldn't, *wouldn't*, ever hurt Olivia."

"Yes, I know," Annie continued. "I wanted you to know that Beth is not under investigation in the murder of Olivia Grant. The results from the crime lab came back. The red splotch on the kimono was not blood. It was plum wine."

Kim let out a breath. Annie could almost feel her relax over the phone line. "Thank you. Thank you," she said. "She is a good girl, maybe not perfect. But good, you know?"

"Yes, I know," Annie said. "Just wanted you to be the first to hear the news."

"Thank you, Annie. Thank you."

Annie hung up and looked back through the forensics report. There was no evidence to pin the murder on Brianna Connors, either, or to corroborate a two-person attack.

She glanced at the photographs of Olivia, Brianna, Drew, Beth, and the bloody crime scene that she'd taped to the whiteboard on the far side of her office. She got up and pulled Beth's photo from the board.

If not Beth Lee or Brianna Connors, then who? Who killed the girl that came all the way from England? And why?

A GIANT WEIGHT LIFTED off Beth's shoulders after her mother called from work with the news. At first she had been scared, but now she was just mad and sad. Deep down, she knew she hadn't been a suspect. Not really. But it still hurt to have to explain herself. She could act tough, but she wasn't *that* tough. Her mom once told her that she was like a porcupine: "spiny on the outside, but so tender and sweet on the inside." The analogy grossed her out, and she wondered when her mom had ever eaten porcupine.

The first thing she did as a "free woman" was text Hay-Tay:

> **BETH**: UR NOT GETTING RID OF ME.
>
> **HAYLEY**: ?
>
> **BETH**: POLICE LAB SAYS NO BLOOD ON MY GEISHA COSTUME. HAPPY DANCE!
>
> **TAYLOR**: LIKE WE'D EVER BE ABLE 2 LIVE W/O U. I'M SO GLAD UR OK & TALKING 2 ME. I NEVER TOLD YOUR SECRET. SWEAR!

BETH: T, I'M SORRY. FRIENDS?

TAYLOR: ☺

And while the group of three girls had finally made up, like they'd all known they eventually would, things were about to get very, very difficult for another Port Gamble girl.

chapter 23

BRIANNA CONNORS WAS BORED OUT OF HER MIND. She'd been hunkered down in that drafty, smelly, abandoned Port Gamble house number 7734, alone for over an hour while Drew went off to parts unknown. Getting food, she hoped. It was so cold that even though she hated the thought of it, the sixteen-year-old decided to scrounge around for some extra blankets. She never let used clothing touch her skin—even if it was labeled "vintage"—but just then she'd gladly take a scratchy old blanket. Even a painter's drop cloth. Anything that would keep her warm. As she moved along the darkened hallway, she noticed her phone on the table. She knew that Drew had said not to use it so the police couldn't track them, but the flashlight app surely couldn't hurt, right?

Brianna turned on the phone and nearly jumped up and down when the screen flickered brightly.

Drew must have replaced the SIM card, she thought and smiled.

But her giddiness dissipated when a strange new text flashed across the screen:

LET ME KNOW WHEN YOU'VE DONE IT.

It was from a number she knew all too well, but the message was confusing. Was this text actually for her? And what was "it"? Brianna scrolled up to see the text history, but there was only the single message. Any others had all been erased.

That's odd, Brianna thought, turned on the flashlight, and found her way to the bedroom.

Peering through the darkness, she saw that the room still had the remains of a bed—and a musty blanket.

Gross! How did I end up in a dump like this?

The door slammed, and though it seemed impossible, the rickety house got even colder.

"Brianna!" Drew yelled out.

"I'm in here."

"I have something for you. I think you're going to like it."

Drew breezed into the room, and Brianna's mood brightened.

"I hope it's a space heater or a hot panini."

"It's better than a panini," Drew said.

"What is it?"

"Hug first," he said, reaching for her in the dark.

Drew kissed her on the forehead and ran his hands up over the small of her back. The effect gave her even more goose bumps. She pushed away, and like a sprung trap, his hands were around her neck.

"Hey, stop messing around, stupid!" she said, trying escape.

Drew grinned. "Game over, Bree."

"You're hurting me," she gasped.

Brianna started to choke as she tried to twist her way from her boyfriend's vise-like grip.

"That's kind of the point," Drew whispered in her ear. "You've called me stupid for the last time. You're the stupid one. You always have been and soon you will be dead."

TO HAYLEY AND TAYLOR'S DISMAY, Text Creeper would not give up. The mystery texter sent yet another message, and this one crossed the line of mere commentary:

CASE FILE #613-7H: PLS MEET ME. WE NEED 2 TALK.

At least the creep was polite, the sisters thought. Of course, it didn't matter how polite Text Creeper was. Taylor and Hayley knew they shouldn't meet him. It violated another one of their crime writer dad's cardinal rules: *"Politeness is sometimes a trick. A killer will pretend to be friendly, or even needy—then, bam! You're buried alive."*

Hayley and Taylor picked up their phones as if they were AK-47s, synchronized, loaded, and ready to fire in tandem. As they sat at the big kitchen table, house number 19 smelling of cinnamon and sugar from an apple pie Taylor had made in her continuing quest to learn how to do one domestic thing better than anyone, the twins started scrolling through the text messages from the freak who had stalked them since Olivia died:

> **CASE FILE #613-7H:** I KNOW WHO KILLED HER.
>
> **CASE FILE #613-7H:** SHE DESERVED WHAT SHE GOT.
>
> **CASE FILE #613-7H:** PLS MEET ME. WE NEED 2 TALK.

Naively, they had believed that if they simply ignored him, he'd go away. Maybe he was a creepy thrill seeker who liked to mess with the heads of young girls. How would they ever know if they didn't meet him and find out what he wanted?

"I'll text him back," Hayley said.

"What are you going to say?" Taylor asked.

"Something short," Hayley said. "I don't know." She thought a moment and worked her thumbs over the characters on her phone. She spun her phone on the table so Taylor could see what she wanted to send:

> **HAYLEY:** OK. WILL MEET U. WATER TOWERS IN PG. B THERE @ 4.

Taylor stared at the tiny screen and then looked her sister in the eye.

"Holy crap, Hayley. Are you sure?"

Hayley nodded. "We can always back out. But I want to get to the bottom of this. Nobody seems to be able to figure out who killed Olivia. So what are we supposed to do? I want to know what's up. We aren't like other people. We can do this."

Despite how hard they tried to be just like everyone else, the fact of the matter was that they were not. Their mom knew it. Savannah knew it. If they could help find Olivia's killer, both twins believed they had to try—even if it meant meeting Text Creeper.

Taylor pushed back her chair and got up. She carried her pie from the counter where it had been cooling to the table.

"What makes you think this freak knows something?" she asked.

Hayley disregarded the question and eyed the pie. It looked pretty good—maybe the best one her sister had made in her never-ending pursuit for baking supremacy. "I could tell you I have a feeling," she finally said. "But when I say that to you of all people, it sounds so lame. But, really, that's all I have. And maybe a little bit of hope."

Taylor wasn't convinced. "Shouldn't we tell Dad? Mom?"

"Dad is clueless," Hayley said, feeling a little disloyal by saying so, but it was true. When it came to whatever it was that was going on with them, he *was* oblivious. She let out a sigh. "Mom's been working so much, we've hardly seen her."

Taylor set out some plates and forks. "Meeting someone we don't know is dangerous. We both know it. God, we've heard stories about the dumb girls who get in a car in a mall parking lot only to be dismembered a half hour later and ditched behind a Jack in the Box."

"I think it was a Taco Bell," Hayley said, correcting her sister. "That's not going to happen to us. We're smarter than those dim-witted girls."

Taylor cut a slice of pie and arranged it on the plate. Apple pieces slid from inside the shell, and she frowned a little. "Those girls probably thought they were smart, too."

"Okay," Hayley agreed. "Look, we're meeting in a public place— our home turf in the middle of the day. There are two of us. You know, like the 'buddy system.' Besides we're not going anywhere with him. We're not getting into his car or skeezy van."

Taylor waffled. Deep down she wanted to settle things too, but she wasn't certain if Text Creeper was going to help them or hurt them.

"I'm not sure," she said, poking the edge of the pie crust with the tines of a fork.

"Too late," Hayley said, pushing the **send** button.

"Pretty flakey," Taylor said.

Hayley looked at her sister. "Us or him?"

"The pie," Taylor said, offering her sister a bite. "Pretty stupid of us, if you ask me."

"Maybe." Hayley took the fork. "We'll see."

IT WAS FIVE MINUTES BEFORE FOUR and both girls were feeling every bit of the angst that they expected would come with meeting Text Creeper.

Their dad was working on putting in an asparagus bed in the backyard. The twins had fibbed to him, claiming they were going to town to hang out for a little while.

Kevin was grateful for a reason to stop digging the trench. The heavy rains, cold weather, and hard-packed soil were making him sweat.

"All right," he said. "Maybe you'll be back in time to help me plant."

"Okay, but don't wait on us," Taylor said.

"Yeah, you don't want the roots to dry out," Hayley added.

"I can cover them with a tarp so you don't have to miss out," he said, half joking and half serious.

Both girls loathed yard work—so much so that Colton did most of it around their place as a favor. And that was *before* he and Hayley had started dating.

The big green town water towers were about a hundred yards from their house. As the girls started down the picket-fenced sidewalk they could see the figure of a man standing on the corner. He wore a dark-blue coat and a baseball cap. He was in his fifties. Or maybe his mid-thirties. It was hard to tell. As they approached him, they saw he had dark eyes and wire-rimmed glasses fitted with transition lenses. Hayley tried to burn every detail of the man's appearance into her memory.

Just in case a sketch artist was ever needed.

"I'm glad we could finally meet," he said, crushing a cigarette butt in the gravel in the shadow of the water towers.

"Yeah. I guess," Taylor said. She wanted to say that littering was against the rules in Port Gamble, but they had bigger issues to deal with than a cigarette butt.

"What do you want?" Hayley asked.

The man's smoky breath pushed at them. "I want to talk to you. And you know about what, don't you?"

Both girls stepped back, committed more than ever never to smoke.

"No, sir, I don't," Hayley said. "I don't know what it is that you think you need to tell us."

Taylor, taking a cue from Hayley, felt more emboldened. "Or why you keep harassing us."

The man shook his head. "I didn't think of it as harassing," he said. "I thought of it more as getting your attention."

"That's what all stalkers say," Taylor said, now on a roll. "People like you think your attention is wanted. It isn't. It is wrong on every level."

"It might even be against the law," Hayley added.

"You seem quite agitated, Hayley," he said.

Was it just a good guess? Hayley wondered. He did have a fifty-fifty chance, but even so, he said her name with such confidence that it was a little unnerving.

"I'm not agitated, and I'm Taylor, anyway," she said.

Text Creeper studied her through his thick lenses, as if he knew that was a lie. But he didn't call her on it.

"Why," he asked, "did you consent to meet with me?"

"Maybe to get you off our backs," Taylor said.

"Maybe because you're curious about things, *Hayley.*" He said Hayley's name tentatively, in a way that indicated he knew who he was talking to, yet playing along. A little game. That was fine with him.

Hayley noticed a gray van parked by the Dauntless Bookstore. Its engine was running. For a fleeting second, she felt a pang of nervousness reverberate through her body. She put her hand to her stomach to quell it. In doing so, she noticed she was trembling a little.

"Let's not stand around here," she said. "People are watching. Let's walk the loop."

Taylor looked at her sister. She wasn't sure what she was getting at. She glanced down the street. No one was watching them. In fact, there wasn't a soul out shopping, walking, or doing much of anything. Port Gamble was deader than dead.

The man agreed, and the three of them crossed the street, away from the van.

"You said you know who killed Olivia and that she deserved it," Hayley blurted out.

The man didn't answer right away. Maybe he hadn't expected to be confronted so soon. Maybe he hadn't expected to be confronted at all. If that had been the case, he clearly didn't know as much as he thought he did about Taylor and Hayley Ryan.

"What are you talking about?" He grabbed hold of Hayley's arm firmly, but not enough to hurt.

As his hand touched her skin, in that second, Hayley saw everything.

Rain. It was last year, right after Colton's mom, Shania, had run over Moira Windsor, the newspaper reporter who had discovered their unusual abilities. A man in a dark-blue coat—Text Creeper. A woman screaming. It was Moira. Moira was hurt from the impact of Shania's car and her fall over the embankment, but she was alive. She was still very much alive. Shania had not been responsible for her death after all.

"Moira, you idiot!" Text Creeper called out. "All you were supposed to do was get me information on the twins by pretending to write a story!" He shook her roughly by the water's edge of Paradise Bay.

"But I tried!" Moira cried out. "I found the tape. Those girls aren't

normal. They can see things. But now . . . I'm sorry." Moira coughed and bent over. "Help me, please. I'm hurt."

Text Creeper hovered over her. "I'll help you all right," he said, pushing her face-down into the dark water. Moira's leg twitched slowly at first, and then violently.

Then she stopped moving.

"Good night, Moira," Text Creeper said. "You were a poor excuse for an assistant. Next time, I'll do things on my own."

"Hayley!" Taylor shouted, pulling her sister's arm free and snapping her back to reality.

"This isn't about Olivia, is it?" Hayley said to the man in front of them. "It's about Moira. And us."

Taylor gave her sister a nervous look.

"Yes, let's focus on you," Text Creeper said, his dark eyes flickering across their faces.

Hayley led him to the playground on the edge of town. It was out in the open, safe, by anyone's standards. Moms in Port Gamble never worried about someone snatching their kids from that park because things like that never happened there.

"You aren't the only ones like you," he said. "There have been others."

Just then, for the very first time, Hayley noticed the knife at Text Creeper's waist. She looked at Taylor and lured her eyes to the glint of steel held in place by his belt. It looked like a sharp knife—the kind used to gut a deer.

Or maybe kill a teenage girl. Like them. Like Olivia.

Her mind flashed to Olivia. Halloween night. Brianna. Drew.

Hayley looked at her sister and screamed without making a sound.

Run!

The man lunged at Hayley, and she did what Colton James had said was the worst possible thing a girl could do to a guy. She aimed her foot where it counted. She kicked him as hard and decisively as she could.

Her aim was perfect. The man cried out and doubled over, and the girls took off.

RUNNING AS IF THEIR LIVES DEPENDED ON IT was the only thing Hayley and Taylor could do just then. Anything else would mean turning themselves over to the man pursuing them—and the deadly edge of his hunting knife.

And there was no way either girl was going to do that.

In two short minutes their world had shifted. The bright sunlight and safety of friendly neighborhood backyards and the town playground had disappeared, replaced by dark, ominous shadows. The glint of the blade as he pulled it out from behind his back was all they saw before they hit the asphalt.

Their legs pumped, faster and faster, past an empty swing set, over perfect Port Gamble lawns, straining against the temptation to stop. Hayley and Taylor knew they had only three options: run, hide, or escape. When they reached the last house and the forest tree line, they didn't hesitate for a second before plunging ahead.

He was coming after them.

Hayley and Taylor thrashed wildly through the forest, their footfalls landing hard against the packed dirt in escalating rhythm with the blood that was jack-hammering through their bodies. They were on the run in a place where screams melted into the green folds of the woods. They knew they should stay together and tried not to look over their shoulders, hoping they wouldn't get caught, wondering what horrors would happen to them if they did.

The lumbering sound of a large body crushing decaying leaves underfoot and brushing past mossy logs told the teens their pursuer was closing in. Then they heard the bristly sound of his thick voice.

"Stop! This is just a big misunderstanding. I only want to talk. I won't hurt you."

Lies. The word floated through Hayley's mind as she imagined his real intention: *Come here. Closer. So I can take this knife and slit your pretty slender throat like a chicken.*

As she tunneled through a tangle of salmonberry bushes, small circles of red bloomed across the white field of her T-shirt.

Berry juice? Hayley wondered. In her heart of hearts, though, she knew it wasn't. Salmonberries are bright orange, not red. Besides, it was autumn, and the berries were long gone.

In the terror of the moment, she paused mid-stride and realized that she and Taylor had become separated. She touched her fingertips to the damp fabric. It was blood. Hers? His? Her sister's?

Hayley could hear the man's heavy breathing, though she was sure he was not near enough to see her. She imagined the stink of his smoky breath and how he'd spout more lies. She was determined not to let him get any closer. Because if he did manage to find her, jump her, grab her, she knew that she would have to fight for the knife and do to him what he planned for her.

Just like a chicken.

As she passed through that thicket, not feeling the thorns or the branches lashing against her face, Hayley wondered one thing above everything else. *Was her sister safe?*

SPRAWLED FACE-DOWN ON THE GROUND, Taylor Ryan froze. She had no idea what was happening, but she tried to remain calm and still. Not move. Not breathe. She even tried to force her own heart to stop its drumlike beating. She'd tumbled over a fallen tree, gashing her right hand on the broken knob of a branch. Crimson muddled the knee of her jeans—Meks that she'd saved all autumn to buy. If this had been any other time, any other moment, she would have examined the jeans for tears. But not then.

Besides the maniac chasing her, only one other thing was on her mind as she crouched in the crook of that fallen hemlock. She wondered about Hayley.

Her twin.

Her other half.

Taylor could feel tears running down her face as she struggled to stay composed in that dank, dark forest. It was dead silent—the kind of silence that she hoped would conceal her location.

He appeared suddenly, from nowhere, begging, cajoling.

"Come out now. I won't hurt either of you," the man called again.

Either of you, Taylor thought with relief. *Hayley must be alive.*

Taylor rolled on her side and took cover in a ratty nest of sword ferns, trying to make sense of what had happened to them and why. First, there were the text messages. Then Hayley had mentioned something about Moira?

The twins had followed their dad's rules, if only partially. They had gone together. They didn't get into anyone's car. They agreed to meet in a public place. They did all of that. They were not stupid. They were raised on Bundy, Manson, and that dopey-looking Craigslist Killer. They understood that evil didn't always look the part.

And yet there she was, hiding from sure death, literally scared stiff. Wondering if she deserved this. If she'd been good enough to the world. If what happened to Moira was their fault. If karma had knocked on their door with a poisoned Edible Arrangement.

Trying to steady herself, Taylor started to stand. A fan of dark-green ferns parted, and a patch of apricot, a color so wrong for the dank cedar- and fir-laden forests of Washington State, caught her eye.

Apricot?

She leaned closer, feeling the earth shift under her feet as icy fear swallowed her into the heavy black soil.

Apricot.

It took every ounce of self-control she had to keep from screaming.

It was a bra. Lacy and torn. A garment in a place meant to conceal it forever.

Taylor touched it with a fingertip, and she knew—she felt—immediately what she had stumbled on.

Brianna Connors. The bra belonged to her.

Twigs snapped, and the sound of boots sloshing through a creek a few yards away ricocheted over the forest floor. *Hayley?*

Then, the voice again.

"I just want to talk to you," he said.

Like hell, killer.

What Taylor didn't allow herself to think was what she already knew. A truth that was deep in the marrow of her bones. He had answers. Answers to questions about their past that nobody else had ever dared give them. He held a piece of the puzzle that had only started to take shape, she now realized.

There was only one way to find out what they wanted to know. But how was she going to make sure she wouldn't be on the losing end of the man's knife?

Exhaling slowly, Taylor paused, then took a deep breath and stepped away from Brianna Connors's lingerie, out into the clearing.

chapter 24

FOR THE UMPTEENTH TIME, Annie Garnett scoured the Olivia Grant file, backtracking to the murder scene as captured by the crime-scene photographers and the cell-phone cameras of the partygoers.

She picked through the dozens of photos and pulled the wide-angle view of the scene from where she had taped it to her whiteboard. Everything was as it had been imprinted on her mind: dead girl on the floor, blood pooled underneath the body and into the cracks between the floorboards, a pile of clothes next to the bed, mirror, dresser, and another pile of clothes across the room on a chair. She had looked at the photo so many times Annie knew she could probably draw it by memory.

Sliding it slightly to the right, the tired police chief retrieved the forensics report and placed it next to the picture. Could she have missed something? The evidence was staring her in the face, but what was it telling her?

Annie looked from the report to the photo and back again. Reading down the list of items, she noticed something that she had disregarded before. The discovery made the hair on her thick, muscled arms rise up. The crime lab had found a single black fiber on Olivia's shoulder, sequins in her hair, and white threads—none of which matched what she was wearing when she died.

Where did they come from?

Annie grabbed the photo on her desk with her right hand and dug around in her top drawer with her left.

Where was that magnifying glass?

As soon as her hand closed around its handle, she held it and the photo under her halogen gooseneck desk lamp. On the chair across the room where the officer had offered up a pair of day-old brown jeans to Brianna, lay a crumpled white sheet. It wasn't an ordinary bedsheet. The camera angle had been such that Annie could just make out a pair of roughly cut eyeholes in the ghost costume.

And next to the bed, closest to Olivia's body, was a sparkly dress. With sequins. There was also one other item on the floor. It was a black cape and mask. It was Darth Vader.

Annie dropped the photo and flipped through the loopy handwriting on the pages of her notebook. Beth had said Olivia had worn a ghost costume to the party. Brianna had said she went as a mail-order bride but changed into a second costume.

Annie couldn't make sense of the disparity. *What happened with those teens? If Olivia had both sequins and thread from the ghost costume on her body, it was possible that she wore both costumes. But why on earth was Olivia wearing Brianna's mail-order bride costume and vice versa when each had her own? And who did the Darth Vader costume belong to?*

As Annie pondered that information, she had no idea that something dark was going on quite literally in her neck of the woods.

chapter 25

"I HEARD YOU SCREAM. ARE YOU ALL RIGHT?"

Taylor Ryan stood still at the edge of the clearing. Her heart pounded so hard that she was going to have a heart attack—even though she was just sixteen, ate mostly the right foods, and was on the school's swim and diving team. She didn't want to die. No one wants to be one of those kids who are mourned with flowery lettering decaled on the back window of a friend's Kia. She had come to face the man and save her sister, whom she was certain had been captured.

But the voice didn't belong to the man who had chased them into the woods. The voice was not menacing. It was full of concern and sincerity. It was Port Gamble's Segway Guy, who had been testing his brand-new all-terrain people mover near the park when all the commotion started. Taylor had never heard the middle-aged man speak before, and she wasn't quite sure she could trust him. She scanned all around for her attacker, but he was gone. She felt somewhat safer, but was terrified at the same time. And still very much out of breath.

"My sister," she said, trying to pull herself together. "There was a man. I think he took my sister."

Jumping off his machine, Segway Guy shook his head. "No. He didn't. He ran off when I arrived. She wasn't with him. I'm sure of it."

Taylor felt a wave of relief. She knew she looked terrible. Blood trickled down her face from the thorns that had clawed at her with the fury of a thousand angry cats.

"Did he hurt you?" Segway Guy asked, powering off his machine and striding toward her.

He was much shorter without his embarrassing mall-cop vehicle. His eyes were kind, and he was there to help her. Taylor felt bad for all the times she and her sister had made fun of him. He leaned closer to examine her. Her scratches stung, but they were superficial.

She shook her head. "No. But I don't know where Hayley is. I thought for sure that he took her or maybe really, really hurt her."

She didn't want to use the words that hung in her throat.

Kill. Stab. Murder.

"I'll find her," he said. "You stay here."

Before Taylor could answer, she heard the snap of a twig.

Branches parted, and Hayley emerged from the green gloom of the woods. She ran into Taylor's arms, and the pair convulsed in tears.

"Do you want me to get your folks?" Segway Guy asked. "House number 19, right?"

"No," Taylor said, looking over her sister. "No. We're fine. But we do need help. We need the police."

Segway Guy nodded. "I was thinking something along those same lines. This kind of thing needs to be reported. No place is safe anymore. Not even little Port Gamble. I sometimes wonder what is happening to the human race that makes people do the worst possible things to each other."

"We don't need the police for *us*," Taylor said, looking back at the woods. "I think I found something they need to see back there."

Hayley, also scratched up, but not nearly as badly as her sister, looked over at the woods.

"What is it?" she asked.

Taylor wasn't sure how to phrase it. She stumbled for the words. "I think . . . I'm pretty sure I found something of Brianna's."

Hayley looked at her twin. "What was she doing in the forest?"

"She's . . ." Taylor struggled to clarify. "I think Brianna's dead."

WITHIN THIRTY MINUTES, half of Port Gamble had convened in the clearing by the swing set and jungle gym made of smooth, peeled cedar logs. Beth Lee and her mother, along with Colton James, Starla, and

Mindee—and, of course, Kevin and Valerie Ryan—were among those who watched Annie Garnett, her deputy, and a K-9 Unit from the Kitsap County Sheriff's Department search the woods. Annie had decided not to call Brianna's parents until there was something definite to report.

A cadaver dog, a tail-wagging German shepherd named Ava, had no trouble finding her way back to where the pretty apricot bra had been discovered in the brambles in the woods. In fact, it took one of Kitsap County's finest canine officers only fifteen minutes on the trail through the woods to locate a shallow grave that held the body of Brianna Connors.

Hayley and Taylor, wrapped in blankets, sat on a bench that faced the playground. The girls had plenty to discuss with their parents later at home, but with just one look between them they had agreed not to tell anyone that they'd willingly met Text Creeper at the water towers. Colton put his arm around Hayley and held her close—which left Taylor in the arms of both parents.

"He just accosted you here?" Kevin asked.

"We were out walking and he came up to us asking for directions," Hayley said. She hated lying to her dad. She just didn't think he'd understand why they would break one of his rules and meet a stranger.

"Yeah," Taylor said. "He said he wanted to know where the playground was. We were walking that way anyway."

"He got real weird, and then we saw his knife," Hayley added.

"Did he threaten you with it?" Valerie asked.

"Not really, Mom. I mean, it looked like he might reach for it. I don't know for sure. We started running," Hayley said.

"Yeah, Mom," Taylor said. "We panicked. Then we got separated in the woods."

"Then Sidney found you?" Valerie asked.

"Sidney?" Taylor questioned.

Valerie pointed to Segway Guy.

Neither girl had known his real name.

"Right," Taylor said, looking at Segway Guy. "*Sidney* found us."

Kevin went off to talk to Annie, and Valerie went over to thank Sidney the Segway Guy. Nobody mentioned what they all thought: that the attacker might be the same person who murdered Olivia. Only Hayley and Taylor knew for sure that he wasn't. What he wanted had nothing to do with Olivia and Brianna. The parents huddled together for a while, watching their children and the thinning crowd in a place where they'd all played together. Things like what happened that afternoon didn't happen in Port Gamble. They just didn't.

TWO GIRLS WERE DEAD IN JUST OVER A WEEK. Even if the temperature dropped by twenty degrees, that day in Port Gamble could not have felt any colder. It was as if time had stood still. The moments after Ava, the German shepherd, found Brianna's grave in the woods behind town melded into that mix of fear and fascination that comes with a horrifying discovery. Some kids tweeted with the hashtag #EasyBreezyDead:

> New town slogan: people are just dying to go to Port Gamble. #EasyBreezyDead

> Never forget Olivia Grant. #EasyBreezyDead

> Probably killed herself. Proves her guilt. Please RT #EasyBreezyDead

Taylor and Hayley followed the tweets from the warmth of their living room in house number 19. Neither thought for one minute that Brianna had killed herself.

"She *was* pretty selfish," Taylor said, looking up from her phone after seeing the suicide suggestion tweet.

"I'll give you that, but no one digs a hole, kills herself, and falls into her grave like she was jumping into bed," Hayley said.

"Right," Taylor said, scrolling though the flurry of #EasyBreezyDead tweets.

"With Olivia, and now, Brianna," Hayley said, "there can be no denying that there's a serial killer running around Kitsap County."

"Right," Taylor said again. "And one of us could be next. Any one of us."

THE BRITISH TABLOIDS had immediately posted their take on the demise of Brianna Connors before the twins had even made it home. Reporters there didn't have the time or the interest to bother checking the police updates to present an unbiased story. From nearly the moment the story broke overseas, as far as they were concerned, Brianna and Drew had been arrested, tried, and proclaimed guilty. No one seemed to care who had killed Brianna—only that she got her just desserts. The headlines screamed:

TABLES TURN ON
OLIVIA GRANT'S MURDERER

EASY-BREEZY GETS HER COMEUPPANCE

DEAD RIGHT: EASY-BREEZY
GOT WHAT SHE DESERVED

The evening news also had a field day with the story, and, tired of following the deluge of hashtags on Twitter, Hayley, Taylor, and Beth watched TV, safe in the Ryans's living room.

"Wow," Beth said, her eyes fixed on the screen.

"Double wow," Taylor and Hayley agreed in unison.

"I hate it when you do that," Beth said.

"So do we," they both said and laughed.

Beth made an exaggerated expression of annoyance. "Knock it off. I want to hear this."

Brianna's mom was on TV, dropping a bombshell in an interview recorded before her daughter was found in the woods of Port Gamble.

Brandy, whom nobody had seen in years in Port Gamble or Kingston, was a phantom mother in more than one sense of the word. Under the lights, she looked otherworldly as she stood in front of the TV camera. There was no doubt her face had gone under a plastic surgeon's knife, and it seemed that her nipping and tucking had gone a little too far.

Hayley and Taylor remembered seeing her last at a Parent's Night in junior high (an event later renamed Guardians' Night, a more inclusive title that made all the kids feel like they were either orphans or in special ed). Brandy Connors Baker seemed to be older back then. Not quite grandma-old, but not too far off.

Apparently, Brandy made the media rounds after Brianna had failed to show up for a shopping trip they'd planned in Seattle.

"Bree loves to get her nails done. She is a girly girl, and I promised her a day of pampering considering, you know, what you all have put her through," she told a KING-TV reporter as a microphone was nearly shoved down her throat.

With the wind kicking up and the clouds threatening to unload, Brandy stood in a rose-colored Versace trench coat and gleaming black boots outside the Seattle Public Library, a striking building that looked like the result of a sight-challenged architect, a fistful of pills, and an Erector Set.

"When was the last time you saw or talked to Brianna?" asked the reporter.

"I saw her a few days ago. It's hard to say. We're so close. The last time I talked to her was this morning. And let me tell you, she was simply crushed by the media attention. You people should get a life. You have fanned the flames and made her the subject of scorn and ridicule all over the world. I got a call from a paper in Hamburg last night. It's a feeding frenzy, and my poor daughter is the shark bait."

Shark bait? There was no doubt in Taylor's mind that Brandy wouldn't hesitate to chomp on her young if she needed a little mid-morning snack.

"Your daughter is the prime suspect in Olivia Grant's murder and you're saying that she's been victimized because of it?"

Brandy looked right at the camera.

"I'm not really sure what I'm saying, because I have no idea what you're asking."

"Do you think your daughter has run away, or do you think something else has happened to her?"

"How would I know? I have no idea what she's doing, but I can tell you that there is no way she would miss out on a mani-pedi with her mother. So yeah, something is very wrong."

"What's very wrong is that Brianna had a mother like that," Hayley said after the segment was over.

"Yeah," Beth replied. "That lady doesn't look like she's too choked up about her kid going missing. Whenever I see moms like that, I'm glad that I have mine."

"Me too," said Taylor.

"Me three," said Hayley. "Whenever I think Mom could be more forthcoming about something or maybe stop talking about the freaks at her work—and I don't mean the patients—I see someone like Bree's mom and I know how lucky we are."

"Forthcoming about what?" Beth asked.

"Stuff," Taylor said. "Nothing big."

Taylor hated lying to Beth, but she knew that as close as the three of them were, they could never, ever share everything.

chapter 26

THAT NIGHT HAYLEY AND TAYLOR, bandaged up and in bed, swiveled open their outlet covers and went over everything that had happened. Foremost on their minds was not the terror of the day—or how they'd led police to Brianna's grave.

Mostly, they talked about Taylor's vision of Moira and what happened after Shania's car had sent her tumbling into Paradise Bay last year.

The night Moira had threatened to expose their abilities, Colton's mom, Shania, had unexpectedly and intentionally gunned the gas and pushed the reporter into the bay. Afterward, Shania had come back from accidentally-on-purpose killing Moira, Colton's mom sat in her husband's black leatherette La-Z-Boy recliner and faced the trio of teens on the sofa.

"We shouldn't talk about this after tonight," Shania had said, clasping her hands in her lap. Every word that came from her ached with sorrow. "It was an accident. Accidents happen. And sometimes what you think is an accident, really isn't accidental at all."

Hayley flashed back to the vision she'd had of the shaking man pressing the button to open the bridge span just as the bus approached the gaping seam. She shook her head and tried to focus again on Shania's words:

"I did what I had to do to prevent Moira from knowing what was really behind the crash and to stop whoever hired her from getting his hands on you. He would stop at nothing to end what started before you were even born. This is bigger than all of us. Bigger than Port Gamble. I had to protect you girls. I can't exactly explain it. It isn't mine to explain even if I could. And if circumstances send me to jail, I'll go. I'm not proud of what I did tonight, but I don't regret it."

But that was then. Before Taylor had seen what Text Creeper had done to Moira. Shania had not killed her after all. *He* had.

"Who do you think Text Creeper is, besides the super-scary 'employer' who hired Moira to find out about us?" Taylor asked her sister as the dark sky started picking up the first hints of dawn.

"I don't know. But what worries me is he's after us and he knows who we are and what we can do. Clearly he knows a whole lot more about our past than we do."

"He said that we aren't the 'only ones.' He said there were others."

"I know. But who are they? Where are they? How did this happen to us?" Hayley asked, hoping the answer would just come to her in a message or a feeling. So far, no luck.

"Part of me wishes that Colton's mom had not erased Moira's cell phone and laptop memory," said Taylor. "We might have been able to find out a lot from her voice messages and emails."

"No, Taylor," said Hayley firmly. "Shania did the right thing—she was very clear that protecting us was top priority, and Moira definitely didn't have *that* on her agenda."

"Well, it leaves us no choice, then," said Taylor. "If we want to find out what Text Creeper knows about what happened to us, we'll have to find *him*."

DOWNSTAIRS IN THE COZY RYAN FAMILY KITCHEN, Valerie and Kevin drank a glass of Oregon pinot noir from a bottle that they'd been saving for a special occasion. This most certainly wasn't that occasion, but the need for a glass was undisputable. It had been a horrible day. They had been mostly silent since the ordeal with the girls, the man, and the discovery of the body.

"I feel so sorry for Brianna's parents," Valerie said. "I can't imagine what they've been going through."

Kevin finished his wine and poured another, his fingernails still grimy from gardening.

"Annie didn't say so specifically," he said, "but I got the impression that whoever had killed Brianna did so elsewhere and then dumped her body there. This whole thing is one damn big mess."

Valerie swallowed her last sip and set down her glass. "Evil can't be forced into neat order, Kevin. You of all people should know that."

Kevin ignored Valerie's last comment. He just couldn't stop. "First Olivia gets stabbed and dies. Next, Brianna and Drew are questioned and made out to be the prime suspects. Then after a bunch of media attention they disappear, whereabouts completely unknown. And now Brianna's body is found out here practically in our own backyard."

Valerie set down her glass. "Find Drew, I guess, and you'll find the killer."

"Unless Drew's dead too."

Valerie looked surprised. "You don't think he is, do you?"

"I don't know," Kevin said, narrowing his focus to meet her eyes. "What do you think, Val? You're good at figuring things out."

She got up and put her empty glass in the sink.

"I have no idea," she said.

Her response was true now. But at another point in her life, Valerie knew her answer would have been different.

VALERIE MAY HAVE THOUGHT SHE'D ESCAPED a series of uncomfortable conversations with her daughters the night before. But bright and early the next morning, Hayley and Taylor found her at the kitchen table, her first cup of coffee not yet touched.

"Mom, we really need to talk," Hayley began.

Taylor continued, "I was looking through our old photos for a school project and I found a bunch of newspaper clippings about the crash. About Timothy Robbinette. And about you when you were lost for two days on McNeil Island. Who's Tony Ortega? What happened to you? You never told us that story."

Valerie looked at her coffee cup, taking a beat to collect herself.

"It was nothing," she said. "I was playing hide-and-seek, and I got lost and couldn't find my way back. As for Tony Ortega, he was an inmate on death row who was later pardoned." Valerie let out a nervous laugh, knowing she had given away too much information. She was holding her coffee cup so tightly that her fingers had turned white.

Both girls knew their mother was lying. She was the kind of person who didn't use a map. She had an internal GPS that was never, ever wrong. Even blindfolded and spun in a circle a dozen times, Valerie Ryan would always be able to get where she needed to go.

"And what about us?" Taylor asked. "You know we're not normal. Remember what happened to Grandpa?"

Valerie thought back to the day that her father almost died. The twins were in their last year at Port Gamble Elementary. It was a beautiful afternoon. She had been cutting a bouquet of rangy white roses that cascaded up and over the trellis by the back door when out of the blue the twins had said they had "a funny feeling about Grandpa."

Chester Fitzpatrick had been suffering from Alzheimer's, and when it became abundantly and tragically clear that Valerie's mom could no longer care for her husband, the family had moved him to Cottesmore, an assisted living facility in Gig Harbor.

At the time, Valerie had shrugged her daughters' worry off, telling them to go play. But the girls' feeling had been so strong and unsettling, they had called Cottesmore to check on their grandfather—who had fallen in the bathroom two hours earlier and almost died from hypothermia. If it hadn't been for that phone call, Valerie's dad would have died then, instead of years later, peacefully in his sleep.

How did they know? she asked herself over and over. But just as she did all those years ago, she refused to face what she wasn't sure she could handle.

"Girls, where is this all coming from? Does it have to do with the man in the woods?" Valerie hoped against hope for an answer she knew wasn't coming.

Taylor put her elbows on the table and searched for the words. *How do we say it? How do we not sound like morons?*

"Sometimes we get messages, and we don't know where they come from. It's more like a feeling than anything else," Hayley chimed in.

Valerie studied her daughters. "What do you mean, a 'feeling'? You're scaring me. That's what I get at work from my patients all the time."

"She means that sometimes we can catch a glimpse of the past, present, or future when we're not even there. You know we can do it. We saw the video," Taylor explained.

"What video?"

"The one of us as babies. The one that Savannah Osteen took of us. We warned her about her sister Serena . . . before she died. You were in the video, too," Hayley said. "You know."

Valerie's eyes started to water. She looked out the window, toward the alley. Tiny tributaries of tears started down her high cheekbones. "I don't want to talk about this, girls. I know you want to. You might even need to. But not now."

Valerie grabbed her coat and keys from the little hooks by the kitchen door.

"Mom!" Hayley said.

"Please," Valerie said. "Don't. Don't dig into the past."

"Talk to us," Taylor said, though Valerie Ryan couldn't hear her.

The kitchen door shut and she was gone.

WHILE THEY WERE MAD AT THEIR MOM, Hayley and Taylor couldn't shake off the anxiety and fear that came from the discovery of Brianna's body. At their mother's and father's insistence, the girls skipped school that day, leaving Taylor to wonder if their excuse would be the best one the attendance office would get all year—better than "Garage-door opener didn't work so couldn't leave the house" or "Mom might be pregnant and I am too upset that I might have to share my room," the top reigning contenders for the title.

The Ryan twins called this one in:

Found the remains of a missing student.

"I really can't think of anything except Brianna," Taylor said as they put on their coats and went outside in the cold. Sitting around the house was bad enough when you're sick, but ten times more boring than when you're completely well. Frazzled, yeah. Scared, sure. But all in all, feeling fine.

"And Olivia," Hayley said as she shut the door.

Taylor nodded. "And their killer."

Port Gamble was always a quiet place. Until lately. The girls took a walk and talked about what had happened in the woods with Text Creeper and Brianna. They also had another piece of business to attend to. Timothy Robbinette might be dead, but they could still track down Tony Ortega. If their mom wasn't going to tell them the whole story, they'd have to find out on their own.

As they turned the corner by the water tower, they watched a white Mercedes coupe turn toward the police station.

For the first time in a long time, the driver was back in town.

chapter 27

BRIANNA CONNORS'S MOTHER entered Annie Garnett's office like a pink-and-purple cyclone—her Look-at-Me signature colors fighting for supremacy in a wardrobe that knew no limits, only extravagance.

"I want to see my daughter," Brandy said, forcing herself in through the doorway. Annie had just picked up the phone to call the Kitsap County Coroner's office and was in mid-dial when Brandy burst in. She gently set down the receiver.

The police chief hadn't seen Brandy in a couple of years, with the exception of the video clip in which she stood in front of the library in Seattle and told a TV reporter that she was devastated by the disappearance of her daughter. When the focus of the investigation had swung toward Brianna and Drew, Brandy had lawyered up and refused to advance the investigation by talking to the police—a stall tactic that could work for only so long. Annie figured that Brandy, like most parents, wanted to protect her child—right or wrong.

"You shouldn't see her," Annie said. "Believe me, Brandy, you don't want to see her."

"I've seen a dead body before. My mother. My father. I want to see my little girl."

Annie searched Brandy's eyes, trying to pinpoint just how much she could tell her. There were reasons why a mother shouldn't see her child's corpse. Nothing could be more devastating than having the last glimpse of your baby looking like *that*.

The final imprint of that image could never be erased.

"Please," Annie said, indicating one of two visitors' chairs. "Sit down."

Brandy shook her head. "I don't want to sit. I drove all the way from

Seattle once I heard on the news that you found her. All the way. Three long hours to get here. Traffic was a nightmare."

"Sit," Annie said, this time less gently.

Brandy undid the buttons of her long pink coat and sat.

"I'm so, so sorry," Annie said, "but your daughter's body was . . ." She stopped, thought carefully, as she tried to summon all of her deep reserves of compassion to come up with the right words to tell a mother the worst possible thing.

Even if it was the worst possible mother.

"Was what?" Brandy asked, tapping her nails on the top of Annie's impeccably tidy desktop.

There was no way of sugarcoating it. "Battered," Annie finally said.

Brandy tried to furrow her Botoxed brow. "What do you mean?"

Annie kept her eyes on the mother across from her. "I'm telling you that she doesn't look like your little girl anymore. She was strangled and beaten."

Brandy didn't flinch, and yet she felt the need for a tissue. "She was buried, correct? I already know that from the news. At least they get to the point."

Annie could be direct too. She knew that being specific could sometimes seem harsh and clinical. That wasn't the kind of woman she was, nor the kind of cop she'd wanted to be.

"Yes," she said stiffly, lowering her eyes, "the news media does a good job of getting the word out, although what they say isn't always accurate. The killer tried to hide Brianna in a shallow grave," Annie said. "She's at the morgue in Port Orchard. They need to determine how she died."

The statement quieted Brandy for a second. *Finally.* Her relentless push to see the body had finally abated.

"We have to be sure it's *her*," Brandy said.

"We're sure. Your former husband identified her."

Brandy made a face—or tried to. She'd been so worked over by a plastic surgeon that it was hard for Annie to determine exactly what her reaction was.

"Oh, he did, did he?" she said, shaking her head. "Nice. Great to see that prick involved in his daughter's life."

Annie's reservoir of goodwill and compassion had been tapped. She wanted to say that she understood it was Brandy who'd been the less admirable of the two parents. She recalled how, on the night of Olivia's murder, Brianna had texted Brandy repeatedly to get her to come to Port Gamble.

But Brandy had missed the ferry.

Worst mom ever.

"Who issues the death certificate? Your office or Kitsap County? I'm a little confused here, Chief Garnett. I don't know who is in charge here."

"I'm in charge of the investigation," Annie said.

"Then I want you to know that I blame you for my daughter's death."

"Me?" Annie asked, her tone more incredulous than she liked.

"You should have caught Olivia's killer before he had a chance to kill again. If Drew is dead too, his father, Chase, will sue you and your soggy little town for letting this happen. I'll bet he'll want answers—and damages too."

Annie let the threat dangle in the air and thought back on the evidence she had pieced together. She didn't want to argue with Brianna's mom. She felt sick to her stomach that the girl was dead.

"There was no evidence to support that theory," she said emphatically. "In fact, we have a pretty good idea that the suspect was not a serial killer."

OVER IN ENGLAND, Edward Grant faced the cameras with wife Winnie standing like a statue by his side outside their home in London. It had rained hard, and the pavement was slick and shiny, adding to the somber mood that came with seeing Olivia's parents on the TV screen. Neither looked well. Grief had grabbed them by the throats and hung on tightly. Olivia's father told the *Sky News* reporter that he wasn't surprised at all by the details that had come out overnight from America.

"I want to be respectful of the American system of justice," he said in his perfectly clipped accent. "But I can tell you without a shadow of a doubt that this latest development has made things crystal clear. The system failed our Olivia. That girl, that horrible Brianna, and her boyfriend should never have been released from police custody. They should have locked them up and thrown away the key. All the evidence needed to do so was there. That girl got what she deserved, but her boyfriend gets off scot-free."

For a second, it appeared that his resolve not to show any emotion was beginning to crack. His eyes watered. "I wonder if the American investigators would have been less accommodating to her and more considerate of justice if the murder victim had been one of their own."

"I want to say something," Winnie said, putting her hand on her husband's shoulder.

The reporter nodded. "Yes, go ahead."

"My daughter and I were very, very close. I don't think I will be able to go on as long as I know that her murderer is out there free in a society that seems to cater to the perpetrator while ignoring the victim."

The camera zoomed in on a small lapel button on Edward Grant's coat. It was a photograph of Olivia with the words: justice for olivia grant.

chapter 28

PUGET SOUND HOSPITAL for the criminally insane was located a few miles north of Seattle's city limits in Edmonds. In the 1960s, the state legislature voted to drop "for the Criminally Insane" in favor of the shorter, less descriptive moniker Puget Sound Hospital. Built of gray and red brick with a neat fringe of Douglas fir trees around its perimeter, the place gave off the vibe of an Ivy League college campus—albeit a campus with a scary student body. There were no guard towers, razor wire, or any of the accoutrements that made the institution look like a prison, even though that's exactly what it was.

That Valerie Ryan would choose to work in such a place might have raised a few eyebrows from those who knew her as a teenager and, later, in college. Those closest to her knew that for Valerie, growing up on McNeil Island had been difficult.

"I'm sure that growing up in the suburbs, like you, was a nightmare of its own peculiar kind," she had told her college roommate, Daphnia. "But just between us, I couldn't wait to get off that island. I'll never, ever go back."

And yet, no matter how far she had tried to run, life's path brought Valerie back to Port Gamble and Puget Sound Hospital, which was, ironically, a lot like the prison she grew up in on McNeil Island.

Valerie spent the morning doing her director's paperwork. The director was out on maternity leave, which meant that Valerie and the other psychiatric nurses had to pitch in. It also meant that Valerie was working double-shifts from time to time, much to the chagrin of her family.

None of the PSH nurses had gone into nursing to be administrators. Some did it for money, but most, like Valerie, had chosen the profession because they truly wanted to help people suffering from mental illnesses of the most dangerous kind.

That morning, Valerie did her best to focus on the work at hand. Yet she just couldn't. All she could think about was the confrontation with her daughters. She'd lied to them. She'd omitted the truth before, but this was the first time she crossed over into the realm of an outright lie. Obsessing over it gave her a massive headache. She took some aspirin, but it didn't help at all. Valerie knew at some point the truth would come out, and when it did there would be hell to pay.

She had not wanted things to turn out this way. She wanted to be the kind of mother who was close to her daughters. Maybe not best friends, but certainly a trusted, respected confidant on whom they could rely. Being that sort of person was next to impossible now that they had asked about Tony Ortega. As much as she hated to dredge up the past, Valerie knew she didn't have much choice. Hayley and Taylor were like dogs with a bone. They wouldn't give up until they found some answers, just like when their grandfather had fallen at the care facility.

"I need to make a phone call," Valerie said to an assistant nurse named Jade.

"Okay, but be fast because I'm supposed to go on break in like five minutes. State law, you know."

Valerie made a note to herself that if Jade ever needed something, she'd make sure her request aligned with state law.

It was easy enough to find the phone number she needed. Valerie logged on to the hospital computer and retrieved it from the emergency contact file for Maria Ortega, Tony's sister. She became a PSH patient after her brother was incarcerated. Valerie hurried from her office down the hall toward the staff lounge, which, thank goodness, was empty. A box of dried-up day-old donuts sat on a table next to a quarter jar that begged for coffee donations.

She sat on the slipcovered black sofa, positioned her phone, and dialed. A man answered on the second ring.

Valerie took a gulp of air. "Tony," she said. "It's Valerie Fitzpatrick Ryan."

"Valerie!" the man said, his voice full of exuberance. "Is it really you?"

"I'm afraid it is," she said.

Just then, Jade poked her head into the staff room and pointed to her watch.

Valerie shook her head and mouthed, "Two more minutes!"

"Valerie?" Tony asked.

"Yes," she said. "I'm here."

"Is something the matter? Are you all right? I've hoped against hope that we'd talk again someday. And now, after all these years, you are calling me."

"I'm not calling to get reacquainted . . ." she said. "You know that I care about you, but this isn't a social call. This is a warning."

"A warning? What do you mean, 'warning'?" Tony asked. "I don't like the sound of that at all."

"I'm sorry. But I need your help."

"Anything."

"If I know my daughters—"

"You have daughters?" he asked.

Valerie thought for a minute. "I do. Twins. Like I was saying, I think my daughters are going to try to find you. I need you to keep our secret safe. Please."

"What you did was a good thing, Valerie."

"I know," she said. "I don't doubt that. But I've never felt completely right about . . . you know, about parts of it. I've never told my family any of it. Nothing."

The line went quiet for a beat. "What makes you think they will come to me?" he asked.

"Two reasons," she said. "They found some old news articles about what happened and, more importantly, because I told them not to."

"They don't listen to you?"

Valerie looked expectantly toward the door, sure that Jade, like a bad penny, would come back around any second. She didn't know how to answer Tony.

"Not really," she finally said, before correcting herself. "I mean, not all the time. I guess they are a little too much like me."

"Meaning?"

"Let's just leave it at that, Tony. Please, don't tell them anything."

Valerie put down the phone and exhaled. She wasn't sure if she'd made things better or worse for herself. She just wasn't ready to tell her girls the truth. She hoped that she would never have to.

chapter 29

TONY ORTEGA HUNG UP THE RECEIVER of the lemon-yellow wall-mounted kitchen phone. If Valerie Ryan was imagining the young man she once knew, then she had forgotten to allow for the passage of time. Tony Ortega's blue-black hair was no longer thick and glossy, but thin and gray. His eyebrows were matching gray caterpillars. His hands bore the calluses of decades of hard work—first on the docks in Seattle and then later as a night custodian at South Seattle Community College. His life was small by many measures. He had a cottage in one of the city's poorer neighborhoods and a job that never could have been called a career. Yet he felt that he was a blessed man.

His wife, Suzie, looked up from her Sudoku puzzle. "Are you all right? What was that all about? It seemed like an important conversation. Definitely not someone trying to sell us vinyl siding."

"I'm okay," Tony said, his voice a little unsteady.

"Really?" Suzie cocked her head, looking into her husband's deep-set brown eyes. She pulled a pair of golden cat's-eye glasses off her nose and continued to study Tony's craggily handsome face, trying to place his expression. She knew her husband of fifteen years quite well.

"You don't look all right," she added. "You look like you've seen a ghost."

Tony walked across the room to the TV and turned off ESPN, his choice of background noise while he read and Suzie played her game. He surveyed the tidy living room, the photos of his stepchildren, and their graduation tassels from high school and college. Tony had hung them on a thin wire strung between two bolts mounted to the wall. He knew that what had just happened—and what was about to occur—was life-changing.

"In a way," he said, kneeling next to his wife, "I just did."

She put out her hands and held his face. "Tell me, Baby."

Tony nodded. He held his breath a moment before speaking. He'd never told Suzie exactly how he had been spared execution and freed from prison. She had heard the framework of the story, of course, and that he had been accused—and found guilty—of killing his father and mother to protect his sister. Suzie loved him for the man that *she* knew he was. He was good. He was honest. She was sure that Tony had never hurt anyone. She didn't know and hadn't asked how he had managed to slip through the legal system. Suzie was just glad that he had.

Tony's phone call, though, seemed to change their status quo. Even sitting in a wheelchair, Suzie could have sworn she felt the ground shift beneath her.

"I told you about the warden's daughter," Tony said tentatively, watching the reaction in her gray eyes. "Remember Valerie?"

She nodded. "Yes, of course. The girl was lost and then she was found. It was a miracle."

"Yes, it was a miracle," Tony said. "But it was so much more than that."

As her husband recounted for the very first time what had happened over those two days when the warden's daughter was missing, Suzie Ortega folded her hands and knew in the bottom of her soul that the miracle was not Valerie being found but what Valerie did for her husband.

As he spoke, Tony could feel the anguish he had held inside for such a long time began to vaporize. Tony wasn't sure exactly why he was telling Suzie just then. He just had to.

While he still could.

VALERIE RYAN WENT TO SLEEP that Tuesday night knowing she would revisit—*relive*—that frightening time when she was a little girl. All of it would come back in her dreams, and there was no stopping it. Some nights, especially when she was younger, she'd purposely stay up late watching TV or, in college, studying at Denny's when she really didn't need to study at all. She'd try anything to avoid the dream.

While Kevin snored next to her, Valerie closed her eyes and gave in to the inevitable.

The dream began with Valerie running. She was a small child, out of breath, running toward something off in the distance. Something or someone was chasing her, pushing her closer and closer to the brightness at the end of the corridor. She was under the prison, her father's prison. Valerie could feel her heart race.

I'm coming!

A slice of light slanted to the floor from an open doorway down a long, dank corridor and she heard a song from an old radio, or maybe a cassette player, somewhere in the darkness.

Valerie looked down at her hands. They were small and cold. Her nails were powder-puff pink, an indulgence her mother had allowed just that once. Her ID bracelet glinted. She was the only child on the island, yet her parents had insisted she wear her name and address on her wrist in case she got lost.

She touched her face. More ice. And though she was freezing cold, she was determined and defiant. She had to be.

The song played louder. *What was it?*

Valerie knew that *she* was doing the right thing. She knew right from wrong, and what they were doing was wrong. She had tried talking to her parents, but it was like running in circles. They didn't believe mistakes could be made in a system that was designed to ensure truth and justice.

But even at nine years old, she knew that they were making a giant mistake. She could feel it.

Valerie hurried toward the light, trying to reach it as fast as she could. She heard footsteps behind her. Closer, closer.

In her dream, she cried out. "Leave me alone! Let him be! This isn't right! This isn't fair!"

She heard the sound of her father's voice, reprimanding her.

"Nothing is fair, child. Sometimes you just have to let things ride out."

Valerie grew up on McNeil Island—a prison island—and she knew more than her share of swear words. But what she said to her father that night was worse than any four-letter word she could have said.

"You know better," she said.

Valerie awoke with a start, arms flailing into her sleeping husband's face.

"What the—" Kevin sat up, rubbing his eyes. "Val, are you okay?"

She tried to shake it off. "Just a bad dream. Go back to sleep. Sorry I woke you."

As Valerie watched Kevin roll back over into slumber, she put her hand on his shoulder and tried to imbue every bit of love she could in that touch. She hated holding things back from him. She detested that some things in her life were off-limits from everyone, even Kevin. And deep down, nothing pained her more than the secrets she kept from her daughters. She knew that they deserved the truth, but by not saying anything, Valerie told herself it would all simply go away.

She was wrong.

UNDER THE VERY SAME ROOF of house number 19, Hayley Ryan had a dream of her own. Like her mother's, Hayley's took place in a dark space and as it grew brighter, a single image came into focus: Darth Vader.

Hayley hated *Star Wars*, *Star Trek*, and basically any of the space shows that most kids latched onto in second grade and kept on obsessing over some thirty or forty years after they'd been popular. And while she immediately recognized the figure in her dream, something about this particular Darth Vader seemed familiar.

"I can do this," Darth Vader said, in that James Earl Jones voice of his. "I can do this for us."

The dream faded to white, and then the imagery went completely blank and Hayley woke up.

Darth Vader?

Gently, Hayley nudged Hedda, asleep by her feet. The little multi-colored dog inched her way up to Hayley's face, reminding the teen that dog's teeth needed brushing. Despite the bad breath, the dachshund was warm and cuddly. Hayley patted her and fell back to sleep, trying to make sense of what she'd seen.

Who was that with the light saber at Brianna's party?

HAYLEY TOLD TAYLOR ABOUT THE DREAM the next morning when they took turns brushing their teeth in the tiny bathroom they shared. Remembering the night before, she had already scrubbed Hedda's not-so-pearly whites.

"He was holding a light saber, but I got the feeling it wasn't really a light saber," Hayley explained.

"Weird," Taylor said, scrutinizing her face in the mirror.

"I think I saw a Darth Vader at the party, but it was later on and he never took off his helmet," Hayley said, turning her attention to her long, damp hair. She picked up the blow-dryer and held it like a gun.

"Well, whatever your dream was about, may the Force be with us. We still need to find out who killed Olivia and Brianna. Plus, we need to track down Text Creeper and sort out the story about Mom being lost at the prison. Nothing came up on Google other than the clips we already read. I vote we check out the prison. She totally lied to us the other day," Taylor rattled off in one of the most take-charge moments Hayley had ever seen.

"The Force is strong in you," Hayley joked and turned the dryer on full blast.

IT WAS SATURDAY MORNING and the house was exceedingly quiet. The floorboards didn't creak, and the wind didn't ricochet leaves off the windows. *So quiet.* Their mother had some errands to do and left early. Their father was away on a research trip. No one was around. Beth was off at a used records store looking for what she called "pure vinyl." Colton was doing stuff with his father.

The girls took their father's car and drove south toward the launch to McNeil Island.

"If no one will give us answers," Taylor said, "we'll get them ourselves."

Hayley agreed. She liked how feisty Taylor was just then.

"About time," she said.

chapter 30

"GRANDPA'S PRISON LOOKS KIND OF PRETTY," Taylor said as she and Hayley stood on the shore facing McNeil Island. The winds were calm, but the November air was still bracing. The girls had come prepared with down vests over fleece jackets—pink for Taylor and aqua for Hayley. "You know, pretty in the way that some ugly things can be," Taylor said. "I'll bet seals have taken over the landing on the other side."

"I bet it really stinks over there, then," Hayley said.

While they'd seen some photographs of the island on the state archives website, they didn't know exactly what they'd find when they got there. They knew only that the prison might hold the answers to questions about their mother and their past. They hoped the place would send them a message, a feeling, or a memory . . .

. . . *a memory that belonged to their mother—one she refused to share.*

Touching objects, going to places where things had happened, and sometimes even being in contact with water seemed to trigger the feelings best. Hayley, more logical than her twin and had read somewhere that tragedy lingers in a place. When something dark and disturbing happens, a residue of that moment stays forever, kind of like hauntings where spirits are bound to a place because of what happened in it. Though Hayley dismissed the whole ghost idea and she would be embarrassed to admit it publicly, she did very much believe that extreme fear and grief left behind an imprint of a feeling.

As she stared across the water, Hayley wondered, *Was it possible for such an imprint to last for decades? Could the trigger be a building? A house? A laptop?*

A prison?

BEFORE IT WAS SHUTTERED by the Department of Corrections in 1989, the Washington State Prison at McNeil Island was accessible by a small but exceptionally noisy ferry that spewed diesel fumes over the water—the kind that would make today's eco-friendly society cringe. *The Sinking Ship*, as patrons called it because it seemed to take on an inch of water by the end of the mile-long crossing, carried family members for scheduled visits with inmates. It also transported family members of the staff and guards who didn't live on McNeil, as well as the children of those who did and attended school off-island.

More than once or twice, the twins' mother had talked about how "getting off the island was the best part of living on it." And when Hayley and Taylor complained about how hard their lives where, Valerie would pull out the Sinking Ship card and trump any argument they had.

"Try living on an island with no TV, no stores, and, oh, yeah, convicted felons. Trust me. You don't know how good you've got it."

Neither girl dared challenge her on that.

In order to get to the island, the twins knew they needed a boat, or someone with a boat. From the creosote-smelly landing, they saw a man tinkering on his boat.

"You talk to him," Taylor said.

"Why me? He could be a freak," Hayley argued, watching him work on the motor of his small cabin cruiser.

"You're older."

"I hate it when you pull rank."

"Well, you *are*. Ask him."

"What do I say?"

"I don't know," Taylor said. "Make up something. Tell him that we're geocaching or something."

Hayley shook her head. "That'll be great. Then he'll want to hang out with us and see what we're trying to find."

"You've been in Port Gamble too long. People aren't as nerdy out here. Trust me."

A few minutes and twenty bucks later, they were on their way across the choppy waters of Puget Sound to the place their mother had grown up.

And where she had kept her secrets.

IT WAS EARLY IN THE AFTERNOON and the island was quiet with the exception of some barking seals along the shore and a flock of seagulls circling overhead. The local paper had dubbed the place "Shuttered Island" when it did a feature story on its closing years ago, and the twins couldn't think of a more fitting name. The place was deserted.

As Hayley and Taylor surveyed the bleak, rocky landscape, their eyes landed on the largest house in the little village planted outside the brick-and-steel walls of the prison.

"Is it just this awful place or do you feel an overwhelming sense of sadness?" Hayley asked.

"More like fear," Taylor said.

The girls walked from the landing toward the house, a big, white two-story that in its prime might have been an amazing residence. It had a river-rock chimney and black shutters. The upper windows were intact, but the lower ones had been broken. Splinters of glass littered the entryway. Some graffiti artist had tagged the door with a spray-paint image of the twist of a noose.

The twins had seen pictures of the house when visiting their grandparents. No doubt about it, it was the place where their mother grew up.

And the place from where she vanished for two days when she was nine.

The door was ajar. Taylor, leading the way, pushed it open.

"Let's find Mom's room," she said. "It's where we'll get the strongest impression."

"Upstairs, to the right," Hayley said.

Taylor looked a little surprised. "She told you that?"

"No," Hayley said. "I don't think so. I just know it."

It had been years since the Fitzpatricks lived there. Decades. There were a slew of other superintendents that followed the tenure of Valerie's father when he stepped down from his post.

The wallpaper from various vintages, none particularly charming, still clung to the walls, although in some places along the seams it was coming undone. The sisters went into the kitchen first. It was a shell. All of the appliances were missing and most of the cabinets. A doorway leading to the basement commanded the inside wall.

"Mom always said a kitchen window should have a view. Makes doing the dishes easier, supposedly," Taylor said, looking out the cracked window over a big, white, cracked porcelain sink. "But not *this* view."

Hayley peered over her sister's shoulder. Late in the day, the prison guard tower cast a shadow over the blackberry and Scotch broom-infested backyard. The remnants of a swing set poked from a spiny thicket.

"Can you imagine Mom playing hopscotch or whatever out there with four guys with machine guns ready to fire?" Hayley asked.

Taylor stepped away from the window. "I don't think they used machine guns, but yeah, I get what you're saying. It *is* weird. It's almost like I can think of Mom in a different way, just by being here."

"How?" Hayley asked.

"I guess I feel sorry for her. She didn't have anyone," Taylor said. She didn't say the words "like I have you" but she might as well have, so implicit was the statement. She and her sister had never really been alone. They'd always had each other.

The living room was an empty space. The walls there were yellow and cream, a patchwork of shadows where paintings or photographs once hung.

"Upstairs?" Taylor asked, though Hayley was already headed in the direction of the darkened staircase.

"First door on the right, you say?" Taylor said. She turned on the flashlight app of her phone to see better in the shadowy space.

Hayley switched hers on too. "Don't ask. I just know it."

The boards creaked with each step, and the girls followed the thin beams of light from their respective phones, worried that a riser might be missing.

"Be careful. We don't want to fall into the basement," Hayley said.

"We won't," Taylor assured her. "Just pay attention to where your feet are landing."

The squeaking sound of an animal and the scratching noise of tiny nails against the floorboards sent a chill down Taylor's spine. She thought of how much she despised rats and mice. Her sister hated them too.

"What do you mean 'time is running out'?" Hayley asked.

Taylor shook her head. "I didn't say *that*. I didn't say anything."

"You did."

"I didn't."

The verbal stalemate ended as Taylor skirted past her sister into what both were now certain had been their mother's bedroom. It was on the same side of the house as the kitchen and it had its own view of the guard tower and razor wire fence and a partial glimpse into the overgrown prison yard. Still, both girls could easily make out where the inmates had played basketball. The court was still there. Out further, past the prison yard, the girls could see the leaden expanse of Puget Sound.

It was all as grim as grim could be.

"I'd hate living here more than Port Gamble on its worst day," Taylor said.

Hayley looked away from the window and around the small room. It was not much bigger than a walk-in closet.

"Country Christmas Festival worst?" she asked.

Taylor smiled faintly. "Yeah, worse than that."

"We need to focus, Taylor," Hayley said, standing in the middle of her mother's lilac room. It was Valerie's favorite color.

Together, the twins thought of Savannah Osteen, of Moira Windsor, of Text Creeper, of their mother's disappearance when she was a child, and of the gibberish twin-talk phrase they'd repeated over and over when they were learning to speak: *levee split poop*. As they did so, the pair kept their blue eyes fixed on each other, trying to feel *something*, hoping to receive a message from their mother's old bedroom.

Yet nothing came. After a few minutes, both became restless.

"Okay," Hayley finally said. "The energy isn't here. We need to look somewhere else. We need to go exactly where she was during those two days."

"The article said she was found in a service hallway, a corridor of some kind that ran under the prison," Taylor said. "There must be a way into the corridor under the prison from here."

Hayley fixed her eyes on Taylor. "The basement," she said.

chapter 31

WITHOUT ANOTHER WORD, the twins made their way down the stairs to the basement. The lights from their phones barely amounted to the glow of a firefly, but down they went. The air grew much colder. Puffs of vapor came with each breath. The basement was huge, bigger than their entire house back in Port Gamble. The center of the musty space was crammed with boxes and other debris.

A trio of rats—or large mice—scurried along the edges of the space, reminding Taylor of an episode of *Animal Hoarders* in which an elderly woman in Baton Rouge collected hamsters. So many were loose in the kitchen that the floor actually appeared to move. On the show, she told her daughter that she had no idea the animals would procreate to such a degree.

"I did my best to keep the little boys from the little girls, but as sure as I'm standing here they somehow found a way to hook up," she had said.

Hayley and Taylor had joked about the stupidity of someone letting their hamsters hook up, a phrase that morphed to a disparaging remark they used for girls and guys on the make. They were looking for a "hamster hook-up."

Down in the basement, a steady stream of cold air came at the girls.

"There's a breeze in here," Taylor said.

"Like an air conditioner at the theater," Hayley said. "On full blast."

Taylor moved her phone's flashlight to get her sister's attention.

"Over here," she said. "It's coming from here." She bent down and held her phone over an opening in the floor. The opening was about the size of a storm drain, maybe a little larger. Cool air blew against her face.

"That's the way into the underground passage," Hayley said, leaning close to the edge. "That's where we need to be."

As she turned, shifting her weight, Hayley slipped. A second later, she was inside the opening, holding onto the edge.

"Taylor!" she screamed. "I'm going to fall!"

Taylor could barely see what was happening. It was so dark.

"No, you won't! I won't let you. Take my hand." She threw herself to the floor and slithered over to the edge, stretching her arm toward her sister. Their eyes met in the terror of the moment.

As Taylor started to pull Hayley out, the edge of the opening began to give way and Taylor felt her body slide down.

"Don't let go!" Hayley screamed.

Taylor's heart was racing. Sweat collected at her temples, and the cold air on her face made her shudder.

"I won't," she said, bearing down as hard as she could. "You hang on."

Hayley dug her nails into Taylor's wrists so hard, she was certain she was cutting her. Yet any less of a grip would mean that she'd fall. And there was absolutely no way she was ever going to let that happen.

"I'm hanging on. I won't let go," Hayley said, inching closer as her sister pulled with all of her strength.

Taylor struggled to heave her body backward, away from the opening in the floor. She used every bit of muscle that she had to leverage her sister out of that spot.

And then their hands separated. Hayley, screaming, fell into the black space under the prison warden's house.

Taylor screamed, too. "Haayyyyleeey!" she shouted into the hole. "Are you all right?"

No answer.

"Hayley! Please! Can you hear me?" Taylor called out again as loudly as she could. She leaned over the hole in the floor and held her phone into the black space.

Nothing.

Her sister was gone.

Taylor got up and looked around for a rope, a garden hose, anything at all that she could use to climb down to Hayley. There was nothing useful. Boxes, rats, a baby blanket. Her phone was down to a flicker, and she knew she had to get help.

"Hayley!" she called down into the hole. "I'm going to get help."

Still no answer.

She closed her eyes and hoped the twin-sense they shared would send a message that would travel through the darkness down below to her sister.

Don't die! Taylor thought, but she didn't say it.

"I'll come back for you. I promise," she said.

BIRDY WATERMAN, Kitsap County's forensic pathologist, hung up the phone. She'd dealt with grieving family members more times than she'd ever care to count. The hurt from a car accident or, even worse, a homicide brought the kind of reaction for which there was no real remedy. She never told the grieving that "time" would make them feel better. There was no "better." But with all the calls that she'd ever taken in her role in the coroner's office, there had never been one quite like the one that she'd just experienced. It simply threw her. She dialed Annie Garnett's direct line at the police department in Port Gamble.

"Chief Garnett here," she said.

"Annie," she said. "This is Birdy. I just had the weirdest call. I mean, in all of my years doing this job. *Really.*"

"I'm all ears," Annie said.

As Birdy talked, Annie made a few notes. At one point, the police chief had to stop and tell Birdy to take a breath. The forensic pathologist had a lot to get out.

"Location?" Annie asked.

"Silverdale Beach Hotel."

"Going there now."

IN THE DAMP DARKNESS OF THE CORRIDOR, Hayley lay on the cold concrete beneath her mother's childhood home. Though she was barely conscious, her brain had kicked into overdrive. Each image that came to her was punctuated by a sudden flash. The first vision was unmistakable. Hovering somewhere between dead and alive in her mind's eye, she saw the Hood Canal bridge. A second later, she saw the back of the little school bus headed toward the Indian Island picnic.

Next appeared a man's face, the same one she had seen in her previous vision. But this time Hayley knew without doubt that he was Timothy Robinette. Then, like a slide show on its fastest speed, she saw Text Creeper giving Timothy an envelope. Next, Timothy alone, looking nervously at the bridge as a storm rolled in and the bus approached. He pushed a button with a trembling fingertip. It was clear that he hadn't wanted to, but had been forced. A fury of raindrops fell like spikes. The bridge deck rumbled as it slowly opened. The bus approached and then dropped into the water.

Then Hayley was underwater.

chapter 32

TWENTY MINUTES AWAY FROM PORT GAMBLE, Drew Marcello went up to the front desk of the Silverdale Beach Hotel.

A young woman with a swirling brunette hairdo that looked like it had been styled by Dr. Seuss smiled from behind the counter as he approached. Her recent customer-service training had emphasized the importance of the smile with each greeting. She was going for the Employee of the Month award, which included a Target gift card and an overnight stay at the hotel. She really wanted that gift card.

"Welcome to the Silverdale Beach Hotel. How can I help you?"

He looked at her nametag. "Hi, Mimi," he said. "My friend said she left me a package down at the front desk."

Mimi smiled again. "Name?" she asked.

Drew leaned against the counter and grinned back. "My friend's or mine?"

"Your name, silly," she said.

"Theodore Roberts."

The phone rang and Mimi pointed at him to wait a second. A moment later she hung up and rolled her eyes. "Guests always want something. We are running a hotel, not a drugstore. Hang on a sec while I go look for your package and for some cough syrup."

She was never going to get that stupid gift card.

Mimi went into the office and Drew hurried behind the counter and jumped onto her computer. He typed in a name. Room 243 came up on the screen.

A KNOCK THUNDERED through the thin door of Brandy Connors Baker's hotel room.

"Room service!" a voice called out.

Brandy looked up from where she was sitting on the bed, its surface covered with her neatly folded clothes and an avalanche of papers. She was in the midst of repacking. She hadn't ordered room service, but the hotel staff had proven themselves incompetent by giving her a street-side room instead of one that looked over the water and Mount Rainier. The stupid young woman at the desk told her that the hotel was full and that there was no way they could move her.

"Don't you know who I am? I'm the mother of Brianna Connors. She was murdered by some freak in Port Gamble and I seriously can't take the stress of that, plus getting a noisy room. Please, dear, move me."

The girl bit her lip and had clicked away on the computer until she somehow opened up a reserved block of rooms so Brandy could get her new, quieter room with a view.

"Just a minute," Brandy said with a sigh, getting up from the bed. "I didn't order anything."

"Complimentary fruit, cheese, and champagne tray," came a voice from the other side of the door.

Brandy loved champagne. She loved free stuff even better. She flipped the deadbolt, moved the lock to the open position, and swung open the door. Her face fell for a second, before she rebounded with a quick smile.

"How come you didn't answer my texts?" Drew asked, pushing himself inside.

Brandy looked startled, but only for a second. "What texts?" she asked, faking innocence.

Drew, looking sweaty, disheveled, and like he hadn't bathed for days, tore off his jacket and threw it on the chair.

"I sent you about a hundred of them," he said, looking Brandy over, then glancing around the hotel room. "I wanted to let you know that I, you know, took care of everything."

"I didn't need a text to know that, Drew. It has been all over the news."

She quickly scanned the hallway. It was deserted.

"Did anyone see you?" she asked.

Drew smiled. "No. I don't think so. I wanted to surprise you."

"You sure did, Baby," she said, shutting the door.

INSTINCT MORE THAN A PLAN drove Taylor toward the water's edge. It wasn't dark yet, but it would be in less than thirty minutes. She looked at her phone, hoping to see at least a chip of a bar so she could make an emergency call.

The phone was completely dead. Not a blip of power remained.

Taylor looked out on the water for the man who had dropped them off, the one who had said he'd be crabbing nearby and would ferry them back to the mainland. He was gone. There wasn't a single foamy ripple on the slate surface of Puget Sound.

"Help! My sister's in trouble!" she yelled across the water.

Taylor turned to face the prison where her sister had vanished in the dark.

Pull yourself together, she ordered herself.

Taylor looked into the blackness of the water, blackness like the hole that had swallowed Hayley in one big, nasty gulp.

Suddenly, a boat rounded the edge of the island.

"Please! Help!" she called once more, her voice now a ragged rasp.

A SPIKE OF PAIN SHOT THROUGH Hayley's body. She opened her eyes, put her hand to her head, and pressed it gently. It was wet. It hurt so much. She thought she was bleeding, but she couldn't see if her hands were wet with water or blood.

She was in serious trouble, and she was all alone.

"Taylor?" she said softly, then louder. "Are you here? Taylor, can you hear me?"

Unsure of exactly what had happened, Hayley got on her hands and knees and started to crawl over the wet concrete floor in the direction of the sound of water running through a pipe. Her leg hurt, but she hadn't broken it. As she moved through the gloom, her fingers touched something long and cylindrical—a cable or wire.

Good, she thought, something to follow. *Something to lead me out of here.*

After about twenty-five yards, Hayley had to stop. Her body hurt like hell. She was pretty sure resting was the wrong thing to do just then, but she just couldn't go on.

I need to close my eyes. Just for a while.

As water from a broken drainpipe collected around her waist, she didn't feel the icy-cold liquid.

"Taylor," she said in a raspy whisper. "Get me out of here."

OUTSIDE, TAYLOR TURNED in the direction of the prison once more. Her sister was alive.

The boat was still there, but it was inching away. Any minute now, Taylor wouldn't be able to see it at all.

She took off her jacket and her shoes. And despite the icy water—water she knew she could survive in for only a short time—Taylor Ryan dove in. As she started kicking and moving her arms at a pace that she'd never once reached during the entire time she'd been a part of the Kingston High swim team, it kept cycling in her head that if she didn't survive at least she'd died trying to save her sister.

Her other half.

HAYLEY ACTIVATED THE VIDEO RECORDING feature of her cell phone. In that hazy moment, she decided that if she didn't make it out of the darkness, she wanted the people she loved to have a good-bye message. She held the phone at arm's length, facing her in the darkness, and starting talking. Her voice was soft, plaintive.

"Dad, I tried to listen to all of your crime tips. Wish now they were survival tips. I'm glad you were . . ." She stopped, realizing that she was talking about herself in the past tense. Right then she knew she had accepted that she was going to die. "Remember when you used to take me for long walks along the beach, not because of any reason other than you thought time alone was a good idea? It *was*. Those were my favorite times. I felt that it was just us. Not me and Taylor. Just you and me. Bye, Dad."

Hayley felt her arm go weak, but she kept on. She had no choice. No one quits before they say everything that needs to be said.

"Mom, I'm not mad. I don't want you to think of that. But I would be a liar if I didn't tell you that it really hurts that you didn't trust me enough with the truth. I could have handled it. No matter what it is. No matter what you've done. Or what I've done. I could have. I love you, Mom."

She was crying then, not able to stop. "Colton, I love you. I always have. If there is another side, I will be there waiting for you. Tell your mother that I love her for all that she did for me and Taylor. Take care of my sister. Not too much, but enough to show that you care. Love always."

The phone battery flickered. Like Hayley, it was fading fast. She was so cold and so weak, she could barely hold on to the phone. She needed to finish what she had to say because it was so very important.

"Taylor, you will always be the best part of me—my other half. I want you to know that you might have been jealous of me, but the truth is that you were always the one I wanted to be. You have the best heart, Tay. You are everything I wanted to be." She stopped, feeling tears tracking down her face. "We can still talk through the wall. I know it. Make Mom tell you everything so that you can tell me. I love you, sister."

Just as the last words slipped from her lips, she dropped the phone and murky darkness descended on her. There was no light to follow. No angel calling her name. Just black. Her last thought was that death could be violent like a storm or soft and easy like the tide.

At that moment, she felt sad and lucky at the same time.

THE LITTLE GIRL WITH THE COLEMAN CAMPING LANTERN in the corridor didn't speak in Hayley's foggy reality. Their eyes met. *Familiar eyes.* Hayley knew the girl was afraid. She kept moving through the dark, her lantern's mantle sending a faint swath of light over the corridor. As she walked, she kept her focus upward.

What was she looking at?

The girl was wearing rubber boots, bright yellow ones that almost glowed against the blackened background of the corridor. Her hands were hidden in large rubber gloves. They were the kind that Valerie Ryan had said she would never use, even if her fingers cracked and shattered from the drying action of dish detergent.

Finally, the girl set down the lantern and reached into the pocket of her lilac robe for a pair of wire cutters. Without hesitating for a single second, she reached up and cut a trio of wires: white, red, and yellow. A shower of sparks fell and she stepped away from it, certain that she'd done the right thing, the only thing. She had saved Tony Ortega, an innocent man.

She had followed the electrical diagrams that she'd taken from her father's office. She knew the corridors that carried water, power, and sewage out of the prison. She knew which line to cut so that the power to the electric chair would fail.

As she stood there, boots and rubber gloves on, pecks of burns on her face from the falling sparks, Valerie had carried out her plan.

chapter 33

HAVING DITCHED HER DARK-BLUE Macy's Woman wool and polyester suit for jeans and a tan-colored down-filled coat from LL Bean, Annie Garnett looked more like a hunter than a police chief, though some would argue they were one and the same. Especially at that moment. Annie and six deputies from the Kitsap County sheriff's office surrounded the Silverdale Beach Hotel just as the sun started its quick dip behind the Olympics. It had been raining on and off all day, but the clouds had parted to eke out a final drop of daylight.

Mimi, the desk clerk, might just get that Target gift card, after all. She had recognized Drew from TV reports and phoned the police. And while Annie was already on her way there after having talked with Dr. Waterman, she was going to talk to Brandy.

"She was angry because the death certificate for her daughter had not been embossed with the official seal of this office. She actually yelled at me," Birdy had said.

"She must have really needed that document," Annie had said.

"Needed it? She would have killed for it."

A police boat from Bremerton covered the shoreline in front of the hotel with searchlights at the ready in the event they were needed. A pair of ambulances had just eased into the east end of the parking lot in case what was about to go down ended in violence. Two canine officers were also on hand—Ava, who had found Brianna's body in the woods, and a younger black lab named Cinder. There was no way Drew was going to get away. Not on Annie's watch. She'd had him in custody the night of Olivia's murder and she felt sick that she'd ever let him go. In a way, she felt that Brianna's death had been all her fault. She *should* have, *could* have done things differently. All the signs were there. As quietly as possible, first in the lobby, then on the floor on which Brandy had been registered, Annie led the deputies to the room.

This was going to be her bust. No one else's. Both of the dead girls had been tied to her beloved Port Gamble and she, more than just about anyone, needed to make the arrest.

She owed it to Olivia's folks. And to Brianna's family.

Annie drew her gun. "Police," she said in her most intimidating voice. "Open the door!"

No answer.

She looked over at her backup and nodded. Next, she took the key card that the manager at the front desk had given her and inserted it into the brass slot. The tiny red light instantly turned green. "Coming in," she said. "Police!"

The door swung open so fast it hit the wall and bounced back as Annie and the others burst inside the dimly lit room. A deputy flipped on the lights, and Annie's dark eyes scanned the entire space. She didn't breathe. With her gun pointed like a laser, she covered every inch.

The room was a mess. Amid clothing, papers, and bloody sheets were two bodies. Both appeared to be nude. The one closest to the door was a male. Annie knew immediately it was Drew. He was on his back, with his left arm dripping blood. A gash over his left pectoral muscle looked like a zipper of red had been undone. The figure next to him, a woman Annie figured had to be Brandy, was wrapped in sheets. Her arm dangled from the opposite side of the bed.

Annie touched Drew's neck and looked up. Her face was as solemn as it had ever been.

"Got a pulse," she said. "Weak, but alive."

"This one too," said Deputy Flinn, bending down to assess Brianna's mother.

Brandy Connors Baker was tangled up in the hotel room's luxurious white sheets, splattered with speckles and streaks of red. Her arm twitched, and the light of the now-illuminated crystal chandelier over the bed caught the edge of a sharp and bloody blade.

"He's got a knife!" the deputy called out.

The erroneous fleur-de-lis tattoo on the right side of his chest twitched. Drew was barely alive. Even so, the police chief wasn't about to take chances. Annie reached over and with the barrel of her gun, flicked away the knife.

"We need a chopper. These two will be lucky if they make it," Annie said.

"We'd be lucky if this punk serial killer dies on the way," Flinn said.

"We don't administer that kind of justice, Deputy," she said. "You know better than that."

Another deputy radioed for a helicopter.

"What do you think happened here?" Flinn asked.

Annie looked at the victims as a horde of paramedics descended over them.

"I don't even want to think about the headlines," Flinn went on, "but this looks like we've got a love triangle here. Drew was with both the mother and the daughter."

"Obviously," Annie said.

"Kid's a regular Don Juan."

She shook her head. "Something like that."

"Grab her ID in case she's got any medical issues," Annie said. "His too."

A deputy picked up Brandy's purse from the nightstand, and then he fished Drew's wallet from his pants pocket. In doing so, a condom fell out.

"At least he practiced safe sex," he said.

"No offense to the victim," Annie said, letting out her feelings about Brandy Connors Baker for the first time, "but I don't think any sex with her could be considered safe. Not unless you like cuddling up to a cobra."

chapter 34

CARMINE ANGELO AND HIS EIGHTEEN-YEAR-OLD SON, Ricky, were fishing for Dungeness crab on the other side of McNeil Island in what had been the worst single haul of their year. It had been a lousy year by anyone's standards. Father and son had been at each other's throats all day, starting in the morning. It was supposed to be a fun outing before Ricky shipped off for army boot camp and then, more than likely, the Middle East. Carmine had chided his son for the past year, telling the kid that if he didn't get his grades up, he'd end up being a house painter or something even worse.

A soldier was worse.

Carmine did not want Ricky to come home in a flag-draped box. He loved his boy with all his heart.

"Dad," Ricky said, looking out at the water. "Check it out."

Across the bow about twenty yards away, they could see a girl swimming frantically toward them. She approached quickly, closing the gap between them. As the waves smacked against the side of the boat, Ricky Angelo managed to lean over and grab Taylor, and Carmine hoisted her up. A second later, she was lying on the saltwater-splashed floorboards of the boat.

Taylor started to cough. *Hard.* She was freezing. She was as cold as she'd ever been. Carmine wrapped an old green blanket around her.

"My sister," she said, her eyes widening with terror. "My sister is in trouble. We've got to get her. We were on McNeil. She fell into a well or something."

Carmine went for his radio. "What were you doing on the island?" Ricky asked.

Taylor's lips were almost blue by then. Her wet hair was tangled with seaweed. She was scared and frozen, but she was alert enough just then to lie. "We were just looking around," she said, shaking. "Just exploring."

As she lay there, Taylor could hear the older man radio for the coast guard. She turned her focus back to her sister as the boat moved toward the old dock in front of the prison.

"Bring that," she said, pointing at a supply of coiled-up rope and the gill net that had been used to no avail by Carmine and Ricky that day.

Jumping off the boat onto the dock, Taylor took two grimy oyster-shucking gloves and a flashlight sitting on one of the benches and headed back to save her sister.

CARMINE, RICKY, AND TAYLOR hovered over the small hole in the basement floor of the old Fitzpatrick house. Even though she was shaking in that way Hedda did after a soaking rainstorm, Taylor felt enough adrenalin to take charge.

"You," she said to Carmine, a man old enough to be her father, "uncoil the rope. And, you," she said, looking now at Carmine's son, "you are going to tie it down over there." She pointed over to the old boiler that sent heat through steel pipes up to the upper floors of her mother's childhood home.

Her mother. In the midst of the turmoil surrounding her, Taylor almost forgot that their mom had been the reason for this disaster. If she had been honest, none of this would have happened.

The Angelos did what they were told. And they did it at breakneck speed. Taylor Ryan, who was half frozen in the water a moment ago, was somehow surging. She was commanding them. She had an authority in the midst of the chaos. She was like that mom who'd made the rounds of the morning news shows when the YouTube video went viral showing her lifting up a car that trapped her daughter.

Taylor was unstoppable.

"Okay," Ricky said, "what's next?"

"You and your dad are going to pull me and my sister up," she said. "I'm going down there to get Hayley."

"You can't do that," Carmine said. "You're in no condition. You're too weak."

Taylor shook her head, her hair now only damp, stuck like glue to the nape of her neck. The man was right, but Taylor wasn't going to give in.

"I don't want to get in an argument about a girl's lack of upper-body strength," she said. "I get it. I know you're stronger than me. That's why both of you need to be up here. You need to get us out."

Without saying another word, the slender teenager put on the oyster gloves, went toward the opening, and kicked the rope into the darkness. She put the flashlight in the waistband of her pants, grabbed the rope, and, just like that, was over the edge.

"Send down the net when I tell you," she called up to the dimly lit faces of the father and son.

THE SOUND OF RATS AS THEY SQUEALED was the first thing Taylor noticed all around her. She stomped her feet, and the emboldened rodents scattered a little—not far, but not underfoot. As far as rats went, she figured that prison rats had to be the lowest of the low. The sound they made and the stench of their feces and urine made her sick. She pointed the light all around, sending stabbing beams into the corridor.

Nothing.

"Hayley! I'm here! Where are you?"

She waited a minute to hear a response, but those disgusting rodents refused to be put on **pause**.

"Knock it off!" she screamed in her now very raspy voice. "I have to find my sister!"

Rats, apparently, weren't good listeners. They kept at it, squealing and milling around, running over her feet.

She followed the corridor until she found Hayley on the concrete slab, her phone in hand, and her eyes open to tiny slits.

"You're alive," Taylor said, starting to cry and wondering why she would fall apart at that moment.

Hayley nodded slowly. "Get me out of here."

Taylor called up into the darkness. "Send down that damn net. We need to get my sister out of this hellhole."

Hellhole. Taylor had never used that term in her life. Yet at that moment nothing else could have been more appropriate.

"Mom," Hayley said. "Mom . . ." Her voice faded into stillness.

"Don't talk," Taylor said. "We can talk later."

When the net found its way to the wet and filthy floor, Taylor dragged her sister into it, lashing it shut with the end of the rope dangling from the basement above.

"Get her up. And then send it down for me. Hurry!"

A RESCUE HELICOPTER FROM KING COUNTY swirled over the dark waters of Puget Sound, scattering choppy black-and-white spray over its frigid surface as it lifted skyward, flying away from McNeil Island to Harborview Medical Center in Seattle.

Hayley and Taylor were on stretchers, cocooned in silver thermal fabric like a pair of baked potatoes from an all-you-can-eat buffet, barely warm. Hayley was in dire straits. She might have been alive, but she looked dead. Her skin was chalk, save for a streak of red across her cheek, an abrasion from when she tumbled into the dark.

Taylor had certainly had better days, but she knew in the end she would be fine. It was Hayley she was worried about. Hayley deserved to live.

She just had to.

"Hang on," Taylor said. "We're going to make it."

Hayley didn't reply. And yet, under her eyelids, her eyes moved rapidly back and forth. The sixteen-year-old was processing something.

Just what it was, her twin had no idea.

Seconds after the helicopter touched down on the slate-gray roof of the hospital, a swarm of emergency-room personnel took over.

"I got this one. Hayley, right?" a young Puerto Rican doctor said, rolling Taylor toward the double glass doors.

"No, I'm Taylor. That's Hayley," Taylor corrected wearily.

And just as the emergency bay doors *whooshed* open, Taylor realized why Olivia had been murdered.

chapter 35

VALERIE RYAN HAD WORKED in the south wing of Puget Sound Hospital for two years, but she had never ventured into Maria Ortega's room. There were many reasons for that. Maria was a barely functioning schizophrenic who mostly just sat and stared at the blank wall and the window overlooking the courtyard. Maria was also not her patient. She didn't know her, so a personal visit was out. Yet after speaking to Tony, Valerie felt a compulsion to see her.

Valerie had passed by room 123 hundreds of times and purposely never slowed, never turned, to see the woman inside.

She just didn't want to. *Couldn't. Wouldn't.*

Maria Ortega had been incarcerated for almost three decades. She was in her forties, but a lifetime of being closed up inside most of the day had kept her skin from the sun. With few wrinkles, she looked to be about twenty-five. She was also small and thin. Many of the patients in the institution ballooned in their weight over time, a combination of drug side effects and helpings of starchy foods designed to keep them feeling full and satisfied.

It was near shift's end and the corridors were quiet, except for the sound of the patient in 113 who always cried out whenever she was being examined by a doctor or nurse.

"You are hurting me! Don't touch me! Don't! I'll tell on you!"

Valerie used her key card to open Maria's room, taking the clipboard with the patient's information and stepping inside. It was a little dark, so she flipped a switch to brighten the space. The walls were white and blank, save for two posters—one of a pair of pandas and another of a sunset over a rocky beach.

It looked like the Washington coast, maybe Ruby Beach, Val thought.

The bed was covered in a rainbow quilt and was perfectly made. Along the top of a bolted-down dresser, with its pair of bolted-down lamps were a water pitcher, a plastic drinking cup, a clock, and a well-worn copy of the Holy Bible.

The place was so quiet, so still, that it felt empty, lifeless. Valerie scanned the room. Her eyes quickly landed on the figure of a woman in a chair, silhouetted in the window facing a row of winter-naked maples. The glass was streaked with rain.

"Maria?" Valerie asked.

The woman in the chair stayed quiet.

Valerie looked over her chart. Maria Ortega was on sedatives. The dosages were high, but Valerie was a nurse who knew that most of the doctors at the hospital had a good grip on what was best for their patients. The hospital was not one of those places in which the insane were warehoused and forgotten.

At least it hadn't been that kind of a place for years and years.

Valerie inched toward the rain-soaked window. Maria appeared to be mumbling something over and over. It was unclear if she was saying words or just running random noises from her vocal chords because the vibrations calmed her. Some patients did that.

"Maria? I'm Nurse Ryan," she said, though after reviewing the chart she didn't expect any response.

Patient can speak but chooses not to. Patient understands commands and readily complies with instruction. Occasionally, patient will speak one-word answers, yes or no.

Maria kept her face toward the window. "I know who you are," she said, in a voice that croaked slightly. Her warm breath condensed on the glass.

That was more than a one-word response.

Valerie felt her heart rate accelerate a little. It was a strange feeling, but one she knew well: fear. Even so, she felt compelled to get closer, to better hear what Maria was saying.

"You do?" Valerie asked.

"Come next to me," Maria said in her crackly whisper.

Valerie leaned forward, and with rocket-like speed Maria grabbed her hand and clamped down with surprising force. Valerie winced a little and tried to relax. To try to pull away abruptly was entirely the wrong move in that type of situation, and the psychiatric nurse knew it. Maria was like a grizzly bear holding on. To get away, Valerie knew that she had to play dead. Her hand went limp, but it didn't help her break loose.

"My brother told me you worked here. Small talk," Maria said. "He says things to me and I pretend not to hear."

"Your brother?" Valerie asked, trying to pull away but not acting like it was urgent that she do so.

"Don't be stupid," Maria said. "You know all about me and my family."

Valerie wasn't sure why she'd gone in there, but what was happening just then had not been her reason. At least she didn't believe so. She tried once more to retract her hand, but Maria would not let go.

"Let go of me," Valerie finally said, calmly.

"I had good reason to do what I did," Maria said.

Valerie shook her head, trying to catch the light in Maria's eyes. She wanted to see a flicker of something that indicated that Maria knew what she was saying and doing just then.

"I don't know what you're talking about," Valerie said.

Their eyes met for the first time in that hospital room, though they'd been connected by circumstances for years.

"You do," Maria said, relaxing her grip but looking right into Valerie's unblinking eyes. "And because of you, I'm here. I wish that you had let my brother die. It was his fault too. He's not without blame. He could have done something to stop it. If he had, none of it would have happened. Your hands are dirty too. *You* put me here."

Valerie Ryan took a quick step backward, away from Maria. Her heart was racing, and she felt a little disoriented. Something was wrong—very, very wrong. She had done what was right. She had never doubted that. She was certain that Tony had not deserved to die.

"I'm sorry for what happened to you," she finally said.

Maria sat stone-faced.

"You shouldn't have started that fire," Valerie said.

Maria shifted her gaze to the parking lot. "I did what no one else would do," she said.

Just as Valerie opened her mouth, Jade, the by-the-book-nurse, burst into room 123. Jade's eyes were full of worry.

"Your daughters are in the hospital, Valerie," she said.

Valerie spun around and collected herself. "What?"

Jade nodded. "Harborview. They've been in an accident or something."

Maria looked over her shoulder. With a smile, she said, "I hope they both die."

Valerie ignored her and went for her phone. Her encounter with Maria had been intense, but *this* news nearly knocked her to the floor. She dialed Kevin's number, and it went to voice mail.

"Honey, meet me at Harborview. It's the girls."

chapter 36

NEITHER HAYLEY NOR TAYLOR KNEW what had been more embarrassing: the fact that they had messed up to such a degree that they were in the hospital or the fact that the hospital gowns they were forced to wear were imprinted with Hello Kitty images. Neither would admit, at least not out loud, that the helicopter ride had been kind of cool. They'd never in a million years admit to that. They couldn't stand the stories of hikers who were stupid enough to get lost and then have to be airlifted to safety. Their adventure to McNeil Island had peeled back a thin layer of what they were trying to figure out, but the cost had been great.

Almost too great.

While they waited for their mom to get to the hospital and read them the riot act, ground them for life, and tell them they had made a mistake that could have ended in the biggest tragedy of a family that had too many already, they sat up in their hospital beds with the TV on. Each girl rolled her eyes as Dr. Phil ranted about how dishonest a drug-addict mother had been to her children.

"You told them that you'd take them to Disneyland, but you used all the money for crack? Who does that?" he asked.

The woman glowered at the bald talk-show host with the boomerang mustache.

"I guess people who bring big ratings to your show do," she said.

Taylor looked at her sister in the next bed. "Okay, Hayley, we thought Brianna's mom sucked. This one here is worse."

The minute Taylor said that, the girls noticed the news crawl that ran along the bottom of the screen:

"Do you think they're talking about Bree's mom and Drew? It can only be *them*, right, Taylor?"

The girls turned from the TV to the window and the sounds of an approaching helicopter.

"This isn't extrasensory crap, Hayley. It has to be them."

A NURSE NAMED CANDIS WALTERS INTERRUPTED the twins' conversation. Her steel-wool gray hair was swept into a suspiciously perfect up-do and her glasses hung from a silver chain. Candis fit neatly into one of the two categories the twins had identified for the nursing staff. She was a warm, friendly chatterbox of a woman—the type that got into nursing to be a nurturer. The other category was "the pokers and prodders." Those nurses seemed to have decided nursing was a legal way to torture people—and it required less schooling than dentistry.

"How are you girls doing?" Candis asked, her kind green eyes sizing up the teens in their matching hospital beds. Both were set at the exact same angle.

"Better," Hayley said, smiling back. "A lot better."

Candis nodded, reviewed Taylor's vitals, and made a note in her chart.

"You're very lucky you didn't freeze to death out there," she said. "You, my dear, are a lucky duck! Do you know that the average person can swim in Puget Sound for only twenty minutes? And that's in August. Not November!"

"I guess I did pretty well," Taylor said. She resisted the urge to say "quack quack" like a vacationer on one of those amphibian vehicle tours in Seattle.

"We just heard the helicopter outside," Hayley said. "What was that all about?"

Candis straightened Taylor's blanket. "You warm enough, dear?"

"Yeah, fine," she said, waiting for the nurse to answer. "Who's arrived?"

Candis made a face that indicated complete disgust.

"That kid from up north," she said. "The one who killed those two girls. He and one of the murder victim's mothers are being rolled in downstairs to ICU."

Taylor played dumb. She and her sister had a pretty good idea what had gone on. Drew had turned out to be a maniac. "What happened?" she asked.

"The cops are sorting it out," Candis said.

"That's good. How are they doing?" Hayley asked.

Candis looked around the room, her eyes flitting from girl to girl. "We're not allowed to give out that kind of info, but between you and me and the fence post, I doubt either one of them will make it. They are both cut up pretty bad. Kind of fitting, if you ask me."

Hayley was interested in her choice of words. She seemed to be, after all, a kind-hearted nurse.

"Fitting?" she asked.

Candis shrugged and shut the file folder documenting their progress since they'd arrived from McNeil Island. Both girls were scraped up a little. Taylor was chilled to the bone from her swim, but was otherwise in good shape. Hayley had cracked a rib, but her leg, which had felt so sore, was fine—bruised but fine. Their condition was nothing short of remarkable, considering their ordeal.

"He cut up that girl, the foreign one, up in Port Gamble. Looks like the psycho got what he deserved. A taste of his own bloody medicine." Candis looked around warily, but went on. "Mind you, I'm not supposed to talk about other patients. But sometimes I just can't help myself. It just comes out of me like a burp. I'll be back in an hour," she said. "Your mom will be here soon. Your dad too. He's coming from the airport."

Hayley nodded. She was glad to hear that. So was her sister.

"Thanks, Candis," Hayley said.

"Yeah, thanks," Taylor added.

Candis smiled at the twins. Their pale skin had regained some color and they looked much, much better.

"You two really are something," she said. "Crawling around in a prison and swimming in Puget Sound in November? Good gravy. Unreal." She winked at them and stepped out into the hall.

The instant Candis had disappeared down the hallway, Taylor looked over at her sister. "Are you thinking what I'm thinking?"

Hayley nodded, feeling a stab of pain in her sore rib from the motion. "Yeah. We're going downstairs."

Taylor smiled. "Uh-huh. That's right."

Hayley slid gingerly to the edge of the bed, and disconnected the IV with the saline solution. "Okay," she said, "but can you double-tie this stupid hospital gown? If it pops open in the rear, there will be another dead girl from Port Gamble—dead from embarrassment."

Taylor went to help her and started to giggle. "Got your back, Hayley. Literally."

Hayley shot her a playful glare, and two minutes later they were headed toward the elevator.

"Let's take the stairs. No one ever takes the stairs," Taylor said.

"Right," Hayley said, "because in a hospital, not many can."

THE TWINS LOOKED THROUGH THE GLASS of the Intensive Care Unit. It was like a force field, a zoo, a separation from the hectic pace of the place and the empty, sad, sterile room that represented the last chance for so many patients. A group of ER nurses sat around a big horseshoe-shaped desk chatting and watching a bank of monitors that displayed all the vitals for each of the patients who were being observed in the ICU.

Standing among them like a redwood in a forest of bonsai were Annie Garnett and her part-time deputy Stephen Shields. The girls recognized him primarily from his second job at the humane society.

"Someone lose their cat?" Hayley joked.

Taylor put her fingers to her lips and kept her eyes fixed on Annie. The police chief was speaking to one of the nurses.

"Can you make out what she's saying?" Hayley asked, leaning as close to the glass as she could without touching it.

Taylor had taken a year of American Sign Language as her foreign language requirement and while she didn't have a knack for signing, she was pretty good at reading lips.

"Yeah," she said. "Annie is telling the nurses that she and her deputy are getting coffee and they'll be back in a half hour. The nurse is saying that the patients are stable but unresponsive."

Annie and Stephen started toward the girls. Hayley jerked Taylor into the first doorway by the entrance to the ICU.

"That was close," she said.

"We need to find out what really happened to Olivia."

"And Brianna. Don't forget her."

"I think I know part of why she was killed, but there's got to be more to the story."

Taylor noticed that they were in the nurses' locker and break room. A row of plum-colored scrubs hung on pegs on the farthest wall. They could hear a shower running and the sound of a nurse washing her hair. She was belting out an Adele song like she was auditioning for *X Factor*.

And she didn't have a chance.

"Let's get out of these gowns and into those," Hayley said, pointing to the scrubs.

Taylor nodded and started to dress. "You take Drew," she said. "I'll take Brianna's mom."

Hayley slipped into a pair of scrubs and tied the belt with a bow. She realized the pair would not be in the same room. Until the police chief had everything sorted out, both suspects would remain in isolation. Even so, she wasn't thrilled with her sister's division of the task at hand.

"How come I get him? He's so creepy," Hayley said.

"And Mrs. Baker isn't?" Taylor asked, annoyed, but still able to keep her voice low. "Come on, we can't argue. We've got the tiniest window of opportunity to see what we can find out."

The only way into the ICU was with a key card, and while neither girl had ever stolen a thing in their lives, they went for the open locker where the nurse in the shower had undressed. Hanging on a steel hook was a lanyard emblazoned with TEAM HARBORVIEW. At the end of it dangled a hospital key card with the smiling photo of a middle-aged woman with cream-colored skin and black hair.

"She's Meagan," Taylor whispered. "Well, I guess you're Meagan now. I've always sort of liked that name." Taylor looked closely at the photo and shook her head. "You look nothing like her, by the way."

Hayley tugged at her sister. "Very funny."

"Okay, Meg, let's go. And remember, the key is to act like you belong here. All right?"

"Got it," she said. "I'm all attitude."

A second later, Hayley swiped the card. They were in.

BLOOD CRUSTED HIS HAIR and Drew Marcello's eyes were shut. Tubes snaked from his arm to a glistening IV unit that hung on a steel hook just over his right shoulder. A heart monitor to his left tapped out a steady beat in a pale green light.

"Drew," Hayley said, keeping her voice low and aimed at his ear. "Can you hear me?"

The monitor kept its steady dull flashing, but Drew remained still and quiet.

Hayley looked up and caught the eye of a nurse, who, incredibly, waved to her from the other side of the room.

She waved back and did what she had to do to get Drew to answer—she gave him a shove on his bandaged shoulder.

"Drew, damn it. Wake up!"

His eyes fluttered a little and, hearing his name, he cracked them open a tiny slit.

"Mom?"

"No, it's not your mom. It's me. Hayley Ryan."

His eyes wandered over hers. "You work here?"

Hayley swallowed and nodded. "Kind of part-time," she said.

"Oh. I'm in the hospital, right?" he asked, his eyes tracking the space all around him once more.

"That's right," she said. "You're gonna make it."

Drew closed his eyes and turned away. "I don't want to make it," he said. "I'm better off dead."

Hayley watched the monitor flicker. She nudged him again. "You need to tell me what happened to Olivia and Brianna, Drew."

He winced a little and shook his head. "Just let me die."

Hayley was practically on top of him. She wanted him to give her answers. She needed to know. They all did.

"Why do you want to die? Because of what happened to Olivia? Brianna?"

In that moment, Hayley didn't have it in her to say what she was really thinking: Because of how you murdered Olivia? Stabbed her? Strangled Brianna? You want to die because that's the easy way out and you're a weak coward?

An alarm sounded. Drew pulled her close and whispered what she wanted to know.

He was still talking when a nurse came in.

"Who on God's green earth are you?

"I'm Meg," Hayley said, looking up at the fortyish nurse who stared at her in the most no-nonsense way.

"Like hell you are," the nurse said.

ON THE OTHER SIDE OF THE ER, Taylor bent over Brianna's mother. Up close, Brandy Connors Baker didn't seem like such a monster. She was no bigger than a girl, really. Taylor could easily make out the tiny incisions that Brandy's oh-so-styled hairline had covered after her latest bout of cosmetic surgery. She remembered how Brianna had once quoted her mom as saying that after thirty-five "a woman needed a face and body makeover" and that "diet and exercise alone were for people without the money to do better."

Brandy didn't *look* better just then. She looked small. Tiny. Weak. So frail. Even though she'd been a witch to Brianna, Taylor couldn't help but feel a little sorry for her.

"I know you," Brandy said, looking up at Taylor. Her eyes were softer than Taylor remembered, though in that moment she conceded that it might be the result of the wooziness that came with the IV pain medication dripping to her bloodstream.

"Hi, Mrs. Baker," Taylor said.

"You're one of those twins. You're friends with my daughter."

Her lips looked dry, but Taylor wasn't about to offer her an ice chip from the container on the tray next to her bed. She wanted to keep her talking.

"I'm sorry about Brianna. I really am."

Brandy looked up at Taylor. "You found her, didn't you?"

She shook her head. "Yes, I did."

Brandy nodded. "Is your sister here, too? You two were always together, as I recall."

Taylor tilted her head and indicated Hayley on the other side of the ER. "Hayley's over there. She's talking to Drew. Or trying to. I think he's still unconscious."

"He's alive?" she asked.

Brandy's heart monitor started to accelerate.

"I think so," Taylor said. "At least, for the time being. The cops were talking about how it didn't look like he was going to live. He lost a lot of blood. You both did."

"He tried to kill me, Taylor. He stabbed me! He said that he hated me more than he hated Bree. He killed poor Olivia too. He killed her by accident. He thought he was killing my little girl."

"I know. I know," Taylor said.

The heart monitor had just kicked into overdrive, the worst beat remix ever. An alarm sounded, and faster than the fatal slash that had killed Olivia, three nurses were on top of Taylor.

ANNIE GARNETT CORNERED Taylor and Hayley just outside of the ICU. She dropped her full coffee cup in the trash, and it landed with a thud. She had always been a gentle giant of a woman, but this time she seemed scary.

"Taylor, I'm not going to blame you for this," the police chief said in a tone harsher than any of them had ever heard. "No one is. But Drew is hanging by a thread and you and your sister's stunt almost killed him. I get that you wanted to find out what happened to your friend. I know that you care about people and you know the difference between right and wrong. But this was a mistake. A big one. I don't know if hypothermia pickled your brain, but I'm going to cut you some slack because . . . well, I've known you since you two were babies."

"I'm sorry."

"We're sorry."

"I know you are. I also get that Brianna's mom doesn't exactly qualify for mother of the year by anyone's standards. But going into the ICU to question her, well, that's stupid and wrong."

Both girls felt their faces grow red.

"Again, sorry," Taylor said.

"I know who's responsible for killing Olivia and Brianna," Hayley said. "If that's any help to you. I mean that with great respect."

"We know Drew is the killer. We matched black fibers from his Darth Vader costume found at the scene."

Hayley nodded. "Right. Drew did the stabbing, but he had an accomplice."

Annie liked these girls, but really, they should leave the investigation to the professionals.

"Brianna wasn't his accomplice, dear," she said. "She was his victim."

"I didn't say *Brianna*." Hayley looked over in the direction of the group of nurses around Brandy's room. "*She* was Drew's accomplice."

"Brandy?"

"Look in her purse. Drew told me that Brianna's mom had waved a big cashier's check in his face. She had laughed at him. He had loved her. Trusted her. She had convinced him to kill her daughter for the insurance money."

"But Drew messed up and killed Olivia by mistake when she and Bree switched costumes at the party," Taylor chimed in, remembering the moment the doctor had mistaken her for Hayley and she had put two and two together. "Olivia was never supposed to die."

"Mrs. Baker told Drew he was never getting a dime because he'd messed up and killed Olivia by mistake," Hayley said.

Annie turned on her heel and headed to the nurses' station. She didn't need a warrant. Her team had taken Brandy's black-and-silver Kate Spade purse from the Silverdale Beach Hotel for medical reasons. The hospital staff had placed her purse and paperwork into a plastic bin.

Annie poked through its contents, a hodgepodge that included a one-way airline ticket to Mexico, four kinds of face lotion, and six lipsticks. And a cashier's check for one million dollars.

The price, it seemed, of her daughter's life.

SEEING TAYLOR AND HAYLEY SIDE BY SIDE in a hospital room was déjà vu for their parents. Hoses and IV lines crisscrossed helter-skelter from each girl to their respective life-support equipment. A large wall clock ticked away the time above the pair of rocking chairs borrowed from a couple of vacant maternity rooms down the hallway that the staff had brought in for Kevin and Valerie.

The scene was not nearly as dire as it had been when the girls were five and had been treated at Children's Hospital in Seattle for thirty-one days after the bus accident on the Hood Canal Bridge. For that, everyone was grateful.

With Valerie behind him, Kevin stood between both beds and blinked back tears.

"I don't know what you were thinking," he said. "Please don't ever do anything as stupid as that again. I can't live without you. Your mom can't live without you."

Hayley met his gaze and glanced over at her mother. She had been crying. Her eyes were puffy and shiny streaks of tears ran down her cheeks.

"We're sorry. We just had to know."

"Know what?" Kevin said, looking completely confused.

"Girls, I'm sorry. I hope you will forgive me." Valerie wedged herself between Kevin and Hayley.

"It's all right, Mom," Taylor said.

Tears rolled down Valerie's cheeks. "This is my fault. I should have told you what you wanted to know. I should have told you everything."

"It's okay. Don't worry, Mom," Hayley said, closing her eyes and sending a question to the person she had seen in the corridor under the prison.

You saved Tony, didn't you?

Hayley looked up at her mother, who remained silent while her tears fell.

When Hayley closed her eyes again, she heard an answer.

Yes, I did.

postmortem

IT WAS OBVIOUS in the weeks and months after Drew and Brandy were arrested for murder and conspiracy to commit murder, that Port Gamble was never going to be the same again. Even before the trial it was clear that Brandy Connors Baker held the advantage.

She hadn't actually killed anyone.

She had a decent lawyer.

She concocted a defense.

"Drew was stalking me," she told a Seattle TV station in a jail house interview. "He was in love with me. I was in total fear all day, every day. I feel like a battered woman," she added.

Drew gave an interview to *Inside Edition*, but most of it was bleeped out.

"That—*BLEEP*—is a—*BLEEPING*—liar! I hate her—*BLEEPING*—guts. Plus she's old!"

Even though the botched crime scene made things difficult for the prosecution, the Kitsap County prosecutor stood firm and offered no deals. Trial was set for June, though most observers expected a series of delays. Justice was never fast, especially when the case was as messy as the one involving two dead teenagers from formerly sleepy Port Gamble, Washington.

Annie Garnett wasn't proud of how things went down with the Grant and Connors cases, but she was able to use the tragedies to increase funding for her department. Her part-time deputy was able to leave his Humane Society gig for full-time employment in Port Gamble. Annie also discovered one thing that brought some relief. While she liked silky fabrics, she didn't care for thongs, after all. Some things literally creeped.

Beth Lee—who was back to wearing her friendship bracelet—entered a student art show in Seattle that winter and won first prize for her drawing, "Girl from London." Kim Lee talked with the property management company about terminating their lease, but she couldn't bring herself to leave. Something would always keep them there.

Colton James let Hayley know that his increasingly absent father wanted him to fish with him that summer in Alaska, and he said yes. Hayley hated the idea. The only thing worse than summer in rainy Washington was summer without a boyfriend.

In London, the news for the Grants was quite good—at least as far as Winnie was concerned. The murder of their daughter had put Edward back in the media spotlight—big-time. Two months after the arrests of Drew and Brandy, the BBC aired the first episode of his new show, *Just Us*, focusing on victims' rights.

NOT LONG AFTER the Drew and Brandy news faded a bit, Hayley and Taylor sat at the kitchen table in front of the Scrabble board. The house was mostly silent, save for the ticking of the mantel clock and the strange dog-purring of Hedda tucked under the table at their feet. Their mom had gone off to Costco to get some things for Christmas, which was the following week.

Their father had just left on a final interview trip to Des Moines, Iowa, to talk to the parents of the murderer for *Killer Smile*.

When Valerie returned, the girls helped carry in the groceries. It had started to snow, and the world seemed especially bleak.

It was as good a time as any to ask about the things that they needed to know.

Hayley put down a bag of Spanish onions. "Mom, what really happened with Tony Ortega?"

Valerie set down her purse and took off her coat. The look on her face was no longer fear but resignation.

"I'll tell you what I know. It has been a long time," she said.

She told them how she had seen Tony playing basketball by himself during his one-hour daily exercise period. One time he looked up at her.

"I can't explain it," she said. "But in that moment when his eyes met mine, I just knew that Tony wasn't a killer. I grew up there on that island. I could sense who was really bad and who wasn't."

She stopped and went to turn on the teakettle, and then returned to her seat.

"What happened when you were lost?" Hayley said.

"Yeah," Taylor said. "And why didn't they just execute him afterward?"

Valerie nodded. "I talked to my father about it. I told him that I didn't think that Tony was a killer, but he told me that the prison didn't make mistakes and—get this—even if they did, it was too bad. I really hated him right then. It just seemed so . . . wrong. I'd overheard my dad saying that a lawyer claimed to be tracking down new evidence to get Tony a stay of his execution, but he wasn't going to get it done in time. I wanted to buy him more time."

"So what did you do?" Hayley asked.

"I know it sounds dumb, but I thought if I could stop the electricity that went to the electric chair I could save him. So that's what I did. I took the schematics from my father's office. We had a passageway from our house to the prison. I used it and did what I had to do."

The girls were silent, processing what it was their mother just said. The teakettle whistled, and Valerie went to fix her tea.

Taylor watched her mother spoon some sugar into the hot liquid. "But Tony didn't die. Why not?" she asked.

"His lawyer came through in the end. Tony hadn't set the fire that killed his parents. His little sister Maria had. Tony never pinned the blame on her. He felt sorry for her. She'd been terribly abused by their father all through her childhood, and the whole family knew it."

Taylor felt like crying. The air in the room seemed so heavy. The image of a red plastic gasoline can came to her just then.

"What happened to Tony?" Hayley asked.

"He was released."

"What about Maria?" asked Taylor.

"She's at the hospital," Valerie said, choosing her words carefully, not wanting to say too much. Just enough.

"Your hospital?"

Valerie nodded.

"Are you taking care of her?"

Valerie dipped her tea bag in and out of the hot water. "No, she's not my patient."

Taylor was relentless. She wanted to know more. "How is she doing?"

Valerie looked away and then shook her head slowly. "Not good. Sometimes the past is so evil, so horrible, you can never get over it. It leaves you kind of stuck. That's Maria Ortega."

"Killing her parents is a ginormous burden," Hayley said, picking at the Scrabble tiles that were scattered in front of her.

Valerie dribbled some milk into her tea. "No," she said. "Not that. I meant what was done to her."

When she returned to the big kitchen table with her mug of English Breakfast tea, Valerie looked down and noticed fourteen Scrabble tiles arranged in three specific groupings:

It was the phrase that her daughters had said over and over when they were babies, and no matter how hard they tried, they couldn't unscramble what they were absolutely sure was a message.

Hayley drummed her fingers on the table.

Without saying a word, Valerie started rearranging the tiles:

Finished, she looked up at her girls.

"You knew all along?" Hayley asked, incredulous that her mom was opening up.

Valerie nodded. "Yes, I knew," she said, her voice full of emotion. "I've always known. You girls can see things . . . know things that other people can't."

"Why didn't you talk to us about it?" Taylor asked. "Mom, you covered it up on the tape. On Savannah's tape we saw you. You hid our message. We gave Savannah a warning in alphabet letters, and you wiped it away."

Valerie took a deep breath to steady herself. "It's because I love you that I didn't say anything. I was hoping it would go away."

"Go away?" Taylor asked.

"Yes," she said. "Like it did for me."

TRUTH IN FICTION

WHILE THE CHARACTERS and the plot of *Betrayal* are fictional, elements of the storyline take some cues from a famous case involving the murder of a British girl in Perugia, Italy, and the subsequent conviction of an American student and her boyfriend for the crime.

Seattle native Amanda Knox was accused of the murder of her roommate and friend Meredith Kercher in Perugia, Italy—a crime committed on Halloween night in 2007. While Knox maintained her innocence, the Italian police and prosecutors thought otherwise. Most of the evidence against Knox in the beginning of the case were mischaracterizations of her behavior. She was seen making out with her boyfriend, Raffaele Sollecito, at the crime scene. She was caught on tape shopping for lingerie right after the murder as if she didn't have a care in the world. She did cartwheels in the halls at the police station. And so on.

The police theorized that the American student was an immoral girl who was involved in some kind of sex game gone wrong. And despite evidence that was severely compromised—or fabricated—Knox and her boyfriend, Raffaele Sollecito, were convicted. The pair served four years of a twenty-six-year sentence in an Italian jail before their murder convictions were overturned on October 3, 2011. Subsequently, Knox returned to America.

Experts agree that bungled evidence at the scene of the crime and an international press corps bent on attacking Amanda's character for the sake of selling newspapers (her MySpace handle was "Foxy Knoxy") contributed to her conviction.

For more information about the nonfiction behind the fiction in *Betrayal*, as well as a discussion guide and resources about the case, visit: www.emptycoffinseries.com.

ACKNOWLEDGMENTS

I CAN'T SAY ENOUGH ABOUT the YA community of bloggers and readers who have made my foray into this exciting new genre the most wonderful part of my career as a writer. When I've been on tour, one of the questions that keeps coming up is, "What's the difference between YA readers and the readers of your adult fiction or true crime?" The answer is YOU. You bring the kind of curiosity and passion to the reading experience that is unique to your genre. (This doesn't matter if you're twelve or sixty.) While all of you who have interacted with me via e-mail, Facebook, Twitter, or in person have been an amazing gift, I am going to single out ten YA bloggers here because my publisher says I can only pick ten! Here they are (in no particular order, of course!): Bunny Cates, Haley Hagen, Amanda Welling, Stacey O'Neale, Lindsay Mead, Jennifer Derasmo, Evie Seo, Jennifer Stone, Liz Bankes, and Jillian Van Leer.

So much to say about the amazing and talented people at Sterling/ Splinter—maybe *too* much! Katrina Damkoehler's design work takes my breath away. Her covers and the beautifully designed book interiors she's created for this series couldn't be more perfect in my eyes. My sincere thanks to Judi Powers, the best publicity person in the business (who also happens to have the cutest dog on the planet, next to my own, of course); Katie Connors, who knows her way around social media like no one else; and Director of Library Marketing Chris Vaccari, who hosted me at the Public Libraries Association convention in Philadelphia this year. Nothing's better than being in front of two hundred librarians! Thanks to Marilyn Kretzer and her foreign rights team for getting *Envy* into the hands of so many readers all over the world. Meaghan Finnerty and Scott Amerman: thanks so much for your hard work on behalf of the series. If I wore a hat, I'd take it off to Cindy Loh, my amazingly passionate (and skilled!) editor who loves each character in the series as much as I do. Cindy has now left Sterling for a brand-new challenge, so I want to say something here about Meredith Mundy, into whose capable hands *Betrayal* has landed. People in publishing often talk about how books are "orphaned" when an acquiring editor leaves and passes a project along to someone else—and how awful that can be. I am grateful for the care that Meredith has shown in this last leg of the journey of getting *Betrayal* in print. All along the process, she has made me feel that she cares about the characters, the spirit of the book, and making it the best it can be. That means a lot to readers, but it means even more to me. Thanks, Meredith.

I'd like to use this space to give a shout-out to Adrian Greenwood, UK Sales Director for Sterling, and his partner in crime on our UK tour, Andrea Reece, publicist extraordinaire. I will never forget the highs and lows of our visit in support of *Envy* last fall. ☺ You both are amazing—Adrian, a charming host even when driving at 100 mph in the countryside—and Andrea, who has the texting skill of a teenager. Special thanks to Jo de Guia at Victoria Park Books, Sarah Marsh and Tricia Kings at My Voice, Christine Everett and Cheryl Siddall at Warrington Libraries, and Judy Hayton and Lucy Belanger at Lancashire County Libraries. Thanks to the Warrington Libronauts too!

There are many people to thank at the scene of the crime, Port Gamble, but first and foremost my appreciation goes to Shana Smith of Olympic Property Management, who has cheerfully supported the *Empty Coffin* series from its inception at the town's ghost conferences.

Cheers to my amazing fans, friends, and readers. At the top of the list for this series: Annette Anderson, Lori and Shane Jones, Ken Jensen, Eve Oney, Ruthanne Devlin, Jim Thomsen, Peter Raffa, Rebecca Morris, Susan Raihofer, Eric Thompson, Tina Marie Brewer, and Suri Marie.

One of the greatest honors of my career is the selection of the first book in the *Empty Coffin* series as Washington State's pick for the National Book Festival later this year. Thanks to Lori Thornton and the Washington State Library for choosing *Envy* to represent our great state.

While all of this is personal, I'd like to take a moment to go a little deeper and share my appreciation for family and friends who have been generally amazing over the years. Thanks to my brother Gary for caring for our father with kindness and humor. Dad is so lucky to have a son like you, Gary.

Finally, gratitude and love to my three girls—Claudia, my love and best critic (toughest for sure!), and our twin daughters, Marta and Morgan, whose existence reminds me every second of the day that the greatest gift of my life is being their father.

Throughout his career, GREGG OLSEN has demonstrated an ability to create a detailed narrative that offers readers fascinating insights into the lives of people (real or imagined) caught in extraordinary circumstances. A *New York Times* bestselling and award-winning author, Olsen has written eight novels and eight nonfiction books, and contributed a critically acclaimed short story to a collection edited by Lee Child—with sales of more than 1.5 million copies. Olsen's debut young adult novel, *Envy*, was selected to represent Washington State in the 2012 National Book Festival.

Olsen's books have been translated into ten languages.

The author has been interviewed on the History Channel, Learning Channel, Discovery Channel, *Good Morning America*, *The Early Show*, *The Today Show*, FOX News, CNN, *Anderson Cooper 360*, MSNBC, *Entertainment Tonight*, *48 Hours*, Oxygen's *Snapped*, Court TV's *Crier Live*, *Inside Edition*, *Extra*, *Access Hollywood*, A&E's *Biography*, and was featured on *Mysteries at the Museum* and *Deadly Women*.

Olsen, a Seattle native, lives in Olalla, Washington, with his wife, a couple of chickens, and two dogs: Milo (an obedience-challenged cocker spaniel) and Suri (a mini dachshund with a huge need to be in charge).

Praise for ENVY

"Gregg Olsen's *Envy* is a riveting page-turner that I could not put down. Like Jay Asher's *Thirteen Reasons Why*, *Envy* explores a serious topic—cyberbullying—in a fantastic, well-crafted story. Can't wait for the next *Empty Coffin* novel!"
>—Nancy Holder, *New York Times* bestselling author of the *Wicked* saga and *Dear Bully* contributor

"Gregg Olsen's *Envy* offers an interesting view on the devastating effects bullying can have, not only on the individuals involved from both sides, but on the community at large."
>—Bree Despain, author of *The Dark Divine* trilogy

"Olsen's characters jump to life and his plots are so intricate you never see the killer coming. . . . [*Envy*] is a definite hit!"   —*RT Book Reviews*

"Based on a few real-life events, parts of *Envy* are completely true. . . . The twists and turns within the plot will surely keep you hooked on this book."
>—*GirlsLife.com*

"This book's timeliness will give it relevance and appeal to teens who themselves regularly experience social ups and downs online . . . with its punchy prose, pop-culture references, and steady stream of unraveling clues."
>—*School Library Journal*

"Olsen writes with authority, drawing inspiration from actual headlines and crime."   —*Publishers Weekly*

"A relatively gratifying examination of the complexity of connections in a close-knit community."   —*Kirkus Reviews*

"The material is sharp, funny and eerie."
>—Eric Thompson, Vigilante Entertainment

"Inspired by a true crime about cyberbullying, this will definitely appeal to the many young people who enjoy this genre."

—Annie Everall, Youth Libraries Group

"Intelligent, multi-layered and very addictive."

—Jenny Downham, author of the critically acclaimed *Before I Die*

"This is truly an attention grabbing read." —*Tattered Cover Book Blog*

"#1—Top Unique Cover of 2011!" —*YA-Aholic*

"It gave me some of the biggest chills and some of the biggest surprises I have ever read. . . . An intense story of mystery, envy, thrill, and betrayal."

—*YA-Aholic*

"*Envy* defies expectations of YA novels." —*Shooting Stars Mag*

"*Envy* is a must-read; just make sure you're not home alone when you read this one!" —*Chick Litaholic*

"A thrilling ride of a book." —*Totally Bookalicious*

"Readers of creeptastic books will highly enjoy this one."

—*Night Owl Reviews*

"Each chapter kept me wanting more." —*YA Booktwins*

"*Envy* is refreshingly bold with its themes. . . . A new, addictive series!"

—*Hippies, Beauty & Books. Oh My!*

"A fresh new voice that expertly encompasses all of the elements of a 'can't put the book down' mystery mixed with all of the things we love about YA novels." —*X-treme Readers*

"An excellent book which kept me guessing until the very end."

—*Bookbabblers*

GO MOBILE!

To access bonus content for BETRAYAL, download Microsoft's free Tag Reader on your smartphone at **www.gettag.mobi**. Then use your phone to take a picture of the bar code below to get exclusive extras about Hayley, Taylor, and other characters from the EMPTY COFFIN series, as well as more information about the books and author Gregg Olsen.

1. Download the free tag reader at: **www.gettag.mobi**

2. Take a photo of the bar code using your smartphone camera

3. Discover the true crime stories behind EMPTY COFFIN!

NEW YORK

An Imprint of Sterling Publishing
387 Park Avenue South
New York, NY 10016